Northern Knight

Book 3 in the Anarchy Series
By
Griff Hosker

Contents

Northern Knight

Published by Sword Books Ltd 2015
Copyright © Griff Hosker First Edition

A CIP catalogue record for this title is available from the British Library.
Cover by Design for Writers

Prologue

Stockton 1125

My son, William, was born in January. This was not a wolf winter as we had endured the previous year but it was cold on the day he was born. That was a good sign. It meant he would grow up to be as tough and as hard as the land into which he was born. The cold, harsh borders in the north of King Henry's lands were filled with enemies. Some enemies appeared to be friends until they stabbed you in the back. The women who attended my wife, Adela, and Faren, who supervised all, kept me well away from the birthing room. It would have been considered unlucky to have me present. I spent the day with my knights, Edward and Wulfstan, looking north from my battlements. It was too cold to practise and I was too nervous. Wulfstan had three children and had gone through this already. He and Edward kept my mind from what was going on below.

"I wonder if the Earl of Gloucester's punitive raid eliminated all of the rebels, Alfraed." Northern barons had allied with Scottish knights to take advantage of the king's absence. We had helped to quell the rebellion and the Earl had headed north with his knights to teach the Scots better manners. He had since returned south to his lands on the Welsh marches. The Scots were not the only enemies we faced.

"I doubt it, Wulfstan. Too many have lands in Scotland and we know that many fled there after the battle of Gretna. They will be building up their strength and biding their time. With the Earl in the south and the King still in Normandy then they can ferment their plots and plans." I would have taken all of our army to march into Scotland and lay it waste much as King William had done when he had first arrived in the north. If there were no knights who dreamed of our lands then we would all be safer.

"Then we must prepare for a spring and summer of raids. Our cattle and sheep have done well over the winter. Now that we keep fodder for the winter then we keep alive many more animals. You did well to conceive the idea. However, the Scots and the dissident lords will seek to take them from us. They want what we have but they do not wish to work for it." Wulfstan cast a critical eye over

1

me. "Have you fully recovered from the wound you received at Durham? We thought to have lost you."

I smiled and pointed to Edward. "Ask my mother there! Edward has Harold reporting to him each week on my exercise and the wound."

Edward was not put out by the implied criticism, "I am concerned, Baron. You have made this manor and those at Norton and Hartburn prosperous. If you were to fall in battle who knows what lord the King would appoint."

"I am fit, Wulfstan. I am fitter than I was before I was hurt. Alf made me a practice sword which is half as heavy again as my own sword. I use it each day to spar with Harold. I am becoming stronger. In fact, it has worked so well that I need to have my armour let out a little for my shoulders are now broader. Fear not, I will be ready for the Scots when they come."

Harold came running up the stairs and we all turned with expectant looks upon our faces. "Is it....?"

"Sorry, my lord, it is not the baby." He frowned. "At least I do not think it is. There is a messenger arrived from York. He has brought you this." He handed me a sealed document.

I took it. "Has the messenger been taken care of?"

"Aye my lord, Seara is feeding him but he leaves for Durham as soon as his horse is rested. He has a message for the Bishop too."

This sounded ominous. I looked at the seal. It was the mark of Robert Fitzroy of Caen, Earl of Gloucester and illegitimate son of King Henry. With the King in Normandy then he was the most powerful man in the land. While my knights and squire watched me, I read the short document. Robert did not waste words.

"It seems that the Emperor is not well and has not long to live. We are to be alert to more raids from the north. We must prepare to travel." Edward nodded. We had both sworn an oath.

I looked south-east as though I could see all the way to Worms and Empress Matilda. I fingered the medallion she had given me. Like Edward, I was a Knight of the Empress and sworn to defend her. I wondered if she would be an Empress still when her husband died. I doubted it for I had been told that the Sallic law governed the Empire and that meant a woman could not rule. It was strange. I had married Adela last summer because the Empress was beyond my grasp and now, she would be a widow; should I have waited? The Housecarls and the Saxons whom my father had led believed that there were supernatural forces determining our lives. Sometimes I agreed with them. This was fate.

"My lord?"

I looked around and saw the three of them staring at me. "Oh sorry, I was daydreaming. What did you say?"

"I said, my lord, how will our lives change as a result of his death?"

"I do not think it should affect us here."

Wulfstan smiled sadly and shook his head. "And there you are wrong, Alfraed. It is as though a stone has been thrown into a pond. We are far from the middle here but the ripples will reach us eventually. Did you read between the lines in the letter?" I must have shown my confusion. He tapped the parchment in my hand. "Matilda can now be heiress to the throne."

"She is a woman."

"But she is young yet and can marry again. She is only twenty-three. She could remarry and have children. She is now the most valuable woman in the western world. She is heir to Normandy, England and Maine. If the right candidate to be Emperor married her…"

Just then there was a cry from below and I heard the wailing of a child. The others cheered and clapped. My son was born. I was happy for the birth but saddened by the thought that someone else would marry Matilda. Someone else would father her a child. I smiled and prepared a face to meet my wife and my son. I was a man torn.

Part 1

The Death of an Emperor

Chapter 1

As spring came we prepared our land and our men for the summer ahead. I held the first session of the year. We collected the taxes. Everyone gained, the Bishop and the King had their share and we, the lords of the manors, reaped the rewards of good husbandry and the management of our lands. Edward and Wulfric journeyed to York to hire men at arms. It was an annual ritual. We shed winter and prepared to summer. We knew that we would face dangers from the north; King Henry's prolonged absence in Normandy determined that. We were seen as the soft part of the land. We had no large armies and yet we were better off than those north of the Tyne and the Solway. The hard work of our people meant nothing to those who wished just to take the fruits of our labours. Although hiring more men at arms was an expense we had discovered that it was a justified one. It kept out people safe and we only hired those whom Wulfric, my sergeant at arms, chose. He had a good eye for warriors.

My son was at that stage in his life where his world was his mother and his wet nurse. I could go and pull faces which occasionally amused him but more often than not he was either sleeping or eating. When he was doing neither of those then he was wailing. Wulfstan had prepared me for the ordeal. I chose that time to take some men at arms and visit the knights who followed my banner. As the winter had been relatively kind and we had had a successful season of campaigning, my knights had added men to their retinue and improved the weapons and armour. A knight was only as good as his armour and his men. I warned them, without divulging too much, that I might have to leave for Normandy at any time. They were happy to follow my lieutenant, Edward. Although not noble born he was a warrior through and through. If he was with me then Wulfstan, who had fought in the Varangian Guard, would be the deputy who would protect my land. The other four

4

knights recognised that. After leaving instructions for patrols along the river and towards Hartness I returned to my home.

I saw a large number of horses in the bailey and I was curious who our visitors were. I was greeted by one of the knights of the Earl of Gloucester. I had served with Sir Hugh d'Amphraville and he was a reliable and noble knight. "The Earl has need of you."

I could see he wanted to speak privately. "Come and we will walk my ramparts." As we reached the top I saw Roger of Lincoln approaching. "We would speak in private."

"I will tell the men, my lord."

When we were alone he said, "The Emperor is close to death. The King has asked for you to take your men and be there at the end. When he dies the Empress will need an escort back to Caen."

"Is he in Worms still?"

"He is."

"Tell me, if you can, Sir, from where does the danger lie? Who are the enemies of the Empress?"

He laughed, "Where do they not?" He held his fingers up as he enumerated them one by one: The Angevin, Charles of Flanders who has not yet forgotten Calais, Louis and William of Clito who has been promised Normandy by the French king. If you add to that those who would relieve the Empress of her regalia and jewels I would say it is an extensive list."

"I am not trying to get out of this but why me? I am certain there are knights in Normandy who would be better and closer placed."

"True but the Empress asked for you and you were the first name which came to the King and to the Earl. Take it as a compliment. You were successful when you returned her to her husband despite the problems and you have more men now." He was of an age with Robert of Gloucester and he smiled. "For what it is worth I think you are the best choice for this task. I have warred alongside you and I have seen that you have an eye for this sort of thing. If anyone can extract her from her predicament it is you."

I inclined my head, "I do take it as a compliment but if I take my men then who is to guard my lands and my family?" Almost on demand my son began to wail from the nearby tower. I laughed, "Do you see?"

He had the grace to smile, "I see, but I am afraid that the King only cares for his daughter now. As you know she is the only heir he has and I am afraid that your own considerations do not matter to the King."

"When do I leave?" I could see that there was little point in presenting more objections.

"As soon as you can. There are two ships awaiting you at Hartness."

I frowned, "Why not here?"

"They brought the new lord of Hartness and his retinue."

"And who is it?" My heart was in my boots for I knew the name, even without it being spoken.

"Baron Raymond de Brus." He saw my face. "Do not worry, Baron, the renegade who was there formerly is only a distant cousin. The new Baron is cut from a different cloth. He is a good man and will be a stout ally for you."

I was sceptical but I would speak with him before I left. "I hope he is for if any harm comes to my family then I care not if I incur the king's displeasure. I shall cut his heart out and raze Hartness to the ground!"

"You mean that don't you?"

I said nothing but turned to speak to Roger of Lincoln who stood at the other end of the ramparts. "Roger, find Sir Edward and Harold. I need them." Sir Hugh joined me, "I am sorry for my words Sir Hugh but the family of de Brus has caused me much pain. They were the reason my father was killed. I serve the King but I will not sit idly by and watch my family hurt."

He smiled, "I understand but you need to be more diplomatic when you speak. I would not betray a confidence but there are others who might."

As I reached the main hall I saw John, son of Leofric, my clerk. "John, entertain Sir Hugh for me. I have to tell my lady I go to do the king's bidding." I saw Sir Hugh's mouth open and close like a fish. I suspect he was telling me to be discreet. This was my family and I would tell them what I chose.

Adela was feeding when I entered. "Seara said we have a visitor. You should have told me I could have had the wet nurse see to William."

"It is a messenger from the King. I am to go to Worms and escort the Empress back to Normandy."

Her face fell. I know not if she suspected there had been a bond between the Empress and I but she was a clever woman. She was also the most loyal wife a man could wish for. Then she brightened. "It is another honour, Alfraed, the King thinks highly of you."

6

"Aye," I said sourly, "Especially when it is a task which others would refuse. There is more. The King has appointed another de Brus to the manor of Hartness." This time she could not disguise her feelings and her hand went to her mouth. "It is a different part of the family but I will have a word with him before I leave. Fear not, my lady. I am not taking all of my men. You will be well protected here and I should be back this six month."

She composed herself. "I am not the frail girl I was. I have survived the wolf winter. Do not fear for me my husband but promise me you will watch out for yourself."

I leaned over and kissed her. "For you I shall."

I sent riders to Wulfstan and my knights. I sent Wulfric, who was my sergeant at arms. He told them that I would be away and they would have to serve under Wulfstan until my return. Harold was already in my castle and I gave him instructions. "We shall be away for some time. We will leave the warhorses here. I am not going to risk a sea voyage and the rigours of campaigning in Germany. If we have to fight then we use our palfreys. Make sure that Dick has enough arrows and we will need lances."

"Yes, my lord. And Lady Adela?"

"I leave Wulfstan and Wulfric here in my place. We do not take all of our men. Twenty men at arms and ten archers in addition to Aiden will do." Even as he left to begin the gathering of our supplies I prayed that Rolf and the other Swabian knights would also be on hand to protect the Empress.

Edward arrived with Wulfstan. Neither knew the reason but, when they saw the messenger I knew that they would work it out for themselves. I spoke in the hearing of Sir Hugh. I wanted him to report to the Earl and thence the King that I was not happy about certain things. "We are to go to Worms and escort the Empress. I leave Wulfstan in command. Wulfric will stay also. We take twenty men at arms and ten archers. I will take Dick and Aiden too. You should both know that the King, for whatever reason has placed a de Brus in Hartness. Our ships leave from there and I intend to let Sir Raymond know that I command in the valley and that he will protect my lands with his life. We will make sure that our people are protected."

I glared at Sir Hugh, willing him to object to my tone.

Wulfstan nodded, "Do not worry; I shall be visiting all of your knights. He will understand. I will make sure of that"

"Good. I have told Harold that we will not need warhorses. I intend to move as quickly as we can. Expect us back by autumn."

7

Sir Hugh looked surprised, "Baron, the Empress will have a retinue..."

"I have travelled with the Empress before. She can travel quickly. If her retinue cannot then we leave them. I am charged with protecting the Empress only! The rest are of no consequence to me!"

We left before dark and reached Hartness at high tide. Sir Hugh came with us. When we reached the manor Sir Raymond greeted us. Despite what Sir Hugh had said I could see the family traits in his face. I hoped that they would not extend to his character too!

"Sir Edward and Harold, get our war gear on the boats. Sir Hugh and I need conference with Sir Raymond." The de Brus knight frowned a little. It was his manor and he was being ordered around. I could see that he did not like it. I nodded towards his hall. "Shall we speak within where it is quieter?"

Once we were inside Sir Hugh played peacemaker. "Sir Alfraed here has been charged by King Henry with protecting the valley. All of the knights in the area around Norton fight under his banner when danger threatens."

Sir Raymond smiled, "Ah I wondered. That is good, Sir Alfraed. I have heard much of you. Your exploits in Calais and Durham are the stuff of legends."

I disliked flattery and I was a blunt man. "Sir Raymond, I would be lying if I said I was happy about your appointment." I held up my hand as he began to speak. "Hear me out and you will understand why. Your cousin, Sir Robert, who held this manor before you abducted the lady who is now my wife and treated her vilely. He harboured the knights who slew my father and killed many of my closest friends. The coward then fled to Anjou before justice could be meted out to him. I am astounded that King Henry would countenance replacing one de Brus with another." I paused for breath. "And now I am sent to Normandy and leave my family close to the grasp of the family who have done me and mine so much harm."

"I swear that I am no threat to your family and I have not seen Sir Robert these many years. I have won this manor through loyal service to the King."

I laughed, "In my experience, your family is very adept at saying one thing and doing another. Your coat of arms should be the mask of Janus."

He coloured and Sir Hugh said, "Baron, you go too far."

I turned my baleful glare at Sir Hugh. "I know exactly how far I go." I turned back to Sir Raymond who had also coloured a bright red. I did not know if it was anger or embarrassment. "I have left Sir Wulfstan in command in Stockton. He will visit you, on my behalf. When I return, if I hear good reports of you then I will apologise for my attitude and my words. Until then I ask you to do as my other knights have done; watch the borders of the valley and keep it safe."

He took a deep breath. "I will do so and I promise that you will see the truth when you return."

I nodded and turned. I heard Sir Hugh speak with Sir Raymond as I strode to the waiting ships. Already the sky was darkening in the east. Night was falling. I glanced around for the headman, Harold of Elwick. I had been suspicious of him when I had met him. Now he was nowhere to be seen and that, with a new lord of the manor was equally suspicious. I could do nothing about it yet but I would seek him out when I returned.

The horses had all been loaded when I reached the two boats. Neither was large and we would be cramped aboard them for the journey down to Normandy. We waited until Sir Hugh joined us before boarding. I left Edgar in charge of the men at arms who were on the other ship, 'La Reine' while Dick and the archers came on board our ship, 'Le Duc du Normandie'. Both captains were eager to get some sea room and we set sail without delay.

This was the first time I had viewed the river and my land from the sea. I could see why the captains had come to Hartness. The walls of the town rose high on a cliff above the sea. The estuary, in contrast looked to be a marshy and dangerous tangle of small streams and sandbanks. I knew, from Olaf, that it was not and the main channel was easy to find once you had sailed it a couple of times. It might explain why we did not have more ships visiting our river. I wondered what we could do about that. More trade meant prosperity for all.

As I looked around the small coastal vessel I realised that we would not be comfortable. There was just a main deck and a hold. Harold and Aiden would sleep in the hold with the horses as would a couple of the archers. They would look after the animals on the voyage. I did not envy them. The smell was bad enough but when you allied that to the pitching motion of the ship it was a recipe for sea sickness. All that we had above the hold was a couple of canvas awnings spread amidships close to the mast. I was just grateful that the journey would take but a few days. With just dry rations and stale beer, it did not promise to be an enjoyable voyage.

"Harold is the armour safe from the salt of the sea?"

"Aye my lord, we wrapped them in oiled sheepskins. They will be fine."

"Good." I stood on the side of the ship facing the coast and watched the river recede into the darkness as the sun set in the west over my valley. Sir Hugh joined me, "Your opinion of the rebel de Brus is well justified you know but not his cousin."

"How so?"

"He is now with Count Fulk and they are in France with William Clito. He plays for high stakes. He is gambling that the King of France will gain Normandy for William Clito and he will regain his estates that way. Sir Raymond fought against Count Fulk's men and earned the high opinion of many of us."

I nodded and, as darkness finally fell, I turned to face the Earl's emissary. "Would you have rewarded the de Brus family with the estate at Hartness, Sir Hugh?"

He had the grace to smile. I saw it in the light from the lantern the helmsman used. "If I am to be honest then, no. I would have rewarded him but not with Hartness. There are many estates further south. Hartness is not rich but it is vital. One day it will be the largest port on the coast."

"Then why give it to de Brus?"

He shook his head. "You must ask the king. I am just a humble knight."

"As I am and Edward here but we have minds and we can think."

My fellow knight smiled, "The trouble is, Sir Alfraed, that you were brought up in the east where there is intrigue and plotting."

"Come Edward, remember when we escorted the Empress home?" He nodded. "There was more deception and self interest than I ever witnessed in Constantinople. But you are correct, Sir Hugh, and I will ask the King."

"He will not thank you for the question."

"Nonetheless I will speak what is on my mind and in my heart. It is my way."

It was not a pleasant voyage and we encountered rough seas. I admired these sailors. When we had sailed from Constantinople to Genoa we had enjoyed blue skies and calm waters. Here it was black skies and grey water. I was just grateful to see the Orne River and Normandy. I would return to my home across the short crossing and travel through England. It was longer but preferable.

We sailed down the river to the castle of Caen. While Edgar supervised the unloading of the men and animals I strode with Sir Hugh and Edward to the castle. I had discovered that the Earl was still in England. I smiled at him as we strode through the streets of the town. "You have another sea voyage to take, Sir Hugh."

"Aye, I am not looking forward to it. Still, it will be a shorter one; just across the Channel and then back to the Earl."

"Is he at his western estates?"

He shook his head, "He is in London. Between you and I, there are factions there who require close attention. Not every enemy comes at you on a horse and wearing armour."

"You are right there," I remembered how a churchman had almost succeeded in delivering Durham Castle to rebels.

We waited for the King in an antechamber. When we were beckoned within the King dismissed his servants and attendants. "Guard the door, Guiscard. We must speak in private." With the door secure he turned to me and, ignoring the other two, spoke directly to me. "I must ask you to go back into the Empire and fetch the Empress and her retinue back to Caen. I know that I ask much of you, Baron, but I believe you are the only man who can do this. The journey will be even more dangerous this time. Then she was the Empress and the Emperor lived. When you bring her back she will be in even greater danger."

He leaned back in his chair and suddenly looked old. "You now have a child, I believe, and you will be able to understand what I am about to say. As a father, you make plans for your children. I sought a good marriage for my daughter. The Emperor of the Holy Roman Empire should have brought her security and power. I was wrong. They had no children and her husband is sickly. I planned for my son to rule after me and the storm took him and the White Ship to his death. Now my daughter is in danger."

He stood and went to the map which was spread across the table. It was elaborately decorated. "Until I become a father again then I must consider that Matilda may become the heir to England and Normandy. She must be kept safe. There are many who would want her dead; my nephew, Clito, and King Louis are two such men. Others would wish to use her. Count Flanders could hold her hostage. My brother, the Curthose, has supporters close to us who would do anything to remove me and my line from the thrones." He shook his head. "There is just my daughter and my nephew, Stephen of Blois, who give me hope."

The hairs on the back of my neck suddenly prickled. Stephen of Blois had been involved in the attempt to ambush the Empress on our journey back to Worms. I could never prove it for he had been in disguise but I knew it. The King had not mentioned him as a threat but I knew him to be one.

"So, as you can see, your task is to be a hard one."

I knew that I had to speak. "I am not objecting to travelling to Worms and bringing back the Empress but would a larger force led by either yourself or the Earl not be more appropriate?"

The King and Sir Hugh looked at each other. When I had asked the question, I had expected an adverse reaction from the King but he looked sad and more than a little uncomfortable. "Nothing would give me greater pleasure; she is my child. However, that could be misconstrued as an act of war by my neighbours and if I did not take enough men then I could be captured and held to ransom. The same would be true of my son, Robert, but he is in England. I have enemies there too." I nodded. That made perfect sense and I could see why an obscure knight from the north of England could be gambled to save a possible future Queen of England.

Part of me thought of my enemies and the risks we would face but I remained silent. My father had put the needs of others above his own his whole life. I would do the same; especially for the Empress.

The King smiled. "However, I have four knights who can accompany you. With only the two of you, you are perilously short."

I shook my head, "Do I have to take them?"

Although the King looked surprised Sir Hugh did not. "Why would you not take more knights?"

"If I am to be brutally honest my liege it is because I do not know them. The two Teutonic Knights who accompanies the Empress were not her choice and it almost ended in disaster for her. I would rather ride with the men I know and trust even though they are few in number. I believe the Empress will feel the same."

"You have surprised me, although not, it seems, my son's emissary."

"That is because he has seen treachery at close hand. I agree with the Baron; better a smaller number that he knows than strangers who may bring their own problems." He turned to me. "And your route; have you decided upon that?"

It was my turn to smile, "I will take a leaf from the Empress' book. I will decide once we are on the road. I will not even tell my men until we are at a junction in the road."

"You trust only yourself?"

"No, my liege, I trust all of my men but I do not trust them to let a careless remark slip out at the wrong time. This way, if it goes wrong, then I can blame only myself."

"My daughter's choice is justified, it appears. We have a knight who knows his own mind and that of his men."

"Your daughter's choice?"

The King laughed, "Aye, Alfraed. She asked for you and Sir Edward by name. You made an impression on my daughter."

This time there was no hurry to leave. The Emperor was still alive. Before we had left the King, it was made clear to me that I was to get the Empress out as soon as the Emperor was buried. Although she was popular she had still, apparently, made enemies. We did not take the knights who were offered but we did take the six spare horses. They might prove to be the difference between success and failure.

As we left the mighty citadel I wondered if it was my imagination or the fears within me which made me suspicious of every sour face which turned our way. I had no doubt that there were spies in Caen. Were they reporting our departure? Although there had been no hurry to leave the castle once we were on the road I intended to ride as hard as we could. Later we could slow down but if someone was trying to get ahead of us then we would hear them as they hurried along the road to catch us.

There were just thirty-five of us who left Caen. It had been more than the last time we had crossed to Germany but still not enough. Five of my men at arms were new men but all of the archers had served with me for some time. Gille of Gainford was also new. He was the nephew of Sir Guy. As Sir Guy had his own son as a squire Gille was keen to train to be a knight and Edward had been satisfied with him once they met. He was determined that he would train him better than he had Alan. I kept telling him, as did Harold, that he had done as well as he could but it was just fate. He would not listen.

Edward and I rode at the fore whilst Aiden and Dick ranged ahead to scout out danger. The last time we had stopped at Rouen and Rheims. That time we had had the Empress with us. Her presence had determined our route. I did not wish to let our enemies know where we were. We would avoid such places. I could trust no one on the road. We kept to the main road only until the first night when we camped by the road in a sheltered dell. My fears were proved to be based on fact when we heard the thundering of hooves along the road. I had two sentries on the road and they stepped out with nocked bows to stop the rider who hurtled down the darkened road. Their Norman was limited and I heard the rider hurling abuse at them.

I reached him and his face changed when he recognised my surcoat. I vaguely recognised him. I had seen him in the castle. "Where are you going in such a hurry?"

"I am on the King's business! Let me pass!"

"Show me proof."

"What?" I could see that he had hoped to bluff us and force his way through by using the name of the king.

"If you are from the King then he will have given you a document or a seal. He would not expect you to risk being stopped would he now...?"

I got no further. He kicked out and struck Will the Wanderer in the chest knocking him over. He then slapped his horse's rump. It was a bold move and it was a quick move. In most cases he would have escaped but he reckoned without Griff of Gwent and Alan son of Garth, my archers. Their arrows threw him from his saddle. "Harold, Gille, get his horse."

The body was brought back to us and, when we searched him, we found a document which was unsigned but which informed Lord Alain of Flanders that Alfraed of Norton was heading for Worms and the Empress with thirty men. There was a spy in Caen. This was just the messenger. He would have been ordered by someone who was much more powerful. I had no doubt that there might be others but we had delayed the message. After taking his weapons, armour, valuables and helmet we covered his body with leaves and finished our disturbed sleep. The armour and helmet were unlike ours and could be of use if we needed a disguise.

The next day we disappeared from view. We took to small greenways and forests. My woodsmen hid our trail and Dick and Aiden kept us from prying eyes ahead. I headed for the one place on the whole road where I knew I could be safe. We reached La Cheppe without any warning.

Sir Guy du Cheppe was also a knight of the Empress and the castle at La Cheppe had been his reward from the Emperor for saving his wife's life. When we had last been here, it seemed a lifetime ago, the remains of the old burnt out castle were a scorched and blackened pile. Now he had built a fine wooden castle and his banner flew proudly from its tower. It was not a large castle but it guarded the western end of the Empire. Sir Guy was a knight whom I would trust to guard my back.

He stood with his hands on his hips as we clattered across the wooden bridge and into the outer bailey. "I wondered when you would get here."

I dismounted and clasped his arms as all warriors do who have faced death together. "But how did you know I would come here at all?"

He laughed as he led us towards the second gate and the keep. "All of the Empire knows that you are coming to the aid of the Empress once more." He lowered his voice so that my men at arms would not hear. "There is a price on your head, Alfraed of Norton!"

"Who wishes me dead so badly?"

He enumerated them on his fingers, "Flanders, France, Anjou why even Lothar and Konrad's fellows seek your head." He gave a rueful smile and laughed, "Oh to be so popular. Come you shall spend the night with me and enjoy a roof over your head instead of the greenwood."

"How do you know we have not enjoyed comfortable nights?"

"We would have heard of your route and your armour would not show flecks of rust!" He was as clever as he was brave.

My men ate with Sir Guy's warriors while we ate in his hall. It was not yet a Great Hall but it was comfortable and well made. He filled us in on the events further east.

"The Emperor is not yet dead but the wolves are circling. He has named his nephew, Frederick as the heir to his estates but he is unlikely to gain the throne. Thanks to the Emperor's problems with the Pope it seems likely that Lothair of Supplinburg will be named Emperor. Oh, they will have an election but the Pope will decide who the new King of the Romans is to be. The election will be a formality. This time the Pope will have his own man ruling the Empire."

I nodded, "Then the Empress should be safe for a while."

"I am afraid not. Lothair hates Henry. He can do nothing about him but he can humiliate him in death by taking the Empress hostage. She is a useful bargaining counter. Already there are suitors lining up to propose the moment that Henry dies!"

"You cannot be serious!"

"I am afraid so. Tell me who ordered you to rescue her? King Henry?"

"Yes."

He nodded and leaned back, "But the Empress requested it. She fears for her life and trusts only you."

"Yes, how did you know?"

"My uncle and I visited Worms last year to visit with the Emperor. The Empress had a word in private. The Emperor had the wasting sickness even then. She said she feared for her life and asked if you still lived. When I said I did not know she became sad and said she would send a message to her father."

"Rolf and the others; they are still at her side?"

"They are there with her but there are but three of them and their ten men at arms. They may be fine warriors but they cannot stop the numbers who would try to take her."

"Then we had better leave in the morning. Perhaps you were wrong about the price on my head. We had no trouble getting here."

"That is because you were hidden from view. Once you pass my uncles' castle at Bar then all the world will know where you are. You were lucky to cross France once; with the Empress and her retinue it will be impossible."

I took this news in and wondered how I could possibly achieve what I wished. "You and your uncle; how are you viewed by this Lothair?"

"He does not like us. The Counts of Aachen and Stuttgart have his ear and they will gain power at my father's expense. The trouble is that my uncle is an honourable man."

"As are you."

He nodded, "As am I. It is lucky I came back richer. I have more men at arms now and a squire. We shall come with you as far as Bar and I will see what my uncle says."

"I do not expect you to risk all for the Empress."

He showed me his palm where we had taken our blood oath. "We swore an oath if you remember and I will not be foresworn. We have cast the dice; let us see what occurs."

Chapter 2

When we reached his magnificent castle the Count of Bar looked considerably older than the last time I had seen him. Events had taken their toll of him. He guarded the western edge of the Empire and he now had enemies at his back too. However, his castle was built of stone and it would take an army and siege engines to bring it to surrender. Here our men and arms and archers had plenty of room for he had a large warrior hall. He took Sir Guy, Edward and myself to a west facing tower. He called it a solar. There we sat with his two sons to discuss events in the Empire.

"Your visit, Baron, is a double-edged sword. On the one hand, I am more than pleased that the Empress' life will be safe in your hands but, at the same time I know that my family will incur the wrath of Lothair."

"Then we will leave, Count. I would not, for the entire world, put you and your family in jeopardy. If it were not for you we might not be alive."

"No, Baron, honour demands that we help you. There are responsibilities to power as well as rewards." He turned to his nephew. "You swore an oath to protect the Empress. You have to go with the Baron."

"What of La Cheppe?"

"We will protect that for you." He leaned forward. "I must warn you, however of the dangers you face. Lothair will do all in his power to stop you leaving. If you do manage to escape with the Empress and reach here then you will have to run the gauntlet of Louis of France and Charles of Flanders. I can only protect you within Lorraine. Beyond that…"

I smiled, "Count, you have given me hope! I feared that our journey would end somewhere in the Empire. With your nephew and his men at my side then I believe we can overcome whatever comes our way."

Edward looked unhappy about something, "Baron, we have a long way to go and then to return. We will need more horses or these will be dead on their feet before too long." He looked at the Count. "We could not take the Count's horses so where shall we get them?"

"Your man is right, Baron, but you may well be able to get horses in Worms. Unless the Emperor is dead the Empress will still have influence. I would get as many horses as you can when you reach there. You should also buy as many supplies before the Emperor is dead. Use her influence while she has it. Once the Emperor is dead then you will need to sleep with one eye open!"

I nodded, "They are both good suggestions. Thank you, Count, and we will leave first thing in the morning. I would not wish to bring any more attention to you than we have. Besides which I feel that we ought to get to Worms as quickly as possible."

"Then my sons, Geoffrey and Raymond, will escort you as far as my borders. It will deter any would be attackers."

It was a powerful force which left the Count's castle. Dick and Aiden were accompanied by some of the Count's scouts. They did not understand each others' language but they were all woodsmen and they communicated somehow. We were approaching the borders of the Count's land when they all galloped in. My men reported to me while the Count's scouts reported to Geoffrey and Raymond.

"My lord, just beyond the borders there is a force of knights awaiting us. They are the men of Flanders. I recognised the livery."

I had wondered about this. While we were protected in Lorraine by the Count of Bar's men we would be safe but once beyond the borders then we were fair game. They would wait until we were a smaller conroi and then attack. "How many are there?"

"It is hard to say. When we spied them the Count's men rode back here."

"Just a guess then, Dick."

"I saw twenty banners."

"That means at least twenty knights. Add another hundred men at arms and we are outnumbered." I stroked my beard. "Archers?"

"We saw a company of crossbowmen. I would say no more than twenty of them."

"They outnumber our archers then?"

Dick laughed, "My lord, we are archers! They will fill their breeks when our arrows rain upon them."

I nudged Scout to join the Count's sons. "It seems they know you will be returning home. Thank you for your help thus far."

Sir Geoffrey laughed, "If you think that we will turn back at our borders and let our kinsmen be slaughtered then you do not know us, Baron."

Sir Raymond nodded, "Besides our borders are notoriously badly mapped."

"You are sure?"

"Our cousin did well when he fought with you. We will take our chances."

I looked at the sky. There were about two hours until dusk. "Good then let us walk into this trap. Dick, come here, this is what I want us to do."

Once everyone knew exactly what I intended I sent Dick and the archers, along with Aiden off to the north of the road. I sent Sir Geoffrey and Sir Raymond with their men at arms to the south of the road and then I led my knights into the trap so carefully laid by the Count of Flanders.

It looked as though we were unsuspecting but we were not. Our casual gait belied the careful preparations we had made. I had Edward to my left. Behind us were our squires. They were laughing and joking as I had ordered. Then came Sir Guy and his squire. Edgar led my men at arms and those of Sir Guy. They rode in a four-wide column That was deliberate. They were our largest force. They had to fight as one. The last three would guard the baggage when the trap was sprung. The rest would form a solid phalanx to come to our aid when we were attacked. It was eerily reminiscent of the ambush when we had had the Empress with us. The difference was that we had no woman to protect and we had no traitors fighting in our ranks. There was a rise ahead. The men of Flanders had hidden behind the rise. I guessed that they had a man watching to signal them for as we rode down the old Roman Road they appeared on the rise with lances and gonfanon. Dick had estimated well. There were twenty of them. I could see a second line of another twenty men at arms. Their flanks had ten crossbows protected by another twenty spears. Finally, I could just see the spears of more foot soldiers behind the men at arms. This was a powerful body of warriors.

Edward said, "Someone wants us dead, Baron."

"Let us try to disappoint them then."

The ambushers steadied their line and came down towards us. They came confidently keeping knee to knee. These were experienced knights who knew their business. Our squires flanked us. Sir Guy and his squire made us six deep at the front. Behind us the twenty-eight men at arms rode in seven lines. I was going to use us as a battering ram to punch a hole in the enemy line.

This was not my warhorse, Star, I was riding but Scout was an intelligent horse and I intended to use intelligence to defeat these men of Flanders. I lowered my lance across my cantle as we trotted up the gentle slope towards them. I saw the crossbowmen to our left level their weapons as the spearmen protected them with an array of spears. If we were foolish enough to charge them then the battle would be over in the blink of an eye. They were not expecting the arrows which Dick rained upon them. They were taken in the flank. Neither spears nor crossbows had any shields and the first three flights of arrows ended the threat from our left. I saw the leader of the knights, with a yellow shield and rampant lion, wave his arm. The crossbows and the spears on their left flank hurried down the slope to begin to harass us. The enemy were so concerned with this column of men which advanced upon them that they did not see, until it was too late, the men at arms led by Sir Geoffrey and Sir Raymond which galloped across the hill to plunge their spears into the defenceless men. A horseman loves attacking archers or crossbows in the flank. The men of Bar needed no urging to fall like wolves on these sheep.

Their leader made the mistake of slowing down to decide what to do. It was a mistake and I took my chance, "Charge!" They should have continued to move steadily down the slope but their leader had been distracted by the appearance of our allies.

I spurred Scout and he leapt forward. I aimed my spear at the leader. He shouted "Charge!" too but it was a lifetime too late. I hunched down behind my shield and concentrated upon the cantle of his saddle. He may have heard of my technique for he tried to turn his horse away from my lance. It was another mistake. His lance went over my head and I stuck his shield square on. He began to fall away to the right. Without a cantle to stabilise him he fell off his horse and beneath the hooves of the men at arms who followed closely.

The men at arms who followed were not as tightly packed as the knights had been and when I saw the next line I had time to turn my lance to the man at arms on my right. I pulled back my arm and risked standing slightly and leaning forward as I punched. It was a manoeuvre which allowed my lance to strike him just a moment before his struck me. The head of my lance tore through his mail and he fell off. His weapon punched me on the side but his fall stopped the penetration as he fell from his horse. My lance broken I sat down and drew my sword. I pulled Scout's reins to the right and rode along the line of men at arms. As I did so I saw that Sir Raymond and Sir Geoffrey had brought their knights to attack the far end of the line of men at arms. My move had brought my knights to the nearer end of the enemy line and the remaining men at arms were like the nuts in a nut cracker.

They found men coming at them from both sides and they panicked. I brought my sword across the man at arms who tried to turn, very slowly, his lance to face me. He had no defence against my blade which tore through his arm and his chest. I continued my turn so that Scout and I were amongst the men at arms, many of whom still had their lances. They should have thrown them away and fought with their swords but their panic meant they clung on to the now useless weapons. I found myself behind a man at arms who was trying to turn his horse; it is not easy to shift eight feet of ash lance held before you and his slowness caused his death. I brought my sword down vertically to strike between his neck and his shoulder. The sword ripped down and almost severed the arm.

As he fell from his saddle I had a clear view to the side where Dick and his archers had wrought such death amongst the crossbows. I saw them still releasing arrows and the knights who remained had had enough and were fleeing. There were still a handful of men at arms who were not fighting and they joined the rout. I used the time to look for my men. Gille was down as was Edward but Harold, Sir Guy and his squire remained on their mounts. Sir Guy's cousins brought their weary horses next to mine.

"A fine victory Baron Alfraed. Had I not witnessed it then I would have thought the story of such a rout the work of a troubadour."

Sir Guy said, "I told you he is like a terrier. He goes for the bull and cannot be shaken from its neck." He saw Sir Edward's empty saddle. "Edward!"

We rode to the fallen knight and his squire. I could see blood. Edward had been hit and wounded. I dismounted and after taking off my helmet pushed back my coif. We had no Wulfric to heal them this time. I was relieved when he opened his eyes. "It is my shoulder, Baron. But how is the boy?"

"I will tend to him in a moment. Harold! See to Gille!"

We took off Edward's helmet and his surcoat. I could see that the head of the lance had entered his left shoulder. The force had torn through his mail and broken the links. It had continued through his gambeson and into the flesh of his shoulder. The head had broken off and its shattered end stuck out. I looked up at Sir Guy, "Do you have a healer?"

He shook his head, "My uncle has a priest who has skill but..."

I nodded, "Then it will have to be me. Have my archers build a fire and fetch water."

Harold appeared with a white faced Gille, "He was stunned when he was knocked from his horse. He will live."

"How is Sir Edward? He took the blow when I was knocked to the ground."

Edward opened his eyes. He smiled weakly, "I am happy that you have survived." He winced as he tried to move.

"Lie still! I am no healer and not as gentle as Wulfric." I took out my dagger. I knew that Wulfric would put the blade in a fire but my men were still gathering dried wood and kindling. I had to risk it. Blood was still coming from the wound. Harold and Gill, hold his arms so that he does not move."

I took off my mailed gloves and wiped away some of the blood with the edge of the surcoat. I saw the edge of the wooden lance. I put the tip of the dagger between the flesh and the wood. I heard a grunt from Edward but that was all. I had to work quickly. I began to pull the wood out with the dagger. At first it would not move. I put my finger and thumb around one of the jagged edges and tried to pull. The first time it was too slippery. I tried again and gripped even harder. Suddenly the end popped out with a spurt of blood. Harold was quick thinking and he jammed the surcoat over the wound.

Dick had got the fire going and his short sword was already in the flames as he began to heat it. I had no cat gut to sew the wound together. We would have to use fire. "Gille, remove some of the links so that we can see the whole wound. Harold, keep up the pressure." I stood for my hands were shaking.

Sir Guy put his arm around my shoulder. "That was well done, Baron. Wulfric could not have done better."

I shook my head, "Wait until I have staunched the bleeding before you heap praise upon my head."

Sir Raymond and Sir Geoffrey had taken their men at arms off when I had begun work and they now returned. "They have fled. They left four dead knights and eight men at arms. Your archers slew all of the men with crossbows."

"If you wish those weapons for your father then I would get them before my archers. They use them for firewood."

Sir Geoffrey shook his head. "I do not understand you English and your hatred of the crossbow."

"It is not hatred. It is scorn. Look what my handful of archers did. I would take five bowmen over a company of crossbows any day."

Dick came over with his sword. "It is red hot sir."

"Hold Sir Edward and keep his body still."

As my men pressed down on him I put the flat of the red-hot sword against the flesh. This time Edward did call out just before he passed out. There was a smell of burning flesh and hair. I held it for a few moments and lifted it. I handed it to Dick to return to the fire. Sir Guy handed me some water which my men had brought from the stream. As I poured it the flesh hissed and steamed. We looked and I was relieved to see that the bleeding had stopped. I had done all that I could. Edward would have an ugly wound but he would live.

"We will camp here tonight and leave for Worms on the morrow." I stood and clasped the arm of Sir Geoffrey. "I thank you and your brother. We could not have beaten them else."

He laughed, "I thought we were going to charge to our deaths!"

"No, my friend; they were bought men with no conviction. Men who fight for a price have no heart. We fight for something different; we fight for each other and the Empress. God favours such men."

We had been lucky. We had wounds but the archers had won the day. The enemy had relied on their crossbows. They had not scouted well enough and, despite superior numbers, had been soundly beaten.

Dick approached me with a green substance. "Wulfric uses this, my lord. It is a moss. I have gathered it for him before."

"What does he do with it?"

Edgar had joined him, "He puts it on the wound. It must be magic or something for it stops a wound going bad." He shrugged. "It worked with you, my lord."

"Then we shall try it." We put the green moss on the cauterised wound and wrapped a bandage around it. Gille and Harold had removed the armour. When we reached Worms, we would need a smith to repair it.

When Edward woke the next day, and stood we were all relieved. He looked pale but he was a hard man. He insisted upon mounting. We bade farewell to the sons of the Count and we headed east. We had let the Count's sons have the crossbows and all else had been divided. My archers and men at arms had reached the bodies of the enemy dead first and all were richer. The hired swords had brought their thirty pieces of silver with them. My men deserved it. The four horses we had captured included two war horses. I was satisfied.

Sir Guy and I flanked Sir Edward, "You will not do Gille any good if you die protecting him, Edward. You cannot bring Alan back by sacrificing yourself for Gille."

"But he lay on the ground. He could have been killed!"

"As could you! Think on that!"

I think that the attack on us had been carefully planned. We had been half way to Worms and it was an isolated spot. The Count of Flanders must have assumed the larger numbers of knights and the crossbows he had sent would have guaranteed success. He would not be happy when they returned empty handed. The last week of our journey was uneventful. It was a slow journey because of Edward's wounds. Although others had suffered cuts and injuries his had been the most life threatening. It seemed I had a future as a healer should I fail as a knight.

We reached Worms two weeks later and we found that the Emperor still lived. His banners flew above his palace. The three of us wore our Empress medallions as we rode through the gates. It gained us easier access than had we arrived as Normans. Normans were viewed with deep suspicion. The success in England and Italy had made other leaders wary of letting in a handful of knights. I was not certain where we would stay. We left the men under the care of Edgar and they gathered in the main square. There they could use some of the coins they had taken from the men of Flanders and buy beer and wine. The three of us and our squires headed for the palace. We were granted entry through the main gate but warned that we would not be able to visit with the Emperor, nor the Empress as she was with him and his physicians.

Leaving our squires in the inner bailey we headed for the Great Hall. We knew that his lords would be there. As soon as we walked in we saw the Counts of Aachen and Stuttgart with another knight. They stared at us when we entered. The Count of Aachen's face darkened and he, rudely, pointed a finger at us. The strange knight nodded. Having been thus identified I would not back down from a confrontation and I strolled across to them.

I smiled at the Count whom I had defeated in a tourney. "Ah Count, I hope you have recovered from our little bout. You are lucky that it was you who picked up the lance with the arrow in the tip. Had it been me you might have been dead and that would have been a tragedy." Of course, he had prepared the lance himself and we both knew it. I was letting him know that I knew of his perfidy.

His face became even redder and his companion said, in an attempt to calm things down, "This is a sad time for us all. The

Emperor clings to life by a thread." He smiled, "This is Count Lothair of Supplinburg. He has come to ensure that prayers are said for the life of the Emperor."

I nodded, "Aye, we all pray for that." I looked at the man who would become Emperor of the Holy Roman Empire. He had a cold and calculating face. He reminded me of a hawk. He did not smile but then I had seen few real smiles amongst the knights I had met. Rolf and his Swabians were the exception.

The Count did not smile but said, "And what brings two Norman knights all the way from Caen? Surely you can have no interest in the life and death of the Emperor."

"But we do. The Emperor rewarded all three of us when we last visited and we hoped that our prayers and our presence might help the priests and physicians. Every prayer, no matter how small, may be of use. However, the three of us are also here to give comfort to the Empress. You must remember that the Empress made us members of her order of knights. It is only natural that we should visit and give her our support and," I stared at Lothair to let him know I was speaking with him, "our help should she need it. For her life means more to us than our own and we will defend it with all the power available to us."

The Count of Aachen adopted an innocent look, "Why should she need help? She is our Empress and the people love her dearly. We protect our own."

I nodded, "As do we."

Just then Rolf, Carl and Gottfried came bounding over to us, totally ignoring the three counts, "I knew you would come!" Rolf grabbed me in a bear hug and almost lifted me from the ground. These three were the only genuine knights in the whole room.

The others shook Guy and Edward by the hands. Edward winced, "Steady on Gottfried, I am not healed yet."

The three of them turned to glare at the counts and led us off. When we were out of earshot Rolf asked, "You were attacked?"

"Aye, the men of Flanders ambushed us."

Rolf spoke quietly, "We heard that men were looking for you. We could not leave the Empress, you understand?"

I nodded. "We would not have expected you to. We are men and we take our chances. We came here for the Empress said she had need of us." I gestured for them to come closer. "The King has asked us to bring her home when it is over."

"Aye, the Empress has asked us too. We will not stay here. We serve the Empress. That Lothair is even slier than the Count of Aachen."

I was relieved. Our chances were greatly increased with the men of Swabia alongside us. "How is the Empress?"

"She is under great pressure. Once the Emperor has been bled she will leave his side. Come we will wait in the antechamber."

"We were told we had to wait in the Great Hall."

Gottfried smiled as he smashed his right fist into the palm of his left, "They have learned not to argue with us."

There were two guards protecting the entrance to the Emperor's rooms. When they saw Rolf, they nodded and relaxed a little. We waited outside with the two servants who hovered there. "Is there any hope for the Emperor?"

Carl shook his head, "They have no idea how to cure him. They have drained off so much blood that he cannot have much left in him. Each day he is thinner and shrunken even more. The man is dying. If he were my horse then I would have ended his life already." He paused, "And I like my horse!"

"And after?"

"And after there will be a rat race to see who can reach the top of the greasy pole!"

"I thought as much. Do you have any idea how many of the retinue of the Empress we will have to protect?"

"No and they are what worries me. We can protect the Empress; she can ride and she is not easily afraid but her ladies and her servants are a different matter."

"Then let us begin now to make arrangements. Sir Guy, go with the squires and see how many horses you can buy in the town. Better to buy in ones and twos and then we will need somewhere to keep them out of sight. For the moment take them to Edgar and Dick. They will watch them for us." Sir Guy left. I had chosen him because he was not Norman and we would be less likely to be cheated.

We waited for an hour in the antechamber. We told them of our journey home and the border battles. "And that sounds much more exciting than our lives. We just watch for assassins. If we did not have each other with which to practice then we would be useless as warriors."

"Do you have men at arms and squires?"

"No, but we intend to hire some men at arms. How many men did you bring?"

"Between us we have forty, including archers."

"Not many to protect an Empress."

"No Rolf, but they are all trusted men. I would not ask for more."

The doors suddenly opened and the Empress Matilda came out flanked by the physicians. I could see by her face that she was both angry and upset. "Is there nothing but draining blood which can be done? It seems to me that it is blood he needs putting in not taking from him!"

The elder of the doctors gave her a patronising shake of the head, "Empress, we have done this since the time of Hippocrates. It will work but it takes time."

"You have done this for the last year and all I see is a weakened husband. Come up with something else or I shall find other physicians!"

She looked up and saw the five of us standing there. Her face changed from a scowl to a smile, instantly. "You came! I prayed that you would."

I gave a bow and said, "We swore an oath. Why would we not come?"

She glanced around her at the courtiers who had followed the physicians from the Emperor's chamber. "Come let us retire to somewhere we can speak."

She led us to another wing of the palace and we entered her drawing room. She dismissed the two servants who waited there. She sat.

I spoke gently for I did not wish to upset her more but I needed to know how the land lay. "So, there is still hope for the Emperor?"

She shook her head, "No, Alfraed, he is dying. If they stopped bleeding him then he might live for longer but each day he is closer to death." I nodded, there was little to say in such circumstances. I did not think that I would have the luxury of dying in my bed. There were advantages to being a warring knight and not a sickly Emperor. "Did you have trouble reaching me?"

"Edward here was wounded by the men of the Count of Flanders. I fear our return will be as fraught with such danger."

She smiled at Edward, "I am sorry you suffered pain for me, Sir Edward. Fear not Baron, I will not hold you up when we leave."

I could not remain silent. "But your ladies and your servants might."

She shook her head, "No, for I take just two with me, Judith and Margaret. They are both Norman and are as tough and resilient as I

27

am. We will not need a carriage or a wagon. We will travel on horseback as you do."

I felt relieved. "Good. Now we need somewhere for the men to stay while we wait... well while we attend your majesty. We could camp close by the cavalry field if you wish."

"That will not be necessary. I have a small estate some five miles to the south and west of here. It is large enough to accommodate you and your men but..."

"But you would like some of us closer to hand."

She clapped her hands in delight, "You read my mind, Alfraed, but I would not expect any of you to sleep outside my door as Baron Alfraed once did." She patted the couch upon which she sat, " this will do I believe."

I turned to Rolf, "There are five of us."

Edward shook his head, "Six!"

I smiled, "Six then. We each do four hours on duty. With the travelling time to the estate this should be enough resting time. One of us will always be in attendance."

"Good." She rose and went to a chest by the door to her chamber. She lifted it, "Each time you return to the estate you should take some of this." She revealed her imperial regalia and her personal jewellery and treasure.

Edward whistled at the sight of so many jewels and crowns, "That is a king's ransom."

"Or an Empress' at any rate. There are those who would take what is mine from me. If we store this at the estate then its disappearance may go unnoticed." She held up her Imperial Crown. "This will need to stay until the funeral."

An official came to tell her that there were dignitaries from Denmark who wished to express their concerns. She rolled her eyes. After giving us the directions to the estate she left us. I pointed to the treasure before us. "We had better take some of these with us now. It seems to me a huge amount of jewellery. We are a big enough target without this. Every knight, lord and bandit will be after this treasure."

We took the small leather pouches containing the jewels and we each took one. Even then we had barely taken the top layer from the chest. We gathered our men with the eight horses Sir Guy had managed to buy and we headed west out of town. We left Rolf to have the first shift and moved towards our home for the next week or so. I smiled as I saw the looks as we left. They assumed we were going home; they did not know us. We were here to stay.

Chapter 3

The estate had been a fortified manor at some time in the past and had an old warrior hall. It was perfect for us. Ernst, who was the caretaker for the Empress, was a little taken aback when we arrived. Gottfried explained it all to him and our gold helped to ease his mind. We were not robbers.

"I will take the next shift. If you give me your armour, Edward, I will get it repaired." Already we were preparing for our departure. I had no idea how long we were staying it could be a day or it could be a month. We had to be ready to fly whenever that was. I summoned Dick, Aiden and Edgar.

"We may have to leave in the middle of the night. Dick and Aiden, I want you two totally familiar with every road and trail out of here. We may be pursued; in fact, I am certain that we will be pursued. You will have to be able to get us away from here unseen. Edgar, organise guards. We too, as well as the Empress, may be a target. Our enemies may decide to eliminate us and here it is an isolated spot. We stay vigilant. The men do not go into Worms. The last thing we need is for the men who serve the Count of Stuttgart to begin to whittle down our numbers. And make sure that all the horses Sir Guy bought are sound and broken in. We may well have to use them for the three ladies."

We explained the arrangements to Sir Guy. "When I was in the town I noticed bands of what can only be described as bandits. They were on every corner and in every ale house. They are like crows gathering over a corpse."

"Then when we go on duty we take our squires with us. We are too few to risk losing any."

I took Harold with me as I headed back into Worms. We already knew a good armourer from our previous visit and I dropped off the mail. By the time we reached the Empress' chambers it was time to change the shift. Rolf took me to one side. "It is as well you have brought Harold. There are many armed knights in the palace. When the Emperor dies then we will have to be on our guard."

"Is it imminent?"

"I do not know." He shook his head, "We are lucky, Alfraed, when we die it will be so sudden that we know nothing about it. I would hate to have to lie there and think about the mistakes I had made in my life and worry about the hereafter. Especially when surrounded by bloodsuckers and leeches."

"Where is the Empress now?"

He pointed to the inner chamber. "She is resting." He smiled, "You will have to endure the feast tonight! She will need a bodyguard."

I groaned. I hated having to eat amongst the lords and ladies. I preferred the company of my men or my family. I was not a sociable person. I took off my helmet and lowered my coif. "This will be a long night, Harold."

He shrugged, "When I think of the nights I froze in Sherwood then I will accept this, my lord. This seems quite a pleasant place in which to wait."

"You are right, I forget sometimes what a pampered life I had before I reached England."

"Do not worry, lord, you have made up for it since!"

The Empress came out followed by her two ladies, Judith and Margaret. Both were older than she was but not by much. She smiled when she saw me, "I feel safer already. These are my ladies in waiting. They will return to Caen with me."

I nodded, "I hope you will not find the journey too arduous, ladies."

"Do not fear, knight, Judith and I will not slow you down. We are Norman and we know how to ride."

I coloured. How had they known my fears?

Matilda laughed, "Do not tease Alfraed, Margaret; he and his men are the wall of iron which will protect our frail bodies. And now let us go down to meet those who play the false smiles of sympathy."

Harold and I followed the three of them to the Great Hall where the tables had been prepared. With so many visitors the room was packed. I saw that the Empress had arranged for five seats kept for us at the head table. It meant she was cocooned by her ladies on one side and Harold and me on the other. She would not have to make small talk. She was making us a barrier.

The room rose as we entered and was silent. The Empress sat down and then nodded to us; we sat. I will say that the servants at the palace were very well trained. The food must have been waiting just outside the hall for the moment we sat an army of liveried servants hurried in and began to place the wooden platters on the table. I watched as Judith and Margaret each took food from different platters and nibbled before nodding to the Empress. She chose only from the food they had tasted. I turned to Harold, "We must also act as food tasters. You try from that platter and I will try this."

I picked up a piece of mutton and ate it. Although it tasted greasy it did not appear to be poisoned. As the Empress reached over for a piece she murmured, "You learn quickly, Baron."

"Is it always like this? Do you constantly fear for your life?"

She looked sad as she gave a slight nod, "It is the reason I wish to return to Caen. There I can eat without fearing poison. I can sleep without guards and I can know that the smiles I see are real." She nibbled at the mutton and then wiped her hands on her napkin. Margaret poured some wine and drank a little. She wiped the rim and passed it to the Empress who nodded her thanks. She sipped and said, "Watch the Counts on the opposite side of the table. The three of them are as close as thieves."

"Why does Lothair of Supplinburg hate you and your husband so?"

As she spoke I stared at the three of them. "Lothair thought that he would be elected and he was not. He has the Pope's support and when Henry dies then he will become Emperor but he festers for he thinks of the years that Henry and I ruled. He will try to pay me back for the years he has waited. He is the only one who has not even shown false sympathy for my poor husband's condition."

"Then why allow him to stay?"

"Because as a Count of the Empire he has every right to be here."

"But he will try to stop you leaving."

"Oh yes. He will definitely try to bring harm to me."

I studied their faces. I had fought the Count of Stuttgart and knew that he was devious. The Count of Aachen was a plotter. This Count of Supplinburg appeared slightly more honest and yet he was the deadliest of the three.

I had been wrong. It was not a long night. The Empress stood after having partaken, albeit lightly, of each of the courses. "I will now retire, please stay and enjoy the hospitality of my husband's hall. I will see how he fares."

We followed her from the room and I felt eyes, like daggers, in our backs. "Come, we will see how poor Henry is."

When we entered the room, it smelled of candles and of death. The physicians we had seen before were gathered in a huddle. One of them approached Matilda as we neared the bed. "We have, as the Empress demanded, stopped bleeding the Emperor."

"And?"

"And he has a little more colour but his condition is not improving."

"But he is no worse?"

"No, highness."

"Then go back to you books and find a cure. I will visit with my husband now."

The gaggle of physicians hurried out. The Empress went to a jug of water and dampened a cloth with it. She tenderly swiped his face. She stood silently for a moment and then leaned forward to speak quietly in his ear. She kissed him lightly on his forehead and turned to us. I saw that she had wept a little.

"They have used drugs to make him sleep. He does not appear to be in pain. Let us return to my rooms." As we passed the guards she said, "Abelard, let no one enter save the doctors. No one!"

He nodded, "Yes highness."

Once we entered the antechamber to her room she flung herself down on the couch and began to sob. Margaret and Judith comforted her while Harold and I looked helplessly at each other. Margaret stood and came towards us as the Empress' sobs subsided. "It shows the faith she has in you, my lord that she weeps openly before you."

"I thought that she and the Emperor were estranged."

"No, my lord. They were never enamoured of each other; it was a political marriage but they were fond of one another." She shook her head, "If the Emperor were a dog then he would have been put out of his misery long ago. There is no dignity in this long lingering death." She saw my look of surprise. "I would have given him a draught myself to ease his pain were it not for the fact the finger of blame would be laid at the door of the Empress and she has even more enemies than the Emperor."

We had been in the corner speaking quietly and the Empress rose. "I am sorry for my weakness."

"You are a woman first, your highness and then an Empress."

She nodded, "Now let us talk of after. My ladies know that the journey will be hard. What are your plans; I know that you will have made some."

I took a deep breath. I had been thinking, while watching the three Counts at the feast how we could escape. I did have an idea but it would need the compliance of the three women. "I know that you can all ride but can you ride as men? Can you straddle a horse?"

Judith giggled. "I had a husband once, I think I can straddle!"

When the other two laughed I felt relief. "I will have three surcoats made for you and buy helmets. You need not wear armour but I will disguise you as men at arms. No one notices men at arms and you can ride in the midst of my men. When we leave they will look at our faces at the head of the column. You three, in the middle, will be invisible. The swords you will wear will be uncomfortable but this will just be until we are out of Worms."

"You would ride through Worms? In full view of our enemies?"

"If they try to prevent us leaving it may be the safest way. Once we are past Worms then my men will take us down secret routes but if we pass through Worms seemingly without you then we will be safe, at least for a while, and they will not try to stop us. If we left with you in plain sight then Lothair of Supplinburg would prevent us from leaving."

"I think it will work but how will you hide our hair? Would you have us shear it?"

It was my turn to smile. I showed her my helmet. "Do you see how we have a cap within the helmet to cushion blows and to prevent chafing? You will not need protection for you will not be fighting and your hair can be tied up underneath the helm and it will be a good fit."

"You could have us wear a coif beneath the helmet and that would hide our lack of beards."

"Not all of my men wear such facial hair but it is a good idea. I will make the arrangements tomorrow."

There was a knock at the door and when we opened it Edward and Gille were there. They looked at us expectantly.

"We have had a quiet evening. I hope you are rested."

"Aye, my lord."

I bowed to the three women. "Then I shall make the arrangements tomorrow. Good night." Taking more pouches of the jewels, we slipped out of the Empress' quarters.

When we left the palace, it was night. Although not yet midnight it was late enough that there were few people around. As we reached the gates to the city I noticed more guards on duty than there had been. They let us out and the gates slammed ominously behind us. It was just a few miles to our bed for the night but I kept glancing around. Something did not feel right. We could see nothing for it was a cloudy night and there was no moon.

"Harold, you are a man of the woods, does everything seem as it should be?"

"No, Baron. I cannot put my finger on it but it feels, uncomfortable and threatening. There are no noises in the woods to our side."

"Draw your sword."

I pulled my shield around to my side. It was pitch black. The only way we knew our route was by the stones before us. Our horses' hooves clattered and that was the single sound we heard. The hiss of my sword as it slid from the scabbard was hidden when Scout neighed. There was danger ahead.

I turned to Harold and whispered, "Ambush! Ride like the devil himself is after us."

I leaned forward over Scout's mane and spurred him. He leapt forward. There were half a dozen cracks as crossbows were released. I felt one as it pinged off my helmet. The rest flew above us. We had sprung the trap but not yet escaped it. I heard German shouts behind us and the sound of hooves on the road. Suddenly four horses loomed up out of the dark. I jerked my reins to the right knowing that Harold would tuck in behind me. We would rely on our shields and fight those to our right. I ducked beneath the sword which swung at my head and stabbed forwards with my sword. I heard it tear across the mail of armour. As I pulled it back I heard a grunt of pain. I barely had time to bring up my sword to block the next sword strike. Fortunately, we were travelling faster than the ones who had sprung the ambush.

I felt something strike my saddle. As I glanced behind me I saw Harold finishing off the man at arms I had wounded. It was too dark to make out who they were but I could see from the moving shadows that there were at least ten men chasing down the road. This would be a race to the estate of the Empress.

"Harold, ride as fast as you can and keep your head down!"

"Aye my lord."

He came level with me and I spurred Scout. The two horses were used to running alongside one another and they settled into a ground eating rhythm. It was so dark that I was disorientated. Had it not been for the Roman cobbles beneath Scout's hooves then I would have been lost. I was thankful that the natural woodsman in Harold came to our aid. "My lord, I can smell wood smoke. We are close to the hall!"

I took a chance and began to yell, "Norton! Ho! Norton!"

I glanced over my shoulder and saw the mailed men were less than thirty paces from us. They were gaining, slowly but surely. They had big powerful horses. I wondered if we would make the safety of the estate. Harold rarely let me down and from what he had said we were tantalisingly close. I saw a lightening of the woods to our left. It was the road which led to the gates. As we began to turn into it I saw two of my archers release arrows. I heard Edgar yell. "Keep going, my lord! We will protect you!"

Despite his words I could not leave my men to fight my battles. I wheeled Scout around as I heard the shouts from behind and the clamour of arms. My men had run from the hall in ones and twos. They jabbed spears at the men who desperately sought my life. One man at arms managed to knock my man at arms, Peter of Totnes, to the ground and he charged at me. I brought my shield horizontally across my body as I swung my blade at him. His sword smashed into my shield making it and my arm shiver with the shock. He rode into my blade with such force that it almost tore it from my grip. It ripped through his mail, his gambeson and his stomach. He fell from the horse and lay writhing on the ground.

The others had had enough. Leaving four of their number behind the rest fled. Rolf and Sir Guy ran up to me. "What happened?"

"They waited in ambush not far from Worms. They were after me. We saw more guards at the gate than there should have been."

Sir Guy reached up to the cantle of my saddle and broke off two bolts. "It seems that God watched you this night. Here are two crossbow bolts. A hand span higher and you would now be dead, my friend."

"We will need to escort the Empress' protectors from now on."

Once we had searched the dead and thrown the bodies into the ditches we went into the hall. Carl said, "They had nothing to identify them. The coins, however, were not from Flanders, they were imperial silver."

I laughed, "It seems our value is diminishing. At least Count Charles pays gold for our corpses."

Rolf shook his head and he had a worried look upon his face. "This is no laughing matter, Baron. We have barely arrived and already they seek our death."

"Rolf, we knew this would happen. It is my fault for not taking precautions. But we have survived and now we can be on our guard."

We put the jewels with the ones we had brought earlier and I explained my plan to them. "I will ride in with you tomorrow, Gottfried. We will take all of the men at arms. Let us have a show of force. I will order the spare surcoats and helmets. Carl, if you come with us then you might hear news of the perpetrators of this ambush."

Sir Guy said, "It is obvious."

"Is it? There are three candidates unless you think they are all acting together. I am not certain that this Lothair would want us dead before he is Emperor. If he is elected then he can kill us legally. No, I would know who seeks us dead now."

Rolf nodded, "And then you would do something about it."

"Better to strike first than wait for the knife in the night."

When I was awakened I felt as though I had barely slept. Edward was returned and Sir Guy was on duty. My archers had escorted them for the changeover. While I ate Dick and Aiden told me the results of their exploration. "The main road has many roads and trails leading from it." Dick took a piece of charcoal from the hearth and, using the wooden table, drew a map. "If we leave by the main road, which I believe is your intention?" I nodded, "Then here," he drew a circle, "the road turns and there is a trail to the south and one to the north. If we turn north then any pursuers will either carry on or think we have gone south."

"North is in the wrong direction."

Aiden grinned, "Aye my lord but the trail north forks a mile or so further on and then swings to cross the road again. Then it heads south west. We followed it for ten miles. There it meets another Roman Road which heads west."

"Good! You have done well."

When we reached the gate of Worms I looked more carefully at the sentries who stood there. Were they the same ones who had watched us leave? Their numbers were much less now, in day light and yet they should not have been. It confirmed that there was a conspiracy. I suspected the Count of Aachen. He appeared to know Worms well. He had been here on our last visit. As we left the horses in the main square Gottfried and his man at arms continued on to relieve Sir Guy. We had left Edward sleeping. His first duty had tired him. He was still recovering from his wound. Carl and two men at arms headed for a tavern and the gossip while Harold and I made for the market area. With the surcoats ordered and the helmets purchased we walked back towards the main square.

I noticed just how many armed men there were. Each day, more arrived as the death of the Emperor grew closer. We heard the sound of hooves approaching and we moved towards the side of the square. The horses sounded as though they were travelling at speed. A column of knights and men at arms hurtled through the square scattering stalls and those who could not get out of the way fast enough. Harold shook his head, "What was that about, my lord?"

"I am not certain but the livery looked to be that of Stuttgart. I didn't recognise any of the knights." I had fought the Count and two of his men at a tourney when we had last been in Worms. "If I had recognised the knights then it might have been an attempt to intimidate me."

Carl hurried across the square to meet us. "Come, we should go." He had a serious look on his face. "I will explain when we are on the road."

Once we had left the gates he told us what he had learned. "The three counts all have their forces spread just outside the walls. Last night might have been a coincidence for the men of Aachen are camped close by that road."

"That was no coincidence but carry on."

"Archbishop Adelbert is coming here to speak with the Empress."

"You make that sound as though it is significant."

"It is. The Emperor gave the imperial insignia to the Empress for safekeeping. A new Emperor cannot be elected until the insignia is in the Archbishop's hands."

"And the Archbishop is Lothair's man."

"Now you see the significance. If Lothair can get his hands on the insignia then both the Emperor and the Empress are no longer needed. They could be removed. Hence the number of soldiers in the town."

"And what about those riders who just charged through the town?"

"They are trying to show the burghers that they rule this place. The Empress is popular and they are trying to isolate her."

"Then we had better plan to leave sooner rather than later."

When Harold and I returned to relieve Rolf, we found that he was standing guard outside the chapel. He nodded, "The Archbishop is within." He pointed to a door leading to another antechamber. "Our friends, the three counts, are in there." He smiled cynically, "They said they would use the chapel to pray for the Emperor when the Archbishop had finished speaking with the Empress."

I quickly told him what Carl had discovered. His face fell, "Then we do not have long."

I shook my head, "I think we should plan on leaving tomorrow."

"But the Emperor is not dead." He shook his head. "We cannot. As much as I would like to it would be even more dangerous to flee. Our enemies could proclaim whatever they wished. The Empress and the Archbishop must be at Henry's side when he dies."

This was an impossible situation. Whatever we did the Empress would be in danger. My thoughts were interrupted when the Archbishop came out. He was holding a small casket. I guessed that this contained the imperial insignia. I found myself being scrutinised by this representative of the Pope. "This is the young knight I have heard so much about; the one who rescued you." He made the sign of the cross, "The church blesses you Baron Alfraed. We are much indebted to you."

Just then the door behind us opened. I could feel six eyes staring at my back. The Archbishop looked beyond me and smiled, "And now I must speak with these three scions of the Empire. Come my sons; let us go into the chapel and pray for the Emperor."

As we led the Empress back to her quarters I saw that she had been weeping. Once in her rooms she said, "It is done. The moment that Henry dies then I lose all of my power. His estates will go to his nephew and I will be sent to a nunnery."

I laughed, "No you will not! You have six knights who will take you back to your father. We have the surcoats being made even as we speak. Half of your treasure has been taken already and by the time dawn breaks it will all be gone. You and your ladies just need to be ready to go as soon as the funeral is over."

"But he is not dead!"

"But he is close, is he not?"

"Yes, but how did you know?"

"When I was in Constantinople I had to stand guard over a strategos who was dying from the wasting sickness. He died during my watch. He looked much as your husband did towards the end. Have you been in yet this afternoon?" She shook her head. "Rolf, you and your man at arms head back to the estate. Have supplies readied so that we can leave quickly. We will see how the Emperor is."

The two of them put the pouches of jewels beneath their surcoats and left.

"Where are your ladies?"

"They are within."

"Get them, we shall need them." When they joined us I said, "When we return have any of the clothes you wish to take with us prepared. Harold and I will take them with us."

"We are leaving?"

"Not yet but, unless I miss my guess, it will not be long. We may have to adapt my plan."

The long faces of the physicians told their own story. "Empress! We have not bled him but he is worsening!" There was a priest hovering nearby. His assistant was swinging a censor while he intoned prayers above him.

Suddenly one of the physicians put his hand on the Emperor's chest. "I fear he is dead!"

Another said, "Hold a glass to his mouth. Sometimes his breathing is so shallow that he appears dead."

They held a glass and a tiny amount of moisture formed. "He lives still."

The door was suddenly opened and the Archbishop stood there with the three counts. The Archbishop frowned when he saw Harold and me there while the Count of Stuttgart almost erupted like a volcano. "What is that Norman doing in the presence of the Emperor?"

"He is with me, Count and I am still Empress whilst my husband lives."

The Archbishop smiled, "Peace. We should all close our eyes and pray for the soul of the Emperor."

The others might have closed their eyes but I would not. I trusted not one of them.

The Emperor was tough and he clung on to life but, an hour after the Archbishop had entered the room, he died. In England we would have said, *'the King is dead, long live the King'* but here there was no natural successor. The Archbishop blessed Matilda and said, "We are sorry for your loss."

She nodded, "If you would all leave me I would like to spend a few moments alone with my husband."

I knew that I was included and we all left the room and stood in the antechamber. The Archbishop must have been well prepared by the others. "What will you do now, Baron Alfraed? Return to England?"

I saw his three companions watching me intently. "I will ask the Empress what she wishes me to do."

Count Lothair snapped, "She is not Empress any longer."

I was not certain about the protocols but I was fairly certain that the title would still be hers; more importantly she had to have a title for her own security. "Correct me if I am wrong but until there is a new Emperor, who is married, then my lady will still be an Empress."

The Archbishop was a shrewd man and he knew that I spoke the truth. He nodded, "Let us not concern ourselves with titles. A great man has died let us think on him and his soul."

As soon as Matilda left the room I made sure that Harold and I flanked her. I did not think they would do her harm but I wanted none of them any closer to her than they had to be.

When Edward relieved us, he told us that the gates were now manned by the men of Lothair of Supplinburg. "Did they stop you entering?"

"No, but they tried to frighten me." I smiled; that was impossible. "I laughed at their pathetic attempts. I am not certain, however, how we will manage to leave without a fight."

"I have that in hand." Harold and I took the clothes the women would need and we left. As we neared the gate I saw what Edward had meant. It was like a siege except here the danger was from within. Two knights held up their hands. "Where do you think you are going?"

"Back to the estate of the Empress. She wishes us to return these clothes to her estate. She has need of black for the funeral."

I could see that I had confused them. I held up the medallion. "This is the authority of the Empress; we need to pass."

One of them sneered, "Only until after the funeral Norman and then you have no protection."

I smiled, "God will watch over me!"

I was pleased that my men had made all the necessary preparations for flight. When Rolf and the Swabians heard about the men at the gate they were angry. "Alfraed, let us return tomorrow. We will stay by the Empress until the funeral. There is no danger to us but there is for you and your men. You cannot leave during darkness."

"What about Edward?"

"We will keep him with us until daylight. He can pick up the surcoats and we will stay by the Empress until the funeral."

I was going to argue but Sir Guy said, "It makes sense. The more they see you the more chance there is of a confrontation and the Empress' life would be in even more danger. Let them think they have cowed you. Do not let a stiff neck bring disaster."

I nodded my acceptance. They were right.

We spent the rest of that night packing jewels and coins into bags placed in the saddles of our horses. We would spread them out. I expected to lose some but the Empress had nothing else to show for her time as Empress; we would take her treasure home for her.

We kept out of the town for the next day. We had nothing we could do there for everyone was busy with the funeral arrangements and I did not wish to aggravate the situation. We stayed at the estate. The horses had all been well rested and, more importantly, well fed. Sir Guy had sent a rider back to his uncle informing him of the death of the Emperor. I hoped we could still rely on him but, if we could not then we would find another route to take the Empress to safety. There was a grindstone at the hall and all of our edged weapons were sharpened. I had the surcoats for the three women all ready for them. The hard part would be to get them to safety. I had, with the help of Sir Guy and Edward, conjured a plan which we hoped would allow us to escape. If it failed, then it would be a bloodbath.

Chapter 4

We set off for the town before first light. I took only my men at arms. They looked resplendent in their surcoats with matching shields. My archers and Aiden had other work ahead of them. Sir Guy and his men at arms entered Worms by a separate gate. I hoped that our enemies would not notice such small numbers. We were admitted for the whole of Worms was filled with mourners there for the funeral of Henry, Holy Roman Emperor. We dismounted and formed a line on the road leading to the cathedral. As a mark of respect, we took off our helmets. When the body passed us, we bowed our heads. Empress Matilda followed, dressed in black and with head bowed leading a jet-black war horse on which the Emperor's sword and helmet hung. Judith and Margaret were with her and Rolf followed with his knights and men at arms.

The service took an interminable length of time. I was keenly aware of the passage of time. Many of the people outside drifted off leaving just soldiers standing. That in itself was ominous for we saw the surcoats of Stuttgart, Aachen and Supplinburg. It made our numbers appear even smaller. The soldiers of the three counts outnumbered us by over eight to one. We could not predict when the funeral rites would end but we had to time our departure well or else we might all die. Although I did not think anyone would begin trouble before the Emperor was buried I just did not know.

The Empress Matilda left the cathedral and she passed amongst the thinned crowd, with her ladies, distributing coins to the needy. When she passed us, she glanced up and gave a half smile. The imperial nobles and the Archbishop followed next and I saw them give us stares. They were not friendly looks. We were now the enemy and, with the Emperor's death, fair game. So far it was all going to plan but it could still go awry. Once the last of the mourners had passed we followed but instead of heading to the palace we went towards the western gate and headed down the road leading to the west and Normandy. I knew every eye was upon us. I also knew that our enemies had spies who would be ensuring that we left their city. We rode leisurely down the road. After five miles we stopped, ostensibly to check our girths but in reality, to waste time.

I had planned everything but I hated this part of the plan. Sir Guy and the Swabian knights would be escorting the Empress from the palace to her estate. All eyes would be upon them. They had to leave quickly before night fell. The people of Worms would understand that the Empress needed to be on her own to grieve, away from the sad memories of the palace. If it was after dark I had no doubt that Lothair would try to capture her. He could not do so with her people waving and watching.

We waited until Aiden arrived. He appeared without warning from the trees to the north. "There are thirty men at arms, lord and they are to the south of you between you and the estate of the Empress. They are keeping pace with you."

"It is as we thought. And the Empress?"

"Another fifty men follow her."

"Do they wear a livery?"

"No, Baron, they are the sweepings of the gutter."

That made sense. When the Empress and her guards were killed then it would be put down to bandits. It would also explain the theft of the imperial regalia which the counts would have assumed she had with them.

"Good, ride to Dick and warn him."

He hesitated, "Do you not need me, Baron?"

"I do but the Empress and the others need you more."

As he rode away I donned my helmet. My men followed suit. We rode west on the same course we had started. This time we rode faster. I almost smiled as I imagined the problems the men who were following us would have. We were travelling on a wide Roman Road and we rode three abreast. They had to ride in the forest and would be lucky to ride in single file. Our earlier speed would have lulled them into a false sense of security. After two miles, I raised my spear and the whole line turned. We plunged into the forest and headed south east. Our move was so sudden that the first man at arms I killed thought that I was one of his own men. He turned to greet me as I punched my lance into his chest. We were attacking them on the side away from their shields and it was too easy. Our lances punched, stabbed and slaughtered the ragged line of men at arms. They were led by one knight and Harold killed him. He jabbed with his lance and took the knight in the throat. The lance broke and the knight died. Aiden's sharp eyes and skills had saved us and ensured that our would-be attackers died to a man.

We could afford no witnesses and my men at arms slit the throat of every man we had downed. We took what they had and hobbled most of the horses. The others we led as we headed towards the estate of the Empress.

When Matilda had left Worms, she had had four knights and a handful of men at arms to guard her. The fifty bandits would already be counting their money. They knew that they outnumbered those within the estate. It would not be a battle it would be a sneaky assault in the dead of night. They were attacking under cover of darkness and against a force which was better suited to an open battlefield rather than the confined spaces of a hall and a forest. They reckoned without Dick and his archers of Sherwood. We came across the first of the dead bandits a mile from the estate. As we neared the hall we saw more of them. Whoever led them had realised his problem and the survivors formed a shield wall close to the hall. There were still many of them.

I lowered my lance and we charged. It was not a solid line which charged them; the trees stopped that but these were not knights, nor were they men at arms. I jabbed my lance at an axe wielding giant who tried to take Scout's head. My lance shattered as it smashed into his head. I drew my sword and swung at the warrior with the spear who braced it against a tree as he tried to defend himself from me. I smote the haft and it broke in two. I halted Scout and brought my blade across his throat. A handful of these hired killers ran from the woods towards the hall. Sir Guy and his men at arms flooded from the hall and their lives were ended quickly.

As Rolf and his Swabians came out I heard the screams and shouts in the forest as the last of the raiders were slaughtered. When Dick and Aiden reached me with broad grins upon their faces then I knew that we had won. We had no time to lose. "Quickly, let us leave while we may."

The Empress and her two ladies came out dressed in helmets and surcoats. At close range, they would not pass for warriors; they were too thin and waif like but, in a column of real warriors, they might pass unnoticed. We now had more than enough horses and we would be able to ride hard and fast, changing horses when we needed to. By dawn I intended to be at least forty miles away from the estate of the Empress. I knew we would be followed but a chase would tire our pursuers. If we could reach Bar then we had a chance; a slim one but a chance nonetheless. The three ladies were placed in a circle of my best men at arms. The three were almost invisible amongst the giants who protected them.

With Dick and his archers well ahead and the Swabians, Edward and Edgar guarding the Empress, Sir Guy and I were the rearguard. Aiden was off in the woods, disguising our trail and watching for

44

pursuit. The work Dick and Aiden had done paid off and, as afternoon drew on, the next day, we found ourselves forty miles away from Worms. We had bought ourselves some time. However, even with spare horses, our mounts could go no further and we camped just off the trail. We had a fifth of our men on guard at any one time. The only ones who slept well were the three ladies. For the rest of us it was two hours sentry duty and snatched sleep.

I was on watch with some of my men at arms when I sensed someone approaching. I drew my sword and then breathed a sigh of relief when I realised that it was the Empress. She had the sense to come close to me and speak quietly. She was the daughter of King Henry; she knew that sound travels far at night. "Thank you, Baron. You have given us a chance to escape."

I smiled and pointed to the trees, "We are not out of the woods yet."

She giggled and was suddenly a young girl again. "It seems like years since I laughed."

"We have hope, at least. We will be pursued and we will have to fight but the odds are more in our favour than they were."

She gripped my arm, "Will men die?" I nodded, "Because of me?"

"We all die, my lady. It is how we die that is important." She wrapped her cloak around herself even more tightly. "Why do Lothair and the others care what happens to you? You are leaving Germany. What harm can you do them?"

"When my father was ill I was sent to rule the parts of Italy where there was dissension." She shrugged, "I enjoyed the work and the people appeared to like me. They were sad when I was summoned back to my husband's side. You saw yourself that those in Worms liked me. I think they fear me because I am popular."

"But Sallic law means that you cannot rule."

"I know but their fear is that someone will marry me and become Emperor because of my popularity. That will be my fate. Someone will be chosen by my father and I will have to marry them."

I felt sorry for the Empress. She had had no choice in her husband and now was like a prize animal to be auctioned to the highest bidder. I saw too clearly why they wanted her. It was not to do her harm but to force her into a marriage. I would make sure she reached Caen safely then her life was in her own hands.

"You had better get back to your bed, my lady. We have long days ahead and you will need your rest."

She turned to go back to the fire. She looked over her shoulder, "What of you and your men? Do you not need rest?"

"We are hardened to the rigours of the road. Do not worry about our men. They are all sworn to protect you. The only way anyone will get to you is if we all lie dead around you."

"I pray that will never happen, Alfraed."

I nodded, "As do we."

While we broke camp the next day I sought out Edgar. "I want three of our best men at arms assigned to protect the three ladies. From what I have learned the aim is not to harm the Empress but to capture her."

"It leaves us short, my lord, if I have three good men out of a battle."

"Nonetheless that is my order. Impress upon them that they keep them safe even if it means deserting us."

"Aye my lord."

As we rode west I smiled at the efforts of the three ladies not to show their discomfort. My men and I were used to the hard saddles we used. We had all ridden for eight hours a day for many years. The ladies could ride but our saddles were not easy on the posterior. I watched as they surreptitiously stood in the saddle to ease the pain for a few moments and then saw them wince as they regained their seats.

Aiden and my archers were spread out both ahead and behind us. Already we were beyond the trails that they had discovered and we were riding the main road to the south and west. One danger was that it would bring us perilously close to France and King Louis. He would not seek the Empress' hand but he might use her to buy the support of a potential suitor. This was a dangerous game we were playing. We had to negotiate a maze and the obstacles could be deadly. I turned as I heard hooves thundering up the road. Aiden galloped up to me, "My lord, there are horsemen behind us."

"How far away?"

"A mile or two."

"How many?"

"At least fifty."

"Find Dick and the archers, bring them to me." As he galloped off I shouted to the others, "There is pursuit. We ride hard until my archers return." I turned to Guy. "If they catch us then we turn with our men at arms and charge them. They will not expect it and it will buy us time." He nodded.

I spurred Scout to reach the horses with the lances. They were strapped in bundles of ten. I unstrapped a bundle. I grabbed one and the rest fell to the floor. My men at arms stopped, grabbed one and continued to ride hard. We did not have the luxury of being able to stop and choose the best weapon. I kept glancing over my shoulder to see where the pursuit was. When this road had been built the Romans had cleared both sides of trees. Over the last six hundred years the forest had grown back and what had been a place safe from ambush was now a potential death trap as bushes had grown in ditches which had not been maintained and trees had spread their branches across the road.

Roger of Lincoln was the last man for he had picked up the last lance. "Baron! They are less than half a mile behind."

I nodded, "Harold, tell Sir Edward to keep going. We will try to delay them. Have Dick and the archers make an ambush."

"Aye my lord."

As he rode off I slowed down Scout. "Rearguard, about turn." The turn took time and I saw the enemy horsemen. They were coming in a column. Their speed meant that there were gaps. "A line of five men!"

I was in the fore with Sir Guy and his squire. Roger of Lincoln and Peter of Totnes were the other two. We lowered our lances. "Charge!"

The enemy had no lances. It is hard to ride with a lance. They had been pursuing us and hoped to take us with their swords. They saw what we intended and drew their weapons whilst pulling around their shields. What they did not manage to do was to form ranks. We did not have much speed but we were knee to knee. The leader was before me and I saw his banner behind him. He was one of the Count of Aachen's men. I pulled back my lance and punched hard. I had no lance coming towards me and my shield was protecting me from his sword. The spear drove through his mail and into his stomach. He rolled from his horse taking the broken end of the lance with him. I used the stump to knock his squire to the ground where his falling banner managed to force another rider into the woods.

Our sudden charge had taken them by surprise. I drew my sword and smashed it against the shield of a knight who approached me. I saw a lance come from behind and the German was skewered. Although we were outnumbered the German men at arms did not know that. They just saw a wall of men and horses. With the leader and the banner down they were confused and I saw them halt. I reined Scout in and stabbed at a confused looking man at arms. My sword punctured his shoulder. He turned and rode east. I saw others joining him.

"Back to the column. Ride!"

As I turned I sheathed my sword and I saw that two of Sir Guy's men at arms had fallen. We passed their bodies as we headed west. Their horses galloped alongside us. Sir Guy and I were at the rear of the column. Three of my men still had lances. They would be a valuable commodity if we continued to be attacked; we could not replace them. I looked over my shoulder. The horsemen had reformed and now pursued us. Our turn had told them of our numbers. We did not ride at the gallop. We did not want to weaken our horses. The cobbles over which we rode would warn us if they closed.

Sir Guy flicked his head to the side. "Will your archers be in position?"

I nodded, "But do not expect to see them. We will know where they are when the men behind begin to fall."

"It is a pity there are only ten of them."

"There will be eleven. Harold is as good an archer as any and those eleven can release forty arrows or more in the time it takes for a column to pass them. It is a surprise we can spring so long as we have arrows."

I heard hooves closing and glanced behind. They were less than a hundred paces from us now. "Be ready to turn on my command. They are closing."

I saw that they all drew their swords, as Sir Guy and I did. I had held my shield loosely and I now tightened it against my side. I caught a tiny movement to my left as we turned to descend slightly. I looked again to see what I had spied and I saw the first of the arrows from Dick and my archers as they released them at less than fifty paces. They struck with such force that even when their shields stopped them the power made the riders reel. The ones who did not stop the arrows found the arrows deeply embedded in their bodies. As we came around the bend and down the slope I saw that Edward and Rolf had disobeyed me. The dismounted men at arms were arrayed behind them with a forest of spears. My men knew what to do. They split in two and rode behind the human barricade. We turned and faced the enemy. They could not outflank us for we occupied the eaves of the forest. They tried to pull up as the German men at arms stabbed forward with their spears. I was happy to see that my three bodyguards had, at least, obeyed orders and the three ladies were mounted and safely behind the horses of the dismounted men at arms.

I kicked Scout forward and rode at a man at arms who was trying to turn away from the spears. I swung my sword at head height. It bit through his coif into his neck. He tumbled to the ground. Edgar brought his mighty sword down to split the helmet and skull of a second man at arms. With Dick and the archers continuing to release arrows into the backs of the pursuers the inevitable happened. The survivors fled. They had left so many dead along the road that I knew they would not return. Others might come but this conroi would never dare to face a foe such as us.

"Dismount and change horses. Despatch the enemy wounded. You have done well!"

They all cheered and the men at arms slapped each other on the back. We had routed a superior force. Already the men at arms and archers were searching the bodies for the spoils of war. Such was our life. One moment your life was in danger and you had the prospect of a brutal death and then you were victorious and loving life.

I took off my helmet and pushed my coif from my head. I was pouring with sweat. "Edgar, make sure that there are no injuries amongst our men. Even minor cuts need healing."

"Aye, my lord. This is where we miss Wulfric."

"It is. When we return to England we will see about hiring a healer."

"If we get a priest who can heal it will ease the men's minds, my lord. They fight harder if they know a priest will give them the last rites."

"I will think on it." I led Scout to the spare horses.

The Empress and her ladies had dismounted too. They approached. "Can we do anything to help, Baron?"

"We will let you know. How are the saddles this morning?"

Margaret gave me a rueful smile. "When we reach Caen, I swear I will never ride a horse again. I know not how you do it each day and wearing mail!"

I laughed, "You get used to it and I fear we have many leagues to go. I can offer you no comfort until we reach the land of the Count Du Bar."

The Empress watched as the dead men were thrown into the ditches. "And can we expect more of this?"

"Not for a while. They have a long journey back to report their failure. I have no doubt that others seek us but these must have been the closest. We now have another five horses. The more horses we have then the more changes we can make and a faster journey."

Margaret groaned, "And that means longer in the saddle."

I nodded, "I think at least three more days before we reach Bar and we shall now be in the saddle for every moment that the sun shines."

"And when we reach Bar then we will be safe, Baron?"

"No, Judith. The dangers will increase for ahead of us will be only enemies. To the north is the Count of Flanders and to the South is King Louis. We will not be able to out run them. We will have to outwit and out think them."

Judith looked at the Empress and shook her head, "My lady is he always this cheerful?"

Laughing, the Empress Matilda said, "He is always this honest and that is what I love about him. It is refreshing after the false smiles of the court. Fear not ladies. These men will ensure we reach safety. Of that I have no doubt."

I was remarkably accurate with my forecast and Aiden and Dick returned three days later to tell us that they had seen the castle of Bar in the distance and, more importantly, that they had met the Count's knights who were watching for us. As we headed west I rode with my knights and we discussed what we would do after Bar.

"Sir Guy, will you be halting at La Cheppe or continuing west?"

"My heart tells me to follow you to Caen but I will speak with my uncle first." He shrugged, "Whether I like it or not I live in the Empire. And we are so close to the French border that I fear my uncle and I may have to accept the over lordship of Lothair of Supplinburg even if we are unhappy about the fact."

"And Rolf, what of you three?"

"We and our men serve the Empress." He laughed, "We are her army."

"I think she needs to recruit more."

"As you know, Alfraed there is a world of difference between hiring swords and finding worthy men. You were more than lucky with Edward here."

"I know. Then the question we need to answer is, which route do we take after La Cheppe?"

50

We rode in silence. I saw, in the distance, the sturdy castle which promised us safety and security for the first time in many days. Sir Guy said, "I would suggest a ride north west to Rheims and then a dash to Normandy."

It was a good suggestion. Rolf said, "I agree but you should know that Rheims is part of the land ruled by the Count of Aachen. We dare not risk the town."

"Then, Sir Guy, I will have to take the advice of your uncle. It seems that we have three routes to safety and all are dangerous." I slowed Scout down, "Do not let the Empress know of our fears. It can do her no good."

Edward said, "I admire the three of them. They have not complained and they have not slowed us down. I have fought alongside men who have whined more!"

Rolf nodded, "I hope she finds a good husband now. She has been used as a pawn already. It is time she made her own choices."

The Count looked relieved to see his nephew. He was a courteous old knight and he bowed and scraped to the Empress. With no daughters of his own it was obvious to me that he had transferred that affection to the young Empress. While she and her ladies were taken to a bed for the first time since we had left Worms, the Count took me to one side.

"I fear, Baron Alfraed, that a net is closing upon the Empress. She is valuable. The Count of Flanders is considering taking her to be his bride. He would then have a claim to both England and the Empire. So many of the counts of the Empire desire her that it is terrifying." He looked, for the first time since I had known him, worried.

"Do we bring danger by our presence?"

There was a flicker across his face which showed he was worried and then he said, "Of course not."

I smiled. He still reminded me of my father. "Fear not Count, we will stay no longer than we have to and I will not endanger Sir Guy anymore. He can remain at La Cheppe."

I saw the relief on the old knight's face. He had a sense of honour and he had been torn. He clasped my arm, "You are an honourable knight. My nephew could do worse than emulate you." he put his arm around my shoulders as he led me to his hall. "My sons told me of your skill as a leader. King Henry is lucky to have you."

I shrugged, "The safety of the Empress is my only concern."

He shook his head, "I do not envy you the next part of your journey. No matter which way you go there will be danger."

"The question I ask you, Count, is where will be the least danger for us?"

"Avoid Rheims. The Count of Aachen has yet to extend his hand. He is powerful and he is an ally of the Count of Flanders. It would not surprise if he did not capture the Empress merely to give her to Charles. It would increase his power. He has no desire to be Emperor but he would influence whoever holds that office."

I nodded, "Then we go south and risk Louis."

"It would have been my suggestion too. If you do survive then this will have been the most remarkable of journeys."

Chapter 5

We left the Count and the safety of his castle two days later. We had dallied there longer than I would have liked but we needed horses shoeing and armour repairing. From what the Count had said the latter part of our journey would be much harder than the former. Sir Guy would leave us at La Cheppe. It was the Empress who forbade him to follow us.

"Sir Guy, you and your men have done more than enough. I would not have you risk your lands. The Baron and my Swabians will be enough. If not then it is God's will that I be taken and forced to marry another." I felt a thrill as she smiled at me when she spoke those words. She believed that we would survive and that she trusted me. I hoped I would justify her faith.

We stayed one night in La Cheppe and Sir Guy escorted us north to the junction of the French and Imperial borders. He had found a place which was far from the nearest French castle. "I feel I have let you down, my lady."

She had smiled and handed him a pouch. "Here is a token of my esteem. Buy knights and men at arms. I am no longer the Empress but I would have the Empire protected by knights such as you."

Once we left Sir Guy I felt almost naked. We had lost ten good warriors and we were heading into unknown territory; the land of the French. The Empress and her ladies still rode horses but the need for a disguise was gone. They travelled as ladies. We had managed to get them three side saddles and that made life much easier. If we met the French then there was a chance that her Imperial status might help us.

The land through which we passed had more open spaces where we could be seen from a greater distance. At those times, we kept the archers closer. Although we had not exhausted their supply of arrows we could not be profligate with them. I wanted Dick within earshot should we be attacked.

Our aim was Rouen. It was Norman and it had good defences. We would be safe when we reached its solid walls. We had over sixty miles of France to traverse. Although I intended to avoid any castles and towns the road did not help us. We would have to camp once more and to keep a good guard at night. We stayed well to the south of the road to Cambrai and Flanders. I began to believe that we might make it unobserved. The weather helped us for it was dull and drizzly which hid us from view. It was as we passed Laon, late one afternoon that we were spotted. The rain deserted us and the sun shone down upon us, glinting from our armour and our weapons. We had travelled as far from the borders of France and the enemies in the Empire as we could but had we gone any further north then we would have risked running into the men of Flanders.

A column of men left the castle and the town. They headed towards us.

"Do we run, my lord?"

I shook my head, "No Edward, there is little point. Our horses are tired and they will be fresher. Empress, we shall have to rely upon your charms."

"You have done what you can, Baron. Now we shall see what the daughter of Henry can do."

It was a column of twenty men. Four knights and sixteen men at arms. Although we outnumbered them I knew that there were far more within an angry shout of us. I smiled. The leader did not.

"Why do you cross the land of the Baron of Laon without permission?"

"Our mission is peaceful. We are here to escort the Empress Matilda who is returning to her father following the funeral of her husband the Emperor."

The knight looked suspicious. The Empress said, "I am sorry that we did not do your master the courtesy of visiting with him but I am still grieving for my dead husband and I would not be good company. And besides we are keen to get to Caen as quickly as possible."

Her smile was enchanting and the knight was forced to give a bow of apology, "I am sorry Empress for your loss. I am certain that you would be more comfortable in the castle than risking bandits ahead."

She smiled once more. "We can be twenty miles closer by nightfall and that means we may be just a day away from a reunion with my father. It is worth the risk."

I suddenly spied an opportunity for confusion, "Besides, the wagons with the Empress' servants and treasure are half a day behind. We would not impose such a large number on you. Better that they camp with us."

I saw an amused smile on the Empress' face. The knight nodded. "My lord, the Baron, will be disappointed but I shall tell him of your decision."

He rode back to the castle. We carried on west, apparently in a relaxed manner. When the knights were beyond earshot I said, urgently, "As soon as we are out of sight I want everyone to ride as fast as possible. Dick and Aiden ride ahead and find somewhere to camp which can be defended."

As my two men rode off the Empress asked, "What was the purpose of the ruse?"

"To sow confusion. They will, of course investigate wagons laden with treasure as well as to ascertain if there are more men than we have. Once they find we have lied they will follow us with all speed. I wish to be as far away from here as I can and in somewhere we can defend. We will be outnumbered and if they choose to take you they would be able to do so on the road."

We trotted quickly down the road. "Can your men find somewhere in a land which is unknown to them?"

"They are both woodsmen and have a good eye for such things. If there is such a place then they will find it."

When night fell I was beginning to doubt my men and then Aiden appeared from nowhere. "Follow me, my lord." We left the road and rode through a break in the trees. It was barely wide enough for two abreast.

"Ralph, cover our tracks and disguise where we left the road."

We clambered up a small bank through some bushes and then through more trees. There was Dick in the middle of an open area. "It looks like, at some time in the past, it was a settlement, lord. There are the burnt out remains of huts. It was all that we could find."

"And it will do. Put up shelters for the women. Aiden put some traps near to the road. I would be warned of visitors in the night."

My men were past masters at setting up a camp quickly and even Rolf and his Swabians were impressed. We did not light a fire. I apologised to the ladies. "I am sorry that there is no fire but I would not alert others to our presence. We will be seen eventually but I would rather it was as late as possible."

"Do not apologise, Baron; you are doing what you must to protect us." We ate the remains of our dried and salted food. The water from a nearby stream was all that we had to wash it down. To make matters worse it was a cold night and hot food would have made sleeping easier. The skies had remained clear after the sun in the afternoon and we were all chilled to the bone. I took the first watch with five of my archers. Sir Edward would take the second. We had found that a two-hour watch was the best for us. It kept us alert and gave us enough rest to continue. I stood with my cloak wrapped around my shoulders and head. I leaned against a tree and peered east towards Laon. As she had before the Empress joined me.

"You should be getting your rest, my lady."

"I cannot sleep. I fear the meeting today has set in motion ideas that I find unattractive."

"But why? We are close to Normandy and have to endure just a day or so more of danger."

"It is the danger when I reach Normandy that I fear. My father will wish me married again."

"Is that not your choice?"

She laughed and covered her mouth immediately. "I wish it were my choice but it is not. The King needs an heir. I am his only legitimate child. He will find some noble lord who is acceptable to him and he will pray that his seed takes."

It was a depressing thought. I wondered now about my wisdom in marrying Adela. I was happy with her but how much happier would I have been with Matilda? Fate has an unhappy knack of giving with one hand and tearing away with another. I realised I had been silent for a long time when she said, "You were lucky to be able to choose your Adela and she was even luckier to have you."

She put her hand on mine and squeezed it slightly.

"Surely there could be a compromise. There must be someone whom you would like who would be acceptable to the king."

She paused and then said, "You mean someone like you?" Shaking her head, she went on, "Whoever marries me must have a lineage at least as old as mine. Even someone whom my father likes would not be acceptable if his antecedents were not from a noble line. Perhaps I should have entered a nunnery."

"That would have been the worst thing you could have done."

I was aware that she was still holding my hand and who knows what we might have said had not Margaret appeared, "Come, my lady. You need your sleep." I wondered what Margaret thought of it all. She was a clever woman and she could make inferences from our posture and our tone.

When the Empress left my mind was in as much of a turmoil as hers had been. I wished she had not spoken to me. Now I had dark recesses of my mind filled with doubts. That was not a good thing in a leader of men.

I had the sentries wake us before dawn. It had not been a comfortable night's sleep and I wanted to push on as quickly as we could. My hopes for a peaceful journey were shattered when both

Griff of Gwent and Aiden rode in; one from the east and one from the west. They both reported the same thing. There were two conroi of Frenchmen converging on us. I had to think quickly. This time I could not use three valuable men at arms to guard the Empress. "Aiden, you and Roger of Lincoln are to watch the spare horses and the ladies. Keep them safe."

They both nodded.

I shouted, "Lances! Dick, you and the archers keep the men to the east from our backs. Rolf, Edward we will charge these Frenchmen who try to stop us."

The Empress asked, "Should we not try to talk with them?"

"If they did talk then it would be to delay us. We charge them and then ride for Rouen. We do not stop again. These two bands are only the first. The word will be in Flanders and in the Ils de France and every knight who wants your treasure will be upon us. It is my decision!"

As the men grabbed lances we formed up in lines of five. The five knights would lead followed by the men at arms. The squires would follow the ladies and the horses. I could trust Harold to organise them. We trotted forward. Scout had been a good choice but this time, I knew, we would be against warhorses and the French would have the advantage. Our only advantage lay merely in our skill and our bond. We were brothers and we had a just cause; the Empress. God would be on our side.

We trotted forward. I could see the gonfanon before I saw the warriors. I spied a glimmer of hope. They were waiting for us. They hoped, I suspected, that we would vacillate and they would catch us between their two forces. Even before we saw them I worked out what had occurred. They had searched the road and missed us. They had to have known we were somewhere on the road and they had tried to trap us. They had split their forces and that gave us a chance. As we crested the rise I saw them. There were, from the banners, ten knights and thirty men at arms. It was a formidable force. With another band following on we had one chance to defeat them and one chance only. We had to spill their knights and send their men at arms packing. My archers would catch us up and, with a head start; we had a slight hope of escape.

"We do this for the Empress! Let us show these Frenchmen that they are no match for the Knights of the Empress!"

My father and Wulfstan had both told me that, sometimes, words were worth a hundred extra men. So, it proved.

I watched as the French hurriedly tried to form a line. It was not easy. They were two hundred paces from us. I spurred Scout and he leapt forward. The others matched my speed but I was still the tip of the arrow. I kept the lance high. It was more comfortable that way. The French line was ragged. They were not knee to knee. We had done this so many times that it was second nature to us.

"Charge!"

We were a hundred paces from them and they had not even started to move. Our appearance had startled them. They tried to move forward but they had warhorses and they took time to move to charge speed. I lowered my lance and aimed for the knight with the dark blue shield and the single fleur de lys. He panicked and I saw it in his horse; he could not decide which way to attack me. I had decided before I had seen him. I would attack lance to lance across his cantle. His vacillation meant that his lance was still coming down when mine struck him squarely below his ventail. My sharpened lance tore into his chest and threw him from his saddle. I hit him with such force that my last lance shattered. I pulled back my arm and swung the stump like a club. It smashed into the head of his standard bearer who fell to the ground. Standing in my stirrup I pulled my arm back and hurled the stump into the men at arms before me. It also allowed me to draw my sword and, as I sat down once more I swung my sword across my body and struck a man at arms on the side of his helmet. Stunned, he fell to the road.

Before me were the crossbows which had yet to be organised. They were so close that they could not release. We tore through them swinging our swords to the left and right of our horses' heads. Those with helmets died as easily as those without for our blows were delivered with great force. When there was no one in front of me; I reined in. Turning I saw that we had demolished the French band. Riders were fleeing to the north and south leaving the road west clear of our enemies. I was as out of breath as was Scout. I was unscathed. How had we managed to destroy such a well armed force? I closed my eyes and said a silent prayer of thanks.

Edward and Rolf rode next to me and raised their helmets. Rolf was laughing. "I am glad I never faced you in a tourney Englishman. I have never seen a lump of wood wielded so well!"

"Save your thanks until my archers arrive. Change horses!"

When Aiden and the horse holders arrived, with the ladies, we all changed to fresher horses. The spares we had accumulated

58

might prove to be the difference between success and abject failure. "Catch the horses of the dead French too."

The Empress was wide eyed, "Baron Alfraed! Does my father know how you fight?"

I nodded, "He does."

"Then he should reward you for I have never seen anything so gallant as that charge."

The archers galloped in. Dick pointed over his shoulder. "They are a mile back my lord but we have barely five arrows left."

"You have done well. Lead once more and we will head for Rouen. We stop for nothing. We reach Normandy in one march!"

My archers must have thinned them out for they came along cautiously. We rode west steadily rather than fast. Aiden watched and saw that they halted where we had defeated their comrades. The bodies of the dead and the wounded warriors must have daunted them. They ceased their pursuit. That was our last combat before, in the late evening, we reached Normandy and safety. We had evaded capture and the Empress was safe. As the mighty doors of the castle slammed behind us I wondered what fate had in store for the Empress. What had I taken her to? We would find out when we reached Caen.

After two days of recovery at Rouen we rode south to Caen. We had an escort of another five knights and thirty men at arms for this part of the journey. It was not necessary for our safety but it was a statement that Matilda was now the daughter and heiress of King Henry once more. It sickened me for it was almost like parading her for potential suitors. The three ladies now rode side saddle and were dressed as fine ladies. The knights from Rouen and their men at arms also looked sparkling and shiny. By contrast our men looked like brigands.

King Henry greeted us on the road so that he and his household knights could lead his daughter through the thronged streets of Caen where her return to her father could be celebrated. After greeting his daughter, he rode next to me and clasped my arm. "Once more I am in your debt. We shall thank you properly, later. Thank you, Baron Alfraed."

Relegated to the rear of the column we were the last to enter Caen. The well wishers had drifted along with the Empress and her father. I did not mind. It showed that our task was complete and we could go home. Edgar took our men and the Swabian men at arms to the warrior hall while we led Rolf and his knights to our quarters in the castle. For Rolf, Gottfried and Carl, this would be their new home; at least until the Empress was married. It is strange to think, now, that she never lost the title of Empress. Even in the dark days ahead when she fought against the tide that was Stephen she was always called the Empress.

"Harold, take our armour and helms to the armourer and have them repaired. I hope we will not need them in a hurry but we cannot be sure."

"Aye, my lord."

"And when you have done that then look in on our mounts. Make sure they are cared for."

I had left fine clothes in the castle and, after bathing and grooming myself, I changed into the better ones I had brought from the east. I had grown in the five years since I had left Constantinople. I would have to purchase new ones soon. Sadly, I realised I would not be able to buy such well made clothes west of the Byzantine Empire. Rolf saw my sad look and misinterpreted it. "Do not fret for the Empress, Alfraed. We will watch over her."

I smiled, "I will not worry so long as you and your brother knights are close by. But I was thinking that I will need new clothes soon."

He laughed, "That is what marriage does to a man. He worries about matters which are unimportant. Now what we worry about is where we will get decent ale in these parts!"

"I am afraid you will be disappointed. It is either cider or wine. If the Empress comes to England you will find decent ale once more."

That evening there was a feast for the Empress and to celebrate her safe return. We were now relegated to a lower table for there were lords and princes aplenty. I noticed, sourly, that all were handsome young men. She was being paraded. The food might have been well prepared but I had no appetite. I had not realised when I had set off that this would be the result. I had thought I was rescuing the Empress for a life of freedom. I was wrong.

King Henry waved me over. I stood behind him and bowed, "My daughter has been singing your praises, Baron Alfraed. You have exceeded my expectations. I had not thought that there would have been so many attempts to kidnap her. My son thinks highly of you and I concur with his view."

"Where is your son, my liege? I have not seen him."

"He is in Wales. They are being troublesome again but this time it is in the south of the country close to his estates. Come tomorrow

morning and I will speak with you. I shall reward you and your
men for their services."

When I rejoined Edward and the Swabians they asked what the
King had said.

"We are to be rewarded for our services and I need to speak
with him on the morrow."

Edward asked, "Will we be heading home do you think?" I
shrugged, "We have done well already. We have fine horses and
much gold. I am not certain that there will be much to be gained
from staying here."

"I fear you are right, Edward." I nodded towards all the suitors,
gathered to woo the Empress. "I think this will be just the start of it.
I do not envy you Rolf."

"We will hunt and we will practise. At least here the Empress is
safe from kidnap. Caen is the most secure castle in the whole of
Normandy."

The King was alone when I saw him. "Sit, Sir Alfraed." He had
a parchment in his hands and he was playing with it. "I always
desired the crown you know. But now that I have it and no heirs it
seems to weigh heavily upon me. William, my son, would have
been your age, had he lived. Things would have been so different
had the White Ship not sunk." He shrugged, "Such is the will of
God." He made the sign of the cross. "Perhaps I am being punished
for imprisoning my brother." I squirmed a little for this felt
embarrassing. He saw my discomfort and smiled, "I am sorry,
Baron. I speak like this with Robert when he is here. Forgive me. I
feel older these days especially when I hear of exploits of knights
such as you. You must forgive a father for thinking of what might
have been..."

He handed me the parchment. "This increases your lands in the
valley of the River Tees and gives you the title of Lord of the
Valley of the Tees. Roger of Ripon wrote a report for me and
informed me that the lands on both sides of the valley have
increased their yield of taxes and animals. That is, largely, down to
you." I was about to protest and he waved his hand. "No false
modesty, sir. There is a manor at Thornaby which had been vacant
because it was impoverished. You can hold that and give it to one
of your knights if you wish. You would profit from the land. I
would have given you Red Marshall too but it is close to the land of
the Bishop of Durham and I would not risk losing the affections of
Bishop Flambard. However, there is a manor at Elton which I have
it in my power to award." He allowed me to read the parchment. I

saw that I was now the most powerful baron and only subject to the Bishop of Durham. It was quite a coup.

"In return, I expect twenty knights from the valley and eighty men at arms as well as forty archers."

"Archers are hard to come by."

"I know but I do not expect that you will have to bring them to muster this year. Apart from Wales, my lands seem peaceful. You and my son have managed to quieten down the ambitions of the Scots and the rebels. With the Palatinate now secure too I hope that the northern border will remain peaceful and prosperous. I must stay here for my enemies gather around me like wolves. Anjou, Flanders, France; they constrict me and conspire against me." He leaned back; a sure sign that the interview was over.

Picking up the parchment I stood, "I will do as you command, my liege, and I will await your orders." Even as I said it I knew how stuffy it sounded.

He smiled, "There are two ships leaving for England today. You and your men can use them to return to England. The castle is crowded and we expect more visitors. Your work is done here and my daughter safely delivered. Go home and enjoy some time with your family." I was summarily despatched. He had no further need of me. I wondered if someone had spoken of the affection of the Empress towards me.

Thus dismissed I went to inform my men. I told Rolf the news and he clasped my arm. "Perhaps it is for the best that you do not say goodbye to the Empress, my friend, eh? Go and see your wife and your son and make more children." Rolf was a wise knight and he watched and listened as all good leaders do. I knew that he was right. It hurt me to do it but I could not allow myself the luxury of saying goodbye to the Empress.

Later, as the two laden ships headed out to sea I looked at the castle of Caen. I hoped that Matilda would come to the battlements and wave but the walls remained devoid of any ladies. Rolf was right. This clean break was for the best.

Part 2

Lord of the Valley

Chapter 6

We reached home in late summer. The journey had not ended in London for we had to march north with our horses and we used the time to recruit more men at arms and archers. With the wars in the west and the north over there were many spare men at arms who sought employment. We even found more Welsh archers. Sherwood had been quiet for some time and that source appeared to have dried up.

I gave Edward the manor of Thornaby. He was delighted. He had been a man at arms for years and suddenly he was a man of substance. He would now have to bear the expense of men at arms but he accepted that burden. Some of the other men at arms we had hired would be serving my other knights and I would need to find another two knights to serve with me. I was not looking forward to that. I had made a wise choice with Edward but Richard had almost done for me. I needed to use better judgement.

As we passed the tiny manor of Thornaby, Edward and I inspected it. Lying across the river from Stockton it had been just two farms and a few huts when we had arrived. The security we had brought meant it had prospered. The wolf winter had cost us one family but more had arrived to replace them. The river sometimes flooded and that brought the bounty of richer harvests. The farmers who lived there would do well so long as they learned to work with nature. There were now half a dozen farms and would bring an income to Sir Edward.

Edward's experienced eye took it all in. "I would have my hall there on the high ground."

"Would you not wish a castle?"

"No, Baron, Stockton is close enough to afford us protection. Stone castles are expensive. I have little enough to spare at the moment. I will have my men begin to hew wood from the river bank tomorrow. We have time enough to build before winter."

"Good. Now let us get to the ferry, I am anxious to see my family."

As we waited for Ethelred I viewed my castle as though for the first time. It was not large. Although we had built three floors in the keep the lower one was below ground. With just one hall and one antechamber it was almost an old-fashioned warrior hall but it had a river running around three sides and it had a curtain wall. We could defend it. It was my castle. In time, it could be enlarged. Perhaps that would be a task for my son, William.

As Ethelred's man pulled us across on the ferry I wondered about replacing the wooden towers at the top of the castle. I had talked myself out of it by the time we had reached the north shore. It would be expensive and it was unnecessary, at the moment. We had other needs now. A bigger stable would be needed and an armoury. Both could be built against the walls of the keep. They would add protection and heat in winter. In addition, I had much to do as Lord of the Valley. The grand title meant more work. It would also mean more taxes for me but my main role would be as defender of the Tees.

Adela and my son came to greet me. He had grown immeasurably since I had been away. Travelling from Caen meant I was dirty and unkempt. I must have frightened him. He burst into tears when he saw me. It made Edward and my men at arms laugh. Poor Adela was distraught. "I am sorry Alfraed, it's just…"

I smiled, "Do not worry. I must look terrifying. When I have bathed, shaved and had my hair cut then we will try again."

She handed him to Seara and threw her arms around me. "I missed you so much. Did you do what the King wished?"

She took my arm as we walked up to my gate. "We did and I am rewarded with two more manors and a new title, Lord of the Valley. But we need to have more knights."

She laughed, "They will come for your fame must be spreading."

"I don't know about that. But we will need to build a warrior hall in the outer bailey. I have realised, since travelling in the Empire, that our castle is small. The keep is good for defence but we need accommodation. Remember the wolf winter? We need to make plans in case we have such a hard one again."

She turned as she heard the horses being brought up from the ferry. "Have you gained horses?"

"We have and treasure too. We will have to try and find some time to spend some before winter arrives. We could hire more servants or buy slaves."

"We have enough of those but we need cloth. We are well provided for in leather and wool but not fine cloth."

"Then we shall buy some."

As I entered my hall I felt the cares of the world fall from my shoulders. I was home and I was happy. My wife's requests were mundane and all the more welcome for that. There was little danger in buying cloth and men did not die building halls.

The next day Edgar and Wulfric took the new men at arms with Edward and they went to hew wood. We would cut enough for Edward and for my hall. I went with Harold to visit Wulfstan and Sir Richard. I would visit the others in due course. I left Aiden with his hawks and his young falconers. Along with his dogs they were his family.

Wulfstan's family was growing and his hall had been enlarged to accommodate both them and the servants he now needed. It was a pleasant afternoon and we sat outside his hall and watched his children play. I told him, in detail, what had happened. I could hide nothing from my old mentor. I saw that he was worried about the need to find more men at arms. "I will see about hiring more men at arms and training archers but the King asks a great deal of us, Wulfstan."

"He is the King and what he says he gets. You have done well, Alfraed, and your father would be proud. You do not command the Varangian Guard yet but you command a mighty force of fine knights. I would be happy to lead them."

"How is the Lord of Hartness?"

"I know you will not wish to hear this but he is nothing like his cousin. He appears to be a good man. He cares for his people and they love him. I have visited with him on a number of occasions and I find him good company."

I knew I had an irrational dislike of him but I could do nothing about that. He was one of my lords and, as such, I would have to learn to have him fight under my banner.

Sir Richard, at Yarm, looked even more prosperous than he had when I had first met him. There were more fields being tilled and his wooden castle had been strengthened and its walls raised. He and his son, Tristan, were practising. Tristan had grown much during the year since I had last seen him. I watched them finish their bout before I approached them.

They were both sweating heavily. Although Sir Richard had defeated his son I could see the latent skill the youth had. "Well done, Tristan. You will soon have the beating of your father."

Tristan shook his head, "He has taught me and all the tricks I know are his. He is the one man I will never defeat."

"Unless you devise ways of your own."

He shook his head, "I am afraid I just use what I have been taught and, besides, at the moment I find the lance too difficult to control."

Sir Richard put his arm around his son. "That is my fault. I am not as skilled in the lance as others. Could you not advise him?"

I nodded and took a spear from a rack. I threw it to Tristan. "But this is not as long as a lance, my lord!"

"And you are not at your full strength yet." They had some sacks filled with straw close to the stables. I shouted to a man at arms. "Fetch three of those sacks over here." When they came I piled them one on top of each other. "Now, Tristan, imagine that this is a man with a spear and he is crouching behind a shield." I jammed the tip of my shield into the ground and rested it against the bales of hay. "I want you to gallop at it as though you were in battle. Rest your spear across your cantle and then, when you are twenty paces from the hay, pull back and punch above the shield."

I saw Sir Richard smiling. He was a good knight but I think he lacked imagination. I was making this more of a game. When they tilted at each other Sir Richard would win every time and Tristan would become demoralised. I thought he might be able to defeat the three sacks of hay.

He charged towards the target. I saw the concentration upon his face as he pulled back his arm. He plunged the spear into the top sack and shouted excitedly. Unfortunately, the weight of the sack pulled the spear from his grasp. I nodded. I had expected that.

"You have not won when you strike an enemy, Tristan. It is after the battle when you cheer. A knight is vulnerable once his lance has broken or it is lost. You could have retained your grip on the spear."

"How my lord?"

"Once you have struck then you twist and withdraw. If your weapon does break then draw your sword as quickly as you can. In a mêlée, there will be other knights around you."

"Thank you, my lord. When will I be able to progress to a lance?"

"Once your arms are stronger. Here, take the hay back to where they are stored and when your father sends his woodcutters out go with them and your target is to cut down more trees than the woodcutters." I turned to Harold, "Go with him and tell him how you train."

He nodded and hefted the sack upon his back. Sir Richard chuckled, "My woodcutters do this all the time he will never out cut them."

"This means he will become stronger."

"Thank you, my lord. I value you your advice."

"I have an ulterior motive. The King has asked for twenty knights form the valley as well as eighty men at arms and forty archers."

"How many do you command now, my lord?"

"We have eight. I need the squires that we have to become knights by next year. Until the weather worsens have Tristan come to Stockton each Saturday. He and Harold can improve each other's skills. We will soon make them both into knights. You have another son; he should begin his training as a knight too."

Sir Richard frowned, "Do we go to war?"

"Not this year but the Scots will only remain cowed for a short time and there are still men who have rebellious hearts." I saw his eyes flick to his wife who was talking to Tristan. "We will leave men at arms to protect our manors. You have six men at arms. You need to double that to twelve and then six can watch your manor. I will tell all of my lords the same. As for archers…" I shrugged, "That is practice for your young men. We now have more people who wish to live in the valley. Although the land is fertile there will be young men who wish a more adventurous life. We can offer them that. Train as many men to be archers as you can. We will go to war again; the question is when."

I gave the same information to the other knights over the next four days. As we were riding back from Hartness, Harold and I paused to look down from the hill close to Hart to view the river and the land all the way down to the hills south of the river. "Baron, I have heard your words to your knights. Do you expect me to be a knight now?"

"In the spring, I will knight you and give you a manor."

"But I am not ready!"

"You think you are not but you will be. When you and Tristan practise you will improve each other's skills. You and he are at the same level in many areas but you have more experience of war.

67

You will tell him of that." I smiled, "I am grateful that you have served me as well as a squire and your reward will be that I will give you the manor of Elton. It is close to Wulfstan and me and small enough for you to grow into the role of lord of the manor."

"But, my lord, I was born the son of an archer!"

"And I am the grandson of a servant. Our course is not set in stone. We make our own future. The King has been kind to me and, I believe, we have deserved the rewards we had been given. I will have a band of knights around me who are as close as brothers. I will have knights that I can trust. You will be such a one, Harold. Set your mind to becoming the best knight that you can be."

He was silent as we headed south.

"And one more thing Harold, have John teach you to read by the spring. A knight needs such skills."

His face which had been filled with joy, now filled instead with dread. John was a good teacher but I remembered that I had preferred the sword to the parchment.

Our winter was not as harsh as the one we had called the wolf winter. The river did not freeze and the snow, while it came, departed with equal speed. Although the cold was harsh we found no frozen families this time. We went in the hills, after Christmas, to hunt the wolves while their sense of smell was not at its best. We killed many. There were still many more left to roam in the remote parts of the land but they preyed on sheep and not man. The world settled into a better routine. Many of the wives of the men at arms were with child. Winter was the time for such things. The long nights were good for that.

We trained hard during those early months of the new year. Winter was slow to lose its grip on the land but eventually it did. As the trees and fields blossomed so did our families who were able to get out into the warm sun. Our children were our future and my son would be a knight. There would now be daughters of knights and men at arms for him to marry. Family helped warriors create unbreakable bonds.

With Easter just a few weeks away I took half of my men and rode down to York. We needed to prepare for summer. We had had peace for half a year since I had returned. I was not certain that it would last. York might have men at arms and we could buy the things we could not make ourselves. John, my clerk, came with us. In truth, he was more than a clerk. He was the one who ran the castle and the lands. Faren had been a housekeeper when she had lived with us and my wife could run the kitchens and the servants

68

but it was John who saw to the day to day running of my lands. He had been honest when he came to me. He wished to be rich. I did not stop him from achieving his aims. I knew that he was a good man and would not cheat me. I was well read enough to check his figures rigorously but he liked money and knew how to make it grow.

He, like Ethelred, had seized every opportunity to increase his coins. He bought tanned hides and had some of the women in the town make them into fine belts and baldrics. He then sold those at a profit to the men at arms. He now sent some with Olaf on his ship, to make even greater profits. He had even bought a sumpter from the manor. We had received a good price and the extra horses we had gained meant we had spares. He now led this horse to York. He had items he had had manufactured; scabbards for swords and dagger, belts and baldrics and leather pouches. The women of Stockton appreciated the extra work and the long nights of winter had been spent productively.

As we neared York I sighed. There would come a time when John would leave my service. That was inevitable. Harold would go to Elton and Edward was at Thornaby. I would miss their company but I knew that change was bound to happen. Such was life; it was a cycle of change.

When we reached York, I presented myself to the Archbishop first. There was a protocol to such things and then I went to the Great Hall to speak with the Lord of York, Geoffrey D'Aubigny. He had come over from Normandy some years earlier and now, in his middle age, he had been given the great castle as his home.

"I have heard great things of you, Baron, and I understand that the King has given you more manors."

"He has. They are both small but we hope that they will grow."

"You are a bastion of the north. I feel safer knowing that the road from the north is protected. How long do you stay in York?"

"There are just seven of us and we leave tomorrow. We wished to buy what we cannot make ready for the winter."

"Then stay here tonight as my guests. There is room a plenty and I have other guests. I had planned a feast tonight in any case."

"Then I would be honoured."

He nodded, "Excellent; I look forward to hearing some of your tales and stories. I will see you this evening."

I knew that the invitation for the feast would only extend to me and to Harold. My men and John would be happy to make their own arrangements. York was the largest place outside of London and it would be exciting for them all. It would do Harold good to mix with nobles. He had learned much since he had joined me and he had more knowledge to acquire. A knight needed to be rounded. He still had some rough edges. It would be hard to expect anything else of someone who had grown up amongst outlaws.

I rejoined my men. "We stay here tonight. Harold and I will be in the castle and you five will be in the warrior hall. John will give you coin for your food tonight."

"Thank you, my lord."

"Keep your eyes and ears open it is some time since we visited York and I would know how my peers fare. When we have seen to our horses we will buy what we need." I smiled at the men at arms, "Today you will be labourers."

The market at York was a busy one. Some of the former market stalls now had a roof and the families slept in the back. John had a list from Adela and the money to buy the things she desired but I was interested in the prices and to see what was on offer. I recognised a few faces, as we mingled in the market, but none were even acquaintances. My knights at home were close, like brothers. The rest of the northern knights were strangers.

John kept purchasing items and the men at arms would lug them back to the castle. I looked at the thin sun in the sky. It was drawing late and I was weary of the market. John suddenly appeared, "That is it, my lord. We are all done."

I noticed the four men at arms struggling with four heavy sacks. "What on earth are they?"

"They are beans, my lord. The farmers can plant them in the autumn, and we will have an early crop. The early spring is a hard time. We can grow and eat when there is little else available to us. What we do not eat, we can dry and they will do during the winter."

I nodded my approval. "Good. And do we give the beans to our farmers?" I already knew the answer to my question.

"We will charge them just what we have paid, my lord. It is a good investment and next year we need not buy any seeds at all."

"Charge them half of what we paid."

"My lord! We will lose money!"

"It is my money and we did well out of our Normandy trip. Half the price, John."

He nodded, glumly. "You are far too kind and generous, my lord!"

The Lord of York had no wife and so the feast was all men. That suited me. I could relax. However, I was acutely aware that we had a lack of women in the valley. My knights needed wives. Adela needed company. If Edward and Harold married then, with Sir Richard's wife, Adela would have ladies close by to visit. Since Faren had left it had been a lonely existence.

At the feast, I found myself next to a new knight or at least a knight I had not met before. He was an affable warrior and looked to be some ten years older than me. I discovered he had a wife and two sons. "I am Raymond of Poitiers, the new Baron of Arncliffe."

Arncliffe was to the north of the Carthusians' monastery. "You are almost a neighbour then?"

He nodded. "I have two more manors but they are further south, close to Doncaster but I have yet to visit them. My main estates are in Blois. The King was kind enough to reward me for my service to him. I know you have also been rewarded; Lord of the Valley. Should you need me and my knights then I would be happy to serve under your banner."

"That is kind of you. How many knights serve you?"

"Altogether there are eight. One of them, Philippe, is my brother. They are in the south evaluating the worth of my estates there."

"Then when you have time you must come and visit me in my castle. It is partly finished but I have two floors of the keep which are made of stone."

He looked surprised, "You have done well for one so young."

"My father brought me up to be careful with my coin and to spend it wisely. A stone keep seemed a good idea. Especially when one lives so close to the Scots."

"I understand there are others who have estates on both sides of the border."

"Aye and they have divided loyalties."

"Well I understand there will be another knight arriving soon. Roger de Bertram has been given Greatham." I frowned. That had been part of Hartness and I had not been told about the change. He saw my frown and smiled, "Do not feel you have been overlooked. I was in Caen when de Bertram was given the manor and I took ship directly. The news will be on its way. He is a good fellow and it means you have another knight to follow your banner."

I enjoyed talking to Sir Raymond who was both entertaining and informative. I learned much about the campaign against Flanders. It seemed that the King had reached an understanding with Count Fulk and the southern borders of Normandy were now much safer. As I left for my bed the Baron promised me that he and his family would try to visit my castle before the weather changed. All seven of us returned north feeling happier about our situation. Harold had enjoyed speaking with the younger knights and, whilst his education had been different, his experiences as a warrior made him popular. John was delighted with his purchases. I knew that he had done some business for himself. I had no idea what he bought but I knew that he would make coin out of it. I suppose when your father was a moneyer then money was in your blood.

Once back in the valley I threw myself into preparing for winter. Although it was still some time off we had learned to be ready for whatever nature had to throw at us. I took Harold to Elton and we met the handful of farmers who lived there. I had expected them to be resentful of this interference from the King. Surprisingly enough they were all happy to have my protection. Many had come from the north where Scottish raids were more regular. I did not introduce Harold as my squire. He was dressed as a knight and they accepted him as one. When I gave him the manor then he would introduce himself properly.

Edward had built a fine manor house. Although it was not a castle there was a ditch running around and the main door was half way up the wall and could only be reached by stairs. He had his lower floor built into the ground and he used it to store his animals. We had not been able to hire more men at arms from York and so Edward, like my other knights, spent each Sunday afternoon drilling his fyrd. They were a last resort but so long as they were trained they were better than nothing.

By the time the harvest was in and the animals gathered in their winter pens we had done all that we could. There were piles of wood drying and every ditch had been cleared so that any winter rain would run off. The bone fire celebration, that year, was one of the best that we had ever had. Some of the young girls of the town had become women over the summer and the wassailing around the fire saw new liaisons spring up. My archers and men at arms had been young men when they had first come to serve me but now they were seeking roots. It bespoke well of the valley that they wanted to live there.

It was the day after when my sentries pointed to the banners on the south of the river. I recognised the banner of Sir Raymond of Poitiers. This was, however, not a social visit. I saw his knights with him.

"Harold, come with me. We will visit with Sir Raymond. I like this not." When we reached the other side Sir Raymond looked angry.

"We have had slavers, Sir Alfraed."

"They did not cross the river here and I doubt that they would have done so at Piercebridge or Gainford."

"No, they are not Scots. They are Vikings from the west. We came here first for we thought they might have crossed the river here and then headed back to the west coast."

"Vikings! We have never had them from the west before. Are they from Ireland or Man?"

"Orkney. At least that is what Bohemond thought."

Bohemond stepped forward, "I served on the western borders. These looked like Orkney Vikings to me." He held out an amulet. "They dropped this near the village they raided. It is from Orkney."

"Why come all the way across the country?"

"It is not far and they can sail their dragon ships up the Ribble and the Lune. I need your help, Baron. You know these lands better than I do."

I nodded, "There is little point in your coming north. Head west and south." He frowned, "That is the shortest route to the rivers you mention. They did not come this way. There are few castles along the way. If they cross the river they have my castles to contend with and beyond that Bowes, Barnard and Brougham. They will not risk that direction. South and west that is where we will find them. Do they have a start?"

"A day."

"I am guessing that they have other slaves they captured along the way. They must have been greedy. Had they stopped earlier we might not have known. We will catch you up. I will gather my men. We will catch them."

Chapter 7

We had to say hasty farewells. I took Aiden and eight archers as well as Wulfric and ten men at arms. I left Star at home. When we crossed the river, I asked Edward to watch my home. "I will come with you, Baron."

"No, my friend, we need speed. Already I am an hour behind Sir Raymond. We will be back within the week at the most. With God's help, we can find them quickly." I hated the thought of having our people enslaved by the Vikings. They would sell them in the slave markets in Ireland or Scotland. Few would ever return home.

We went along the river to Yarm. I wanted Sir Richard to know what we were about. Tristan begged to be allowed to accompany us. I saw that his father was torn. "I will watch over him but this may be a chance to see the improvement he has made." Sir Richard nodded his agreement but I could see that his wife was far from happy. Mothers hated letting their sons go.

He was eager to be away and we rode swiftly west from the manor. Although Sir Raymond had a start on us we knew the roads and he did not. We caught up with him north of Ripon. As we approached the prosperous city Tristan asked, "Why did the Baron not seek help from here? It is closer to his lands."

"He does not know the country yet. He is new. He knew me and I think he expects us to do what he cannot; find his people." We rode towards the column of knights which were heading west along the road.

Aiden came trotting back from the west. He had ridden ahead of us. "I have cut their trail, my lord. They have travelled across country rather than using the road. They were to the north and west of us."

I turned to Harold, "That makes sense. The land is gentle and is not as rocky and difficult to travel upon. The slaves will be on foot but they will have to drop down to the road soon for the gorges are treacherous. We need to ride harder." The men at arms at the rear of Sir Raymond's men heard us coming and the column stopped.

I pointed to the north and west. "The slaves have headed across country. They are just a few miles ahead. They will be on the road before too long." Sir Raymond looked relieved, "Do you know how many Vikings and slaves we follow?"

"No. They took at least two villages and many farms. We had no time to check."

I turned in the saddle, "Aiden, Dick and Wilson, find them."

The three galloped off. I noticed that Sir Raymond had only crossbowmen. "I would use archers if I were you, Sir Raymond. Crossbows defend castles. Out here they are more of a liability."

"But in Normandy..."

"In Normandy, there are many more castles than there are here." I saw the doubt on his face. He would learn that, in England, bows were better than crossbows.

It grew dark and we had still to hear from our scouts. "We will need to make camp."

"Surely we can push on." I knew that Sir Raymond was angry and that was no way to pursue an enemy. It was too risky. I also know that we had to conserve our horses. Vikings were hardy warriors. They needed no horses. We would catch them but it would take time.

"And risk horses falling down ravines or breaking legs? They will have to stop to eat and to rest. My men will find them. We rise early and we pursue them. The rest will do the horses good." I pointed to my archers. "They have no armour and can ride faster than we can. My archers can hold them until we arrive and then your knights can do what they do best."

He bit his lips. He was torn between wanting to ignore my words and continue the chase and listening to what he knew was sage advice. He nodded and we camped. Wulfric quickly organised the camp and the food. He was an old campaigner. It did not matter if the Vikings could smell our fire or see the flames. They were the ones who were being pursued.

A weary Wilson rode in as we had just started our food. "They are ahead sir, just twenty miles away. They are not far from Gisburn."

I suddenly remembered the knight who had told us of the rebellion at Durham. Guy of Gisburn had been allowed to return to his manor. Perhaps this was fate.

"And where are Aiden and Dick?"

"They are watching them. It was dark, Baron, but from their fires Dick estimated that there were sixty or more warriors."

I nodded, "Two boat loads and that means there will be a third boat to take the slaves. You have done well. Eat."

"Yes, my lord," he hesitated, "there are children Baron." I saw the pity in his eyes and I nodded. We would get them back or die in the attempt.

Sir Raymond said, "Your face showed that you know of this place."

"Let us say I have heard of it and there is a castle at Gisburn but it is a small demesne. They may not be able to do anything to stop them but, equally, we might be able to add them to our force. Sixty Vikings are a formidable warband."

"You have fought them before?"

"Not from Orkney but I have fought them. We will need to use lances. They go for the horses knowing that a downed horse makes a knight easier to kill. Hopefully they will not have much mail and our archers will be able to pin them down." I smiled, "And perhaps your crossbowmen will come into their own."

We rose before dawn. We had three knights, three squires, twenty men at arms and a force of fifteen archers and crossbows. I hoped that it would be enough. By the time dawn had broken we were armed, armoured and ready to ride. As soon as we started to ride Sir Raymond saw the reason we had camped. Within half a mile of where we had spent the night we had a gorge cascading to one side of us and precipitous rocks above our heads. Wilson led the column for he knew where they had spent the night. They had obviously moved when we reached their camp but their trail was easy to find. Dick and Aiden would leave signs if there was the danger of an ambush.

Once we passed through the last pass the ground fell away and we saw them two miles ahead. They were on the road and it was descending between the wooded slopes of the valley. I hoped they would not realise they were being pursued but that did not really matter now for we could see them.

"Wilson, take the archers and find Dick. There looks to be cover to the side of the road. Have Dick pin them down until we can get there."

The archers trotted away. They did not use the road but headed into the fields and scrubby bushes which lined the road. They were masters at hiding. I turned to Harold and Tristan. "Get the lances." As they went to the pack horses I took my helmet from my cantle. "We had better arm Sir Raymond. As soon as they see us they will form a shield wall." I hesitated. I did not want to insult him. "If you have never fought a shield wall I should advise you to try to strike between the shields rather than the head or the shield. You have more chance of making a hole in the wall and that is what we must do. If we can break their shield wall then we have a chance."

"These are barbarians. They cannot stand against Norman knights!"

"Do not underestimate them, Baron. They are worthy and ruthless opponents. They will take the legs from your horses if they can."

He did not look convinced but he and his men at arms prepared.

"I would suggest we ride in a line five abreast." He nodded. "Tristan, you ride next to Wulfric in the second line."

"Yes Baron." If he was disappointed he did not show it.

We cantered down the road. Our horses were still relatively fresh and the slope helped us move more easily. The noise of our hooves must have alerted them. There were faces turned to us and then a sudden movement as shields were presented. I was impressed with the speed with which they formed a shield wall. These were well trained warriors. This would not be easy. Their spears protruded and, as we closed to within five hundred paces I saw two lines of spearmen and, behind them, a line of mailed warriors who looked to be the leaders. The slaves, and there were many of them, were penned in by ten lightly armed warriors.

As we lowered our lances I hoped that my archers had managed to get into position. Sir Raymond's crossbowmen were riding with us. They would be of little use until it was all over. I was pleased that Harold was keeping tight to me as was Sir Raymond. Worryingly the knight to the left of Sir Raymond, William of Helmsley, was not and worse, he was getting ahead of both Sir Raymond and me. It was too late to order him back for we were now galloping. I pulled back my shield closer to my body and looked at the warrior I would strike. I stood in my stirrups as I punched forward. Even as I was striking I heard the scream of a dying horse as William of Helmsley's mount was hacked by a Danish axe. William was thrown over the horse's head to be butchered by the warriors behind.

The Viking I had aimed my lance at had glanced to his left. It cost him his life as my lance sank into his shoulder. William's dead horse crashed into the shield wall and Harold managed to spear a Viking in the face. It meant we had created a gap. I continued to urge Scout on and the dead Viking's body fell against the spears of the men behind him and they could not bring their spears to bear.

Dick and his archers began to rain arrow on the unprotected backs of the Vikings. With their centre broken by the four of us and their right flank assaulted by archers the cohesion of the shield wall was gone. We were no longer knee to knee but Wulfric and our second rank were now in a position to bring their lances to bear. I threw my broken lance at the men before me and, as I unsheathed my sword, I pulled back on the reins so that Scout's hooves rose to clatter down on the broken shield wall. Our combined weight came down on a warrior and crushed his chest as though it was a sheet of thin ice.

We could not stop, that would be disastrous, and I yelled, "On! We have them! No quarter!" There were too many of them for us to risk trying to take prisoners. I stabbed down and found the unprotected throats of a blond, bare chested Viking. We were now a wedge which was forcing its way towards the five leaders who stood waiting for us. They were a different proposition. They had mail byrnies and well-made shields. They were also standing on a small mound. We finished off the last of the shield wall. Dick and his archers had done the most damage. There were just the five leaders standing between us and the slaves. The warriors who were guarding the captives would not be an obstacle.

I turned to Sir Raymond, "Bring up your crossbows. Let us see if they can make these last five charge us."

He shouted and his seven crossbowmen arrived. "Sir Alfraed wants you to hit those five."

The leader nodded and the crossbows cracked as they sent their bolts towards them. All of them hit the shields. They were well made shields and did no damage.

"Aim for the legs." That was one advantage of a crossbow. It had a flatter trajectory. The Vikings were not expecting it and, when they had reloaded, the seven bolts hit the Vikings. One was hit by two and he fell to the floor. The captain of the crossbowmen looked at Sir Raymond, I shouted, "Keep going! Do not stop. When they are on the ground we will charge them!"

The five were brave men and they were hard to kill. The crossbows seemed to take an age to reload. I shouted to Dick. "Take out the guards on the captives!"

It did not feel glorious to watch the end of the Vikings but they had risked all for their slaves and they had paid with their lives. Finally, one of the Vikings ran directly at me. I was dismounted, standing next to the crossbows. They had yet to reload and he ran with his war axe swinging. He threw his shield like a giant discus and it smacked into the chest of a crossbowman. I did not wait for his strike. With my shield held tightly I stepped towards the Viking and pulled back my sword. As his axe smashed into my shield I stabbed forward. My sword tore into his mail and his stomach. I punched so hard that the tip struck his spine. I twisted and pulled. As his guts spilled out the last of the Vikings fell dead at my feet.

The men at arms all cheered but I felt sad. It had been an unequal contest. If Sir Raymond's knight had not broken ranks we might have suffered fewer casualties. As it was one of his knights had a broken leg, suffered when his horse had been killed and two of his men at arms had foolishly advanced beyond my men at arms and been hacked to death.

Sir Raymond said as he viewed his dead and wounded, "I see what you mean. I will heed your advice next time."

The captives were delighted to be rescued. It turned out that half of them had been taken from this side of the great divide. "Are any of you from the manor of Gisburn?"

A woman and her daughter came towards me. "We are my lord. Thank you."

"Is it far from here?"

She shook her head. "Just five miles to the north my lord."

"Harold and Tristan, go with these women and ask Sir Guy if we can stay at his castle this night. He may remember you, Harold. If not then remind him of my name!"

It took some time to strip the Vikings of their valuables and pile their bodies on some dead wood. Wulfric kept shaking his head as he organised the weapons and the treasures. "These Vikings are a strange lot, my lord. There was just a dozen who fought in armour and yet every one of them has a piece of silver or gold around his neck. Most of them have these." He held out a small piece of metal on a thing.

I examined it. "Thor's hammer. There are many Christian Vikings now. Perhaps this explains their raid here. They are going back to their old ways."

"They fight well enough, my lord but no discipline."

"Did we suffer any losses?"

"Two horses, my lord. The riders could do nothing about them. The warriors threw their weapons at them to break up the charge. The lads have a few cuts and bruises. Nothing too bad. I'll stitch them up when I get the chance."

Sir Raymond and I set the pyre alight and mounted our horses as the flames consumed this throwback to a different age when Vikings rampaged and pillaged this land. I nodded to Sir Raymond, "Wulfric will see to Sir Tancred's leg when we reach Gisburn. He may not be able to travel back for a few days anyway; at least not on a horse."

He nodded, "I may well ask this Sir Guy if we can stay there for a couple of days. The captives have been harshly driven."

"If memory serves then this Sir Guy has a poor manor. I would use some of the Viking coins to ensure he does cooperate."

He looked at me strangely, "But we are all brother knights!"

"And these are the northern borders. Sometimes it is not the way it should be." I shrugged. "The King spared his life and so he may be grateful."

The castle was tiny. It was one of the smallest motte and bailies I had ever seen. Sir Guy and his wife greeted us. My first impression of Hilda was that she was thin and wasted. She did not look well. Sir Guy looked pleased to see me and that was a surprise.

"Thank you for rescuing my people, Baron," he held his arm out. "As you can see my manor is small but I can accommodate the knights if you wish."

"Thank you, Sir Guy., I will only need shelter for one night but Sir Raymond here has a knight with a broken leg."

"Stay as long as you can. We are poor but I remember the favour you did me and I am in your debt."

I had my men use the rations we had brought for Gisburn did not have an abundance. With winter approaching I hoped that the young knight had prepared well enough. I discovered that his fortunes had worsened since the abortive rebellion. He had been ostracised by those of his neighbours who had been loyal to the King for his involvement and his other friends had deserted him. He had but two men at arms left.

The next morning, as I left with my men I wondered if they would survive the winter. He had spoken to me of going to the east to take the cross and hope for better fortune there. We both knew he would not do it. He had not enough coin for the voyage and his wife looked too sickly. We would have had no ransom had we tried to extract one when he had been captured. It showed me the result of ill advised decisions.

I was brought out of my reflections by the excitement of Tristan. He was bombarding Harold with questions as he relived every moment of the skirmish. He finally asked me one, "Baron, how did you teach your horse to use his hooves? He is not a warhorse."

"No Scout is no warhorse but he has intelligence and I used his natural ability. Get to know your mount, Tristan. It is every bit as much a weapon as your sword or your shield. You did well yesterday."

"But I only used my lance once."

"And yet you hit your target and you did not fall off your horse when you did so. Work with Harold until the ground is too hard to fall upon and by spring you will be a knight."

When I told Adela of the manor at Gisburn she nodded, sympathetically, "When my father had Norton he found it hard to survive. The King wanted his taxes and he did not care if the crops had failed or we had had raids. You have made this a safer place to live and you should be proud of your achievements."

She was right. The north was not an easy place to be successful. After King William had cleared away the old Saxon lords and the villagers it had been a wasteland for many years. Only Durham, with its Prince Bishop had prospered. Now the land and the people were recovering but it only took a wolf winter to set us back.

Adela and I discussed the improvements John was making. "You should make him steward, Alfraed. He knows how to run the estate, I have seen that. The King will call upon you again. I could try to run the estate but it is not in my heart."

"I know that you are right about John. I will speak with him on the morrow."

John was, of course delighted. Surprisingly he did not negotiate too seriously when I discussed his remuneration. When I asked him about that he smiled and seemed almost boyish. "I know that you are giving me a great opportunity and I am young yet. Perhaps when I have done the job for some years we will discuss this again but for now I am happy to be given the opportunity to learn."

The months leading up to Christmas were always filled with the myriad of tasks which we had to complete before the winter. While John organised the food for the winter and the stabling of the animals, the rest of my men cut wood and gathered together all that they would need for the winter. Aiden and his rabbits were in great demand. Cloaks and mittens made from their fur could be lifesavers in a harsh winter. I worked with Harold and Tristan. I needed two more knights and these two were close to ready. I spent each day honing their skills. Harold was older and stronger but Tristan had more natural ability, especially with a sword. It was a pleasure to work with them. Even as November approached I began to think about the two new squires we would need. Tristan and his father would have to look to their own manor but we needed two from our lands. That would be my task over the winter.

Christmas that year was almost benign. I walked my walls without mittens and just a cloak. It was my son, William's second Christmas and he could now walk. He was more of a child now and he recognised me. He no longer burst into tears when he saw me. Life was good. We also held a feast on St Stephen's day and some of my knights and their families crammed into my hall. Edward, Richard and Wulfstan all came as did Athelstan and Osric. It was a joyous time. Tristan and Harold were firm friends now and I looked at Sir Richard as he watched his son. He was now lost to his father. He had made that transition from son to warrior and he could not go back. It did not seem that long ago that had been me and, as William giggled at Edward pulling faces, I knew that one day that would come to me. That Christmas, however, was the most peaceful one I could remember. Sadly, it would be the last one without tribulation for many years to come. That was the Christmas I needed to see into the future. There were storm clouds over the horizon and they would sweep through my land and the whole domain of King Henry. We had no premonition and no warning that Christmas and so we enjoyed peace. It would not last.

Chapter 8

The Scots had had a long time to lick their wounds and brood on their failures. We had had a secure border since the abortive rebellion. The single raid by the Vikings had been our only conflict. I had begun to wonder if we had won. Perhaps we had taught them all a lesson. It was pleasant living in a peaceful, prosperous world. That all changed after Easter. We had held the sessions and paid our taxes. John planned improvements to our lands. William the Mason continued to work on and improve my castle. Buttresses were added; ladders replaced by stairs. I did not mind the expense. It would be worth it if we were protected from harm. Besides we had more money available to spend. Edward and the other knights in my conroi had all had good springs and increased the yields of their lands. They were not the knights who spent all their time hunting and enjoying life. They knew the value of their manors and they worked hard to improve them. I now knew how lucky I was to have such knights serving alongside me.

The days were becoming longer and Adela and I had taken to walking the ramparts with my son. We were all wrapped up well against the chill wind which blew across the sea. William just liked to run. Every time he did so Adela's hand went to her mouth. "He is a boy and they run."

"And they fall!"

"When he falls he will learn. It is life. Do not worry about him."

"I worry about him as I worry about you." She smiled at me and put her hand on mine, "Besides, it will not be long before there will be another child born within these walls."

I had noticed that her cheeks had been flushed of late, "You are with child?" She nodded, "Then that is wonderful news." We had something else to look forward to. Life was becoming good once more and I threw myself into running the manor.

Harold and Tristan had been knighted at Easter and I had taken on Leofric, the falconer, as my squire. He was rough around the edges and he was not a perfect choice but he was willing and he was strong. I needed someone who was good with animals, strong and willing to work hard. Leofric had all of those qualities and he had shown some skill with a sword. Harold promised to guide him and, until Harold chose his own squire then Leofric would serve us both. He had grown considerably since Aiden had trained him as a falconer and, at sixteen summers; he was the right age to begin training as a squire.

Harold and I had had our armour improved by Alf. He had fitted metal plates around our knees and that added protection. When we rode our knees were vulnerable to a blow from a soldier on foot or a deflected lance. Our helmets had been modified. We had had the nasal removed and cheek guards fitted. Both of us enjoyed the improved vision and I could never remember a blow to the nasal. The back was strengthened for we had both been hit there.

The warnings of danger came from Bishop Flambard. Since we had rescued him he had been in constant touch with us. He realised that we protected his lands from the south. He was keen to maintain my loyalty and he sent gifts to Adela and Faren. He summoned me to his castle at Durham. His message, whilst guarded, told me that there might be danger. I took just Leofric while I sent messages to my knights warning them that we might require a muster. Leofric had no armour yet and it was an old palfrey he rode. He was still learning to ride well and the old horse was just the right one for someone starting to ride. I suspected that Leofric would take more time to train than Harold. Harold had grown up in a world of war and danger in the forests of Sherwood. Leofric had grown up enjoying the woods as a place of excitement. He would need to learn how to fight. He was still growing but he had a surcoat. Since we had returned from the Empire Adela had arranged for women with nimble fingers to make the garments for us. It benefitted the town and gave us better surcoats. He had his shield and a helmet but I knew that he yearned for mail. He asked me about it as we headed north on the ride to Durham.

"If I am to fight will I be given armour, Baron?"

"You need to earn your armour. Besides I would not risk you in combat yet."

"What will I do then? Watch while others fight?"

"You will carry my banner and you will watch the horses. Harold did the same. It took him almost five years to become a knight and he was already a warrior. You know hawks and you are stealthy. Those skills will serve you well. I need to make you a warrior and that will take time. You watch, you listen, and you learn. I know you know how to be silent. That was what made you a good falconer." As we neared the bridge over the Wear I said, "If it does not suit you to be a knight then you can return and be a falconer. I shall not mind. Harold was not sure at first. There is naught wrong with the life of a falconer. But you must choose to be a squire and, perhaps, a knight."

"No, Baron, I would like to be a knight and I am sorry for my foolish questions."

"No question is ever foolish it is just the answers which may be."

The last time I had passed through this gate I had been in disguise and it was held by the men of Northumbria. Now I was welcomed by those within. The banner which Leofric held aloft had been sewn in the winter by Adela and her ladies. It was a larger one than before and the yellow of the star was brighter. My name and my banner were known. That could be a good thing but I knew that in combat it would draw my enemies like moths to a flame. It was important to have a rallying point on the battlefield. Our horses were taken from us and my banner left inside the gate of the keep.

The Bishop awaited us in his Great Hall. There were servants present and a clerk, but no knights. "Ah Baron Alfraed, welcome." Leofric was ignored. He was a squire and he was treated like a servant. I smiled at his confusion. It was all part of the learning process. While I was offered a seat, he stood. He was overawed by his surroundings. I noticed his face as he stared at the magnificent tapestries hanging on the wall. Then his eyes were drawn to the high roof. My humble castle had a much smaller one.

The Bishop was a diplomatic man and he began our discourse with pleasantries. "Did you and your people prosper over the winter?"

This was a question he already knew the answer to; Roger of Ripon had collected my taxes before he had visited the Bishop. Perhaps he was being polite or perhaps he was checking on honesty. "We have done well. I have a good steward and he manages to turn small investments into large profits."

"And your church?"

As a reward for saving the city I had been allowed to build a church and the Bishop had given me a priest. Father Ralph was a little more serious than Father Peter but the people liked him. They expected a priest to be aloof and distant. He was all of that. "It is progressing my lord. It will take some time before it is worthy of a visit from you."

"*Where two or three are gathered together, there is my Church.*'" He smiled as he quoted the Bible at me.

"Just so." I wanted him to get on with what he had to say. I disliked preambles of any description. He must have sensed my impatience for he leaned forward, "I have spies who travel the borders. They tell me that the Gospatric family now lives on their Scottish estates." .

"That does not harm us, surely. If they are north of the border then they cannot plot and plan."

He shook his head irritably, "We do not get the taxes for one thing and their lands do not bring us profit but there is a more sinister aspect to this. I believe that they are colluding with the Scots for an invasion."

"And the King of Scotland; is he part of their plans?"

"No, he is not part of it but there are many of his lords who wish to see the lands the King's father conquered, returning to them. They all had a difficult winter. Like you, the rest of the north prospered. It is envy. The Scots wish what we have. They did not plan as well and those rebellious lords would have the lands which produce wheat."

I waited. I could not see how this affected me. We were far to the south of the lands claimed by the Scots. However, if they wished for lands which bore wheat then they would have to come through our valley. Perhaps there might be danger.

He continued, "I know that they intend to attack my lands but I know not when. I cannot keep my men armed for they need to work their fields and their farms. I have few men at arms and, since the rebellion, even fewer knights."

There had been a key phrase in his words, he had said, *'my lands'*. He was not worried about my valley but his own lands and estates which were further north. "I know when they will come."

He shot me a puzzled look, "You do? How?"

I enjoyed surprising people. I knew the times because it was when I would have chosen to attack. "There are two times. The first is in the next month or so when your sheep and your cattle have given birth and they are on the hillsides. The second time is in the autumn when the harvest is in. I would guess that they will attack both times. They are the times when the fyrd cannot be called to arms for they will be busy working in their fields."

He nodded, "You are right. Then what do I do about it? The King will not be happy if he does not get his taxes."

I hid my smile behind my hand. The Bishop was more worried about his loss of his own income. I waved an airy arm towards the north. "There are lords further north, close to Hexham and the New Castle. The Roman wall still prevents many crossing points. The Scots could be stopped there."

"Sadly, much of the stone from the wall has been taken to make castles and after the rebellion most of the border lords were either killed or fled to their Scottish lands. The border is more fragile than it once was"

I knew what he wanted but I wanted him to ask rather than me suggesting it.

"Baron, I would have you and your conroi protect my estates to the north."

"Are they not beyond the Palatinate of Durham?"

He shifted uncomfortably in his chair, "Yes they are but they are south of the Tyne and are part of England. The King would not be happy if they were attacked."

"He would not be happy if I abandoned the valley of the Tees to attack your enemies."

"By protecting the north, you protect the valley." He was a clever man but trying to defeat me with logic was a mistake. I had had my education in Constantinople where I had argued with the greatest of philosophers.

"I am sorry Bishop but I cannot commit my conroi so far from home. The King charged me with the Valley of the Tees and not the Valley of the Tyne. If you are attacked and summon me then I will respond."

"By that time, it would be too late." I could hear the panic inflect his voice. "You have a worthy reputation, Baron, as someone who has a keen military mind. You showed that in your rescue of me. I need a mobile force based north of here." I saw him chewing his lip as he considered what to do. "How about this then? I will pay you and your knights to be based at my estates."

This was a better proposition. I did not need the Bishop's gold but my knights and men at arms did and they would all be stronger because of the reward. "How much would you pay?"

"One gold piece to each knight for each week they were here. Ten silver pieces for each man at arms and five pieces of silver for each archer."

"And the same for the squires."

"Five silver pieces?" I nodded. He smiled with relief. He must be even richer than I had thought for he had not quibbled over the exorbitant amount I had requested. "Then when can I expect you?"

"I will need to ride south and gather my men. We will leave some behind to watch our manors. We will return in fourteen nights."

He nodded, "I have an estate at Chollerford. It controls a crossing of the Tyne and is at the last standing section of the wall."

"Is there a castle?"

"No, but there are the remains of an old Roman fort."

I nodded. That would do. "I will need authority for your steward there and to let the other lords know that I act under your orders. The manor will need to provide for my men."

"When you return then the documents will be ready."

"And a banner signifying that I fight for Durham rather than myself."

"That is a good idea. It will show the barbarians and the rebels that I rule here yet." He would risk his banner but naught else.

As we left and headed south I reflected on the Bishop's words. He thought he had power but he was clinging on to the little he had. He was no Bishop Odo who had ridden about the north imposing his will on all of the land. He had been a true Prince Bishop. Flambard was more a Bishop who yearned to be the Prince. King Henry was wrong to spend so much time in Normandy and neglect the north. His son controlled the west but there appeared to be no one to do the same in the North. We needed a Marcher Lord here as well as in Wales. I knew that one day it would come to hurt us.

We were nearing Norton when Leofric finally spoke. "My lord, does that mean that I will get five silver pennies a week?"

I laughed, "You have got sharp little ears. No, I will be given the coins for you. As your lord, I bear your expenses. You may get some coins but, as John will tell you, running a conroi is expensive. Do not worry Leofric; we will get you a mail shirt made, at least." He was delighted at the prospect.

I was honest with my knights and I told them what they would be paid. Although the thought of spending many months away from their manors was not attractive the coins they would earn was. In addition, their own manors would be spared the expense of maintaining their men. That would be borne by the Bishop from his estate at Chollerford. Most decided to go to war. Wulfstan declined to join us and I did not blame him. With three young children, he wanted to spend as much time with them as he could. He had spent most of his life fighting and he did not need the money. I was happy too. He would watch my lands. The rest all agreed. I chose to take just ten men at arms and ten archers. As Adela was with child I wanted her and William protecting. Harold had yet to hire men at arms and he did not have a squire. He brought just two archers; they were young men who came from a large family. They were good choices.

We said our farewells and left just before May Day. I think the Bishop was relieved to see us return when I had promised. Perhaps he had thought I might change my mind. If he was disappointed in our numbers he did not show it. With just ten knights, thirty-five men at arms and twenty archers we were not a large force but we were all mounted and I was confident that we could discourage any force which came south. With squires and servants, we numbered seventy-five in total. I gave the Bishop's banner to Harold who held it proudly aloft. We headed north up the road which led to Scotland.

Hexham still remained a burnt-out shell. The King's new lord of the manor had yet to be appointed. As we crossed the bridge I looked at the potential for defence. If we had to retreat then this was a good place to stop an advancing enemy. The bridge stood and my archers could stop an assault. Although the river was fordable mailed knights and men at arms would not risk such a perilous crossing.

The manor at Chollerford was not a large one and was just a few miles north of Hexham. The manor house looked as though it had not been altered since the time of King Ethelred. It was a simple wooden house with a drainage ditch running around it. It looked to be profitable. There were outhouses and buildings surrounding the hall in an untidy tangle. It looked as though we would be well fed. I saw cattle, sheep and pigs as well as fowl clucking around the yard. The steward, Ralph son of Athelstan, had a family and they lived in the manor. He read the letter from the Bishop. I saw the sadness on his face. "My family and I will move out, Baron."

"There is no need, Ralph. We will stay with our men. There would be nothing to be gained from having a roof over our head but we will need food." I pointed to the forests which surrounded the manor; there was little land for farming. "I will have my men hunt there but we will need milk, bread and cheese."

He brightened immediately. "It will have to be oat bread, my lord."

I saw Guiscard frown at that. He was the one most recently arrived from Normandy. He would learn. "We can eat oaten bread, Ralph; you have ale too?"

"Yes, my lord, fine ale. It is brewed by my wife." I could see the quality from his girth and his rosy cheeks.

"Then we will have some sent each day." I pointed across the river to the old Roman fort. "We will be based in the old Roman fort."

His wife gripped his arm, "It is said, my lord, that it is haunted and there was a battle near here. St Oswald killed the mighty Welsh King, Cadwallon. The ghosts of the Welsh warriors wander the wall at night."

I laughed, "We are warriors and we will endure the dead. We have sent plenty to their deaths. They do not frighten men who fight for God and the Bishop."

We headed towards the fort which was on the other side of the Roman Road. Surprisingly the outer walls of the old Roman fort stood and looked as though they would not require much work to improve them. Edward nodded. "We can build a sort of gate here my lord and we can make shelters. This is better than I hoped."

"And I. I think it must have been built for cavalry. They look to be stables down there." I pointed to the gate near to the river and the bridge. "I want two men on guard at the bridge at all times. Sir Richard, assign them." He nodded. "Dick and Aiden, I want you and the rest of my archers splitting into pairs. Spend tomorrow finding out what the land looks like and then the day after we begin our patrols. Right, now I want you to go and hunt some meat for tomorrow. It will give you the lie of the land."

Baron Raymond de Brus said, "But we could just stay here. The Bishop only wants us to stop an attacker. There are none."

"When I do a job, Sir Raymond, I do it to the best of my ability. Besides that, I do not want to be surprised. When the Scots come we attack them when I choose not when they suddenly appear." Thus chastened, Sir Raymond nodded and coloured. I looked at Edward and gave him the slightest of nods. I would leave it to him to explain to Sir Raymond the way I worked. I had not had the luxury of getting to know my new knight.

We had enough tents for the knights and Wulfric organised the others to use branches to make roofs for the barracks. I hoped it would not rain over much but we were hardy men and summers were generally dry. When Ralph's wife and children came for us to tell us that food was ready we had already achieved much. We had just begun to eat when our hunters returned. From the size of their catch there had to be plenty of game in these forests. With no lord at Hexham and the Bishop in Durham no one would have hunted for some time. We would eat well.

I had forgotten what it was like to sleep on the ground. Although it took me some time to fall asleep I would soon become accustomed to it. Leofric seemed excited when he woke me. "There are many knights here my lord and I am the youngest squire."

"Good, then you will be able to learn from them! Remember your most important task is to look after Star and Scout. They must both learn to trust you. When I go into battle you need to be close enough to see if my mount weakens and then you bring whichever I am not riding."

"Yes, my lord."

Although I was being strict with him, I liked his enthusiasm. He was young enough to see much of this as a game. My words would make him stronger. I sent Dick to the New Castle with orders to find out the disposition of the garrison. While the rest of my archers scouted I had my knights and men at arms practise some new manoeuvres. If they were disloyal then it might prove problematic. We had to fight as one. If each part worked well then, the whole would have a greater chance of success. "We are mobile and we will use the charge but there will be times when we have to fight on foot." I saw the looks of disbelief on the faces of Raymond and Guiscard. "We have done this before and it can work. With archers behind us and lances held before us we can deter any enemy. If we are outnumbered then it is a tactic we will use. Get your lances and spears and let us try it out."

We spent all morning working out the best way to face an enemy. I placed Edward and Richard on the flanks for they were the most solid and reliable of my knights and I placed my new knights between them along with Sir Guy and Sir Geoffrey. I left a proud Leofric holding my banner in the middle while I mounted Scout and rode at the conroi as though I were the Scots. Although small in number I was impressed with the appearance we presented. Our array of knights would stop an enemy; of that I was certain.

After three days, my archers had explored the land to the north, east and the west. The men at arms at the New Castle, Gospatric's retainers, informed Dick that they had been given orders to protect the river crossing. Dick had no reason to doubt them. He told me that they seemed honest enough. There were not many of them but they could easily delay an invading army. Edward pointed out that they could not stop a rebel army led by their leader, the putative Earl of Northumbria. I knew that but hoped that Gospatric would not wish to draw attention to himself. He would be more likely to have others do his bidding. As he had shown the last time he was a shrewd plotter and had distanced himself from the actual rebellion. I was certain he would do so again.

Had I had enough men I would have placed a small number at the south of the bridge at the New Castle but I had to work with those that I had. I sent a rider back to tell the Bishop of the situation and I advised him to have the road from the New Castle watched. He had enough men at arms to do that. A warning would be all that they would need to give. Secretly I was still convinced they would travel down the road we guarded. The river could be forded at many places. When the Romans had built their wall, they had known they could not stop the old tribes of Scotland crossing the border and raiding but by building their forts and their wall they could stop them taking their ill-gotten gains back. That was my plan. They would try to cross the river first. It would be later that they would try the river fords.

On the fourth day, the scouts reported a column of men heading south. We saddled our horses and, leaving the archers on the crumbling walls of the Roman fort, I led my mounted men to the end of the bridge. The valley rose gently to a high point a half a mile from the end of the stone structure. We rode to the top of the rise. As soon as we were there we saw the banners of the Scots. It was a large, raiding warband.

"Aiden ride to the New Castle and warn them that there is a Scottish warband on the loose." As he turned to ride I said, "Keep your ears and eyes open. See how they react."

He grinned, "Aye, Baron." He knew men as well as he knew animals.

If we could see them then I knew that they could see us. The rabble that approached became more organised as their leaders gave orders. I sought the banners. I was looking for the banner of the Scottish king. I could not see it. Nor could I see Gospatrick's banner either. In fact, I recognised none of them. That was both a good and a bad thing. It meant that we had not fought them before; they would not know us but we did not know them either.

Raymond de Brus' family had estates in Scotland too. "Baron Raymond, do you recognise any of those banners?"

He peered north, "I can see the banner of Fife and Dunbar but none who are Norman."

Harold had the sharpest of eyes. "My lord, there are some knights with plain shields and they follow no banner."

"They will be English rebels who do not wish to be identified." I had seen such deception before.

We had the slight advantage of a slope. "Prepare lances." Our formations had been practised. The one we adopted was a line of knights with the squires as a half line and banners behind and then four equal lines of men at arms. I had chosen the formation because the width of the road allowed it. The old Roman Road had ditches and scrubby bushes alongside. They would either have to knock us from the road or find another way around.

When I saw them forming a line of knights I knew they intended the former. "They mean to try to destroy us with a charge up the hill. Let us earn our coin this day."

We began to trot down the road. I had impressed upon all of my men the need to obey orders. Leofric was directly behind me with my banner and it was his movements with the banner which would give the commands. The Scottish knights rode up the hill towards us. I noticed that they came at us in a ragged line. They were not knee to knee. Our speed increased so that we were cantering. We needed to go no faster for the slope was with us. In contrast, the Scots were whipping their horses as they struggled up the slope which sapped energy from already tired legs.

I lowered my lance when we were just fifty paces from them. At twenty paces, I pulled back my lance and then we struck their line with a shattering smashing of wood. Their lack of discipline meant that we knocked aside the five knights who had faced us and the four who followed were pushed into the ditches. The third line did not even have lances prepared. I saw a knight with a yellow shield try to bring his shield around to his right side. He failed and my lance took him under his arm as his sword failed to break my lance. Edward, Guy and Richard were in their element. They had all done this many times before. My men were constantly at war and it showed. When their spears shattered they drew their swords in one easy and controlled motion. They did not panic. The Scots, in contrast, showed that they might have practised with their lances but they had not fought together. They fought as individual knights.

We had done enough already. The knights and mounted men at arms had been disrupted. If we continued to charge we might kill more Scots but we risked being overwhelmed by superior numbers. I could see a mass of men on foot with spears and they were forming a shield wall already. "Fall back. Leofric, signal retreat!"

We had practised this too. We all stopped our horses, punched forward at the warriors before us and then turned. We had the problem of negotiating the road littered with men and horses. Four Scottish knights were down and would not rise again. Two horses lay writhing with lances in their bodies. Other knights and men at arms crawled into the ditches to avoid the thundering hooves. It would take them some time for our enemies to reorganise.

We had not escaped unscathed. Sir Raymond's horse was injured. I sent him back to the camp. Tristan had also suffered a wound to his leg and he accompanied, reluctantly, Sir Raymond.

"Wulfric bring up eight men at arms. If we have to charge again they can lead."

"Aye, my lord."

We watched as the Scots debated what to do. Harold's sharp eyes saw their intention. "They are sending men into the woods and forests, my lord. They are going to outflank us."

"Sir Edward, take the rest of the men back to the bridge. Harold, stay with me. They cannot see beyond us and we can return to the bridge when they have tired themselves out in a charge."

The top of the hill felt lonely when they left. There were just eleven of us. My men at arms were not worried. I could see that in their posture. All seemed relaxed. This was a calculated move. I wanted to show the Scots that we did not fear them. If eleven men could halt them then they might be more tentative in their attacks in the future.

The Scottish knights and men at arms reformed and began to come at us. Someone had taken charge and they came at us tighter now; they were knee to knee and there were no chinks in their defence. Our retreat would need to be timed well. I knew that they would have their foot racing through the woods. The Scots liked to use lightly armed warriors who had a helmet sword and shield only. They were fierce warriors and the woods would suit them. They would move almost as fast as the horses which advanced up the road.

I waited until the Scots lowered their lances and I shouted, "Fall back!" I did not need to say *'to the bridge'* they already knew that. I could see my knights on the bridge already. We had cleared away the scrubby growth at the end of the bridge and an enemy would have to risk my archers on the walls of the fort and at the southern end of the bridge. As we descended the hill I saw that the Scots had spurred their horses on. It was a mistake for they lost order and their horses were becoming exhausted. They were no longer knee to knee as the more eager knights went to the fore.

"Leofric, signal the charge!"

He signalled the charge and I saw Edward lead my knights up the road. "Two lines along the edge of the road!" I was the last man and I watched as my ten companions split into two lines so that the road was clear for our charging knights. As Edward and the knights charged past me I pulled Scout around and followed them. This time our charge was halted as my men smashed into the enemy. Sir Geoffrey was unhorsed. I rode into the gap and punched my lance through the face of the exultant Scot who thought to finish him off. He tumbled backwards from his horse. We had stopped them and there was no point in risking further losses.

"Sir Geoffrey, lead your horse back to the bridge. We will follow."

I looked up the road to the enemy. They had superior numbers and were now using them. I suspect they thought we had fled through fear. They would learn differently. The rest of their horses had now followed and were galloping down the hill.

"Fall back to the fort."

Once again, the Scots had to negotiate the casualties on the road and we reached the end of the bridge with ease. Dick had taken it upon himself to bring ten archers to the bridge and, as the Scots advanced they were showered with arrows. Three horses and two men were hit. They quickly retreated.

"Well done. Wulfric, have a barrier erected here and Dick have six of your archers watch them."

As my men set about their task I dismounted and took off my helmet. "You did well Leofric!"

"Thank you, my lord."

Sir Richard and Sir Edward took off their helmets and joined me. Edward pointed to the west. "They will lick their wounds and cross the river you know."

I nodded, "But that cannot be today for it is coming on to dark and they will not risk the Tyne at night. They would lose too many men. Tomorrow we place scouts along the river and when we see where they are using to cross we make life difficult."

"This is a large band, Baron. I estimate almost two hundred men." I could see that Sir Raymond was worried by the large numbers facing us.

"But we have hurt them already. They were knights who fell. The bulk of their band is made up of those who fight on foot. They cannot out run us. The knights are the leaders. Without them the rabble will fall back when we attack. The advantage is still with us and our plan works yet."

As we led our horses back into the old fort I pointed to the land which rose gently south, towards Hexham. "There is little for them south of here for twenty miles. Those are twenty miles we can use. If they pass us we can attack from ambush. For now, we wait and see what they will do."

We unsaddled our horses and took off our mail. Some bathed in the river. They were my men and they were showing the Scots, now camped on the other bank, that they were not afraid of them. I stood with my knights. Tristan had his arm in a sling. Wulfric had assured me it was a precaution but advised against having him in the front rank.

"Tristan, you can carry the Bishop's banner the next time we fight." I saw him swell with pride and the nod of thanks from his father. I pointed to the Scots. "They have no archers. If they had then our men would have been attacked when they bathed."

Edward smiled, "Then we can use our archers to keep them at bay."

"But they could cross the river anywhere!"

"Yes, Sir Guiscard, but, if they do, then tomorrow our scouts will be out again and they will soon pick up their trail. We are all mounted and we use that advantage. We can move much faster than men on foot and they have to cross rivers. That limits their movements. It is one reason the Bishop and I chose this as our base." I began to plan our next moves. The enemy might not know what he would do but I had his options in my head. I would plan to defeat whatever they might try.

Chapter 9

We had eaten when Aiden came galloping in. His horse and his breeks were wet. Edward laughed, "Have you been swimming, Aiden."

He had the good grace to laugh. "Aye my lord." He pointed to the north bank. "I came from the New Castle along the northern bank. I saw movements ahead of me and I watched. The Scots are building a raft two miles downstream. I chose the wet road back here."

"And the garrison?"

"I think they were taken by surprise, my lord. They certainly began to prepare for the worst. I do not think they knew of the attack."

"Good. Then get something to eat and after we have eaten we will see about this raft."

Sir Guy pointed to the Scots across the river. "Then there must be almost two hundred in this band for there are still many camped yonder."

"Just because you see fires do not assume that each one has men around it. I have used such ruses before. And besides there is no point in worrying about the odds. We are paid to fight and we will do so. We fight until they go away."

Edward laughed, "Why worry? They are only Scots. They may be brave but they are reckless. They hope to intimidate with a wild charge but if you are resolute then it will come to nothing." Edward was the rock of my conroi. He would still stand when all else lay dead.

I gathered my archers and Wulfric around me. "Dick, choose ten good woodsmen. Wulfric find ten men who can wield an axe and move stealthily. Edward, you and the other knights stay here. Move around as much as you can and make them believe that we are unaware of their raft. Keep a watch to the west. They may have two rafts under construction. I will take Harold. He is a good woodsman. We will not need armour."

We slipped out of the south gate. It was as far away from the Scots as it was possible to get. We did not take horses and Aiden let us swiftly through the woods to the place he had seen raft building. Although they had chosen a spot well away from the bridge we heard their axes as we neared them. We moved even more cautiously then. I was not wearing mail for I did not wish to

97

be seen. I expected to have to do little save watch my archers and men at arms.

The Scots had done well and already the log raft was floating in the water. The Scots who had built it were making it more secure. They could not just launch it and pole across; the current was too swift for that. They would need to use a rope and secure it to the southern bank and then have men haul it across. It was the way Ethelred moved his ferry at Stockton. I waved my men towards the trees across from the place they would need to use to land the raft. I intended to let them cross and then destroy them and their raft. It would discourage further raft building. We hid ourselves just twenty paces from the river bank. We were invisible. Trees overhung the river and tall grasses and reeds rose high to give us cover. The wait gave me the opportunity to identify them. The huddle of men who supervised was the knights. The leader was the Earl of Moray. I recognised William fitz Duncan and his livery. The quartered lions and the blue and white checked fess were distinctive. If these were his men then they had travelled a long way south. There were five of his household knights with him and I counted at least thirty men. They were men at arms and half had mail on. The other half did not and I knew that they would be the ones to haul the raft across.

We were close enough to hear them speaking. Unfortunately, the sound of the Earl was hidden by the guttural Gaelic of the men below his men toiling with the raft. He was giving orders, for one of his squires mounted his horse and rode back along the bank to the main camp. I saw why when four men dived into the water and swam across. They were pulling two ropes behind them. Even though they were strong swimmers they were still pulled downstream and they had to struggle back along the southern bank towards us pulling the sodden ropes with them. They tied the ropes around the bole of a mighty willow and then waved. The men at arms who had mail on began to board the raft. The ones without mail lined the two sides. Half of them had poles, to use on the downstream side while the others took hold of the ropes on the upstream side.

I tapped Dick on the shoulder and he and his archers nocked an arrow. I nodded to Wulfric whose men slipped through the undergrowth to the four exhausted men who were resting on the bank. When the raft was half way across I yelled, "Now!"

Dick only had ten archers but they were less than forty paces from their targets. The ten men hauling the ropes died instantly.

The four swimmers died even as they watched their comrades raise shields to protect those who were poling. The current had the raft and even though the men worked hard they were fighting a losing battle. Dick's arrows did not always find a target but gradually the men with the poles fell into the river. I heard the crack of axes as the ropes were severed by Wulfric and his axe men. The raft with the doomed men at arms drifted away eastward in the dark. Soon it would meet the South Tyne and become even faster. Even if it beached on the south bank the fifteen men at arms who had survived would not be a threat. We waited until the Scots marched back to their camp before we did the same.

Although my men were excited and exultant I warned them against over optimism. "We are still outnumbered and I think they will try to force the bridge."

Sir Geoffrey shook his head. "That would be madness We have archers and the bridge is narrow."

"We have but twenty archers and, as we saw tonight, they have men who can swim beneath the bridge and attack us."

Sir Raymond asked, "Will we be mounted when next we fight?"

I knew the reason for his question. His palfrey had been injured and he would have to ride his destrier. In such a confined space, it could easily be badly hurt and his destrier was his most expensive piece of equipment. "No, there is little point. We face them on foot. If they are foolish enough to charge us across the bridge then they will suffer many casualties. When it is pitch black then I will have logs placed in the middle of the bridge. If anyone tries to move them then Dick and his archers will have some easy target practice."

We enjoyed a peaceful night. We had spoiled their plans and they would, even now be working out another strategy. I knew that we had not hurt them enough to deter them. They had much support amongst the absent rebels. None of those who had risen in the previous rebellion would join this attack but I knew it would have their tacit approval. Cynically, I knew that this was why the Bishop of Durham had sent us north to fend off the attack. He could absolve himself of all blame should the invasion and a future rebellion take place. I was King Henry and Robert of Gloucester's man. We were expendable.

I had Wulfric wake everyone before dawn. The logs which had been cut down in the night had been jammed between the walls of the bridge and would prevent horses charging. I had had them placed irregularly. I knew horses could jump logs. Wulfric and my men at arms had taken some of the poorly made weapons we had captured from the dead Scots and fashioned them into crude caltrops. They were spread between the logs on the bridge. If they used their horses then they would get a shock. Finally, we had taken some of the fat rendered from the pigs we had eaten and that has been poured onto the bridge. It would make the surface slippery. It would not be an easy crossing for the Scots.

I made sure my men ate. A man fought better on a full stomach. I lined my knights up at the bridge. We each held a long ash spear. I could have used my men at arms but it was dishonourable to risk our men while we watched. Behind them I had two rows of men at arms who were also armed with long spears and, behind them, I had my archers. The squires, led by Tristan and his injured arm, held the banners before the gate so that the Scots would know whom they fought. The remaining men at arms I split between the gate of the camp and guarding the buttresses of the bridge. The only ones not fighting were Aiden and those watching the horses. We had to hold them at the bridge end. If they reached the gateway then we had lost for there was no gate; it was just a wooden barrier to stop a surprise attack.

They advanced and they came as I had expected. Their horsemen led. There were forty knights, squires and men at arms. Above them, on the slope, the mass of wild warriors with swords, axes and shields waited to fall upon us and wreak death and destruction once their horses had broken us. I saw the Earl of Moray, William fitz Duncan, with four other knights waiting to lead them down and end our resistance. I smiled. He was not confident. If he was then he would have led the charge himself. He had allowed his younger, eager knights who wanted the glory to charge us. My name and my banner drew them on. I had been a thorn in the side of the Scots and the younger knights were keen to remove it!

The charge would be led by three knights who looked to be the same family. They had a blue shield with three red fesses across them. I saw them shouting to their men and there was an enormous cheer. I daresay they were inspiring them. Then they charged towards the bridge. They would have seen the logs but I assumed they would have thought they could leap them. The pig fat, the irregular placement of the logs and the caltrops would be surprises. Dick and his archers had their arrows jammed into the ground next to them. They would release six arrows in quick succession once they began. There was little point until the Scots were just paces away from our spears. Their arrows would kill indiscriminately. Horses and riders would fall. One hundred and twenty arrows loosed at such close range would hit more than they missed.

"Jam the haft of your spear into the ground and lock shields." Even with our archers I could not guarantee that someone would not get through. If they did then we needed a wall of metal to halt the mass of horseflesh and mail which would be crashing towards us. The Scots had to slow as they reached the logs. One who tried to rush found a caltrop and then some pig fat. The horse reared and fell over the side into the river taking the knight to a watery and ignoble grave. The others slowed and, already, their charge was doomed to failure. When they reached halfway they were so busy looking for traps and fat that they failed to see the arrows which plunged down vertically at them. My archers released four more flights before making their arrows fly horizontally. Horses were hit and enraged. They reared and bucked at the pain they were suffering. Some arrows struck mail and shields but many found flesh. Once the arrows began to fly horizontally the knights were just twenty paces from our shields and our spears.

Despite the rain of death four knights on wild horses made it through the maelstrom of murder we had inflicted upon them. Two of the horses were maddened by arrows which would suck the last vestige of life from them very shortly. Their nostrils flared they charged towards us eager to stop the pain they were suffering.

"Brace!"

We had practised this and the men at arms jammed their bodies behind ours. The four horses were impaled on our spears. Their dying bodies pushed us back towards the gate but their bodies fell like a barrier before us. I let go of my shattered spear, took out my sword and stabbed the stunned knight who tried to disentangle himself from his dying horse. Edward, Sir Guy and Sir Richard all despatched the three other knights. One of them looked to be mortally wounded anyway; he had three arrows in his chest. Eight of the horsemen at the rear had halted for their way was barred and they began to pull back to safety. Dick and his archers kept up their rain of death and another two were hit before they reached the Earl.

"Bring up spears!"

The attack had broken half of our spears. The wild men would attack soon and they would be less easy to stop. Our arrows had brought down horses as well as men. A falling horse stopped a rider as effectively as an arrow. The bridge now had a route of dead horses and knights over which the Scots could advance. The caltrops and the pig fat were no longer a barrier to the men on foot. The men who would charge us next would hide behind their shields. Dick and his archers would have a smaller target and it would be down to the knights to stop them. As the spears were passed up I looked to see if we had suffered losses. The last four knights had failed to strike a blow but I knew that the others would be feeling the bruises from the crashing horses. Our armour and gambesons gave us some protection but we would still know that we had been in a battle when we had finished this day.

The Earl of Moray launched his attack. He had waited until all of his knights who had been wounded had dragged themselves back along with the remaining horses. The bridge was now littered with the dead horses and men at arms. The foot advanced. I had expected a wild charge across the bridge but they came steadily and were led by a dismounted knight. They had bunched together, protected by their shields so that we could not see a gap into which to send an arrow.

I heard Dick, my captain of archers, advise his men. "When they step over the logs and the bodies then there may be a gap. Our arrows are like gold do not waste them. Release when you have a target only."

The Scots had reached half way across the bridge before we had our chance. As they carefully climbed over the carcass of a dead destrier one of them caught his foot in the reins and bridle. He tumbled forward. My archers saw their chance. Three arrows flew into the gap and punched into the next soldier. The Scot who had fallen was struck in the neck by two arrows and the two men at arms who flanked the gap were hit by arrows.

The Scottish knight halted the line while the gap was filled. There would be more carcasses to contend with and they came forward even more slowly. Some of the men in their front rank did not have a kite shield such as ours. They had the old-fashioned round shield my father and the Vikings used. It provided good protection to the body and head but almost none to the legs. Some of Dick's archers pushed their way behind us so that they could release their arrows horizontally. As the Scots climbed the logs, arrows were sent towards legs which had neither a shield nor mail to protect them. Although they only sent ten arrows towards the bridge before they had to return to Dick, five Scots fell. Their fall made up the mind of the knight. He yelled, "Charge!" when they were twenty paces from us.

It was no solid line which hurled itself at us. There were too many obstacles in their way. Now my archers had targets and they released arrow after arrow.

"Ready!"

Our spears were jammed against the cobbles of the road and braced across our shields. Their sharpened, deadly heads protruded before us. This time there were no horses to take the first of the spear heads. As the Scots clambered over the bodies of the horses which were a barrier before us they jabbed down with their own spears. We took the blows on our shields but, more importantly, as they opened their bodies for the thrust they became an easy target for the archers. Inevitably some of those struck were either pushed or fell forward and they were then impaled upon the spears. As spears shattered then my men drew their swords. I saw that the other spears in our front ranks had been broken. I took my own spear and punched it forward at the knight who towered above me. His attention was on the faltering line and my spear found a gap and scored a hit along his side. The head came away bloody as he smashed down with his sword and broke my spear in two.

I drew my sword just as a warrior with neither helmet nor mail leapt down at me with a vicious looking axe. I barely managed to push his axe away with my shield. A spear jabbed out from behind me and stuck him in the chest. As he died before me he spat out a curse in Gaelic.

The knight was still above me, standing on the carcass of a dead horse. I swung my sword sideways. He had expected the blow and he jumped. The body of the horse was slick with blood and he lost his footing. He fell backwards. I was tiring and I knew that my knights would be too. I yelled the command, "Second rank, change!"

We had practised this. The hiatus of the knight's slip afforded us the opportunity. We all turned to the right, presenting our shields to the enemy as Wulfric led ten fresh men at arms and their spears to take our place. We moved behind the rear rank. The new wall of spears greeted the knight as he regained his feet. He urged his men on and they had to try to break this new wall of spears. The results were the same. The men who survived the spears were struck by arrows. The knight realised the futility of the attack and he ordered his remaining men to fall back.

I knew that they were doing so reluctantly when three warriors suddenly ran, full tilt, towards our line. They launched themselves in the air. Their movement was so swift it took my archers by surprise. One of the Scots impaled himself upon three of the spears but his crashing body allowed the other two to land amongst the men at arms. Their swords flashed and men died. I saw the mighty Wulfric raise his sword to decapitate one of them while the other was transfixed by an arrow in the middle of his head. The battle of the bridge was over when the last wild warrior fell.

Wulfric was both upset and annoyed that the last suicidal attack by the three Scots had cost him two of his men. He and his men hacked the three bodies as they lay on the ground. It was a futile gesture but I understood it. Wulfric and his men had a bond and to lose any comrade was a blow.

I strode past them and clambered on to the dead Scottish horse which had acted as a wall for us. I saw the Scots as they trudged back to their leader and the ones who had not attacked. We had not destroyed these raiders but we had hurt them. Sir Edward and Sir Richard joined me.

"Will they return, Baron?"

"I know not, Richard. We have hurt them and we are still as strong as ever. We clear the bridge for they could use the dead to their advantage in the night. Have the bodies of the Scots thrown into the Tyne. We will have to butcher the horses; they are too large to shift otherwise."

Edward rubbed his hands, "We eat well tonight. The men love horsemeat!" My men at arms were strange. They had such affection for their own mounts that they would weep at small injuries but they would happily devour an enemy's horse.

"Collect any weapons and armour."

"They are poor quality."

"I know Richard but we can make more caltrops. They are a good warning system and I have an idea for another kind of barrier too. Edward, take charge."

I walked back to my men, taking off my helmet and pushing my coif back over my head. I saw Wulfric and he still had an angry face. "Have you vented your anger, Wulfric?"

"Not yet my lord; that should never have happened."

"I know but it is in the past. Put it behind you. Have your men collect as many daggers, spear heads and broken swords as they can. Then tell them to take the handles from the swords and daggers and then I want small logs. Ram the spear heads, daggers and broken swords into the logs so that they stick out from every side. They will make a more effective barrier than caltrops and will prevent us from being surprised."

"An excellent idea, my lord." He had suddenly brightened. His anger could now be directed into making a wicked weapon with which to hurt his enemies. It was not my original idea. I had seen them in Byzantium. There the Emperor had many such fiendish weapons.

"Dick, how is the supply of arrows?"

"We have used too many."

"Then send two of our men back to Hartburn to collect more from Tom the Fletcher." Having brought men to watch the horses we had the ability to replenish our supplies.

"Aiden, go across the river and find out what the enemy intend."

"Aye, my lord."

"And Aiden, be careful!"

He laughed, "My lord you will be telling me next how to gut a deer!"

Leofric appeared at my side. "We won my lord! Can I be at your side next time?"

"There will be a time for you to fight at my side but it is not yet." I handed him my sword. "Put an edge on that and ask Sir Tristan to go to the manor and tell Ralph and his wife that we have horsemeat aplenty. If they want some tell them to come and collect it."

This was a bounty we would share.

That night the air was filled with the sound of meat being roasted over open fires. The Scots still camped to the north and I knew that the smell would be doubly galling. It was their horses we ate and the smell of the roasting flesh would be making them hungrier. Aiden slipped back into camp after dark. Wulfric berated the sentries who had not spotted our ghost of the woods. I smiled. It was an incredibly gifted guard who would spot Aiden if he wished to remain hidden.

"I crept close to their camp. I could not understand what they said but they appeared to be unhappy. The knight who led them was arguing with others who wore the same coats."

"You have done well. Are they all within the camp?"

"Aye my lord. They had sentries set too." He cheekily smiled at Wulfric. "I slipped past those as well."

"You have done well. Go and eat." I turned to my knights. "We will see what the morrow brings but be ready to ride out and see if we can intimidate them back to Scotland."

Our new logs embedded with blades had the advantage that we could move them easily and they would not bar our progress across the bridge. They were secured by ropes beneath the bridge. If an attacker tried to remove them they would have to expose themselves to a rain of missiles.

When dawn broke the Scots were still on the slope leading north. I left only my archers at the bridge and, after we had cleared a passage across the bridge I led my conroi of knights and men at arms up the road. I did not want to fight them but I needed them to move. If they chose to attack then I would respond and then fall back to the bridge. Dick and his archers had enough arrows left to cause the Scots a problem. I used the same formation I had done before and we filled the road. The Scots' trumpets sounded as their camp came to life. I noticed that they now had but a handful of mounted men. We had eaten well the night before and would feast on horseflesh for another week at least. Their lost men at arms and knights meant that the Earl of Moray had to rely on the poorly armed men he had brought. This was better than I had hoped. His warriors on foot were armed with swords, axes and daggers. They would not stand against a mounted charge by mailed men.

I halted my line a hundred and fifty paces from them. We all lowered our lances which indicated our intent; we would charge. We were still outnumbered but the Scots faced forty-five horsemen; all of us were mailed and armed with a lance. "For the Bishop of Durham and King Henry! Charge!"

It was ridiculously easy. As soon as we began to canter the Earl ordered a retreat. He and his remaining knights and men at arms led by example and they galloped away. The men on foot were leaderless and they melted into the woods. We caught five of them and two who tried to stand were slain but the rest ran back to Moray, Dunbar and Fife. They had left a great deal in their camp. There were spare weapons and mail as well as food. It was not a great deal of food but we took it anyway. The Earl and his knights had tents and we took those. Unfortunately, every horse, no matter how poor was taken as they fled north to lick their wounds and reflect on their disastrous foray into England.

The men were in high spirits as we divided our gains. I sent Tristan and Harold with four men at arms to escort the prisoners to the Bishop and to ask for the first part of our stipend.

I gathered my remaining knights around me. "I think we will be safe for a few more days, at least. I have no doubt that there will be more raiders, but the Earl of Moray will make them rethink their strategy. I doubt that they will cross again here. Edward, take some men and ride to the New Castle. Tell the Constable that we have sent these raiders packing. While you are there see if the castle could withstand an attack. The rest of us will make this fort more defensible and homelier. Now that we have more tents we can do so."

When our scouts returned to say that there was no sign of the Scots within ten miles of us we took off our armour. There was an old Roman bathhouse by the river. It no longer functioned but we found we could change there and bathe in the river for the Romans had made a small stone breakwater and it prevented the current from sweeping us away. I used it first for I was more used to bathing than the Normans. Once they saw me there then they, gradually, joined me.

Sir Raymond had grown on me a little. He was nothing like his cousin. I had been wrong and Wulfstan had been right. He smiled as he entered the chilly water. "We have had more success than I expected. The Scots seemed remarkably easy to defeat."

Sir Richard laughed. He dropped below the water and as he rose, dripping from it, said, "The more you fight alongside the Baron the more you will realise that he is a leader who thinks. Had we tried to fight on horseback we would have lost but he saw that we could fight on foot. Tristan and I have become richer since following his banner. Hartness will become as rich too."

He nodded, "Already my men are smiling more. Coins in their purses induce such smiles."

I cautioned them. Sir Geoffrey and Sir Guy nodded their agreement as I added, "This is not the end of our campaigns and they will learn. I have no doubt that they will try to employ archers. They will not be as good as ours but they will make life difficult for us. I want every warrior to practise for half of each day. We have a unique opportunity here. Our squires can learn from each other and our men at arms can learn to fight as one. There will still be a place for each banneret to use his own men but the more we fight together the more success we will have."

When Edward returned, later that afternoon from the east, he seemed quite happy about the ability of the garrison to hold out. "It seems that the Gospatric family took their loyal retainers with them. The ones in the castle now are locals who have lived there since the north was emptied by the Conqueror. It is their home and they will defend it."

I was relieved at that and so we began half a month of peace and order. The men practised and all became better warriors. When they were not working at becoming better warriors and improving their skills they took it upon themselves to make things. Aiden and Leofric used some of the bones from the horses to make a chess set. They each carved the pieces. Aiden had decided to use some of the blood from the animals we hunted to dye one half a rusty brown. It looked very effective. Others used the bone to make adornments for their scabbards and their horses. Every man at arm and archer had something to keep his hands busy. The practise took the need for fighting away and the beer we had from Ralph's wife was not strong enough to fire the blood.

The messengers returned from Tom the Fletcher with more arrows and Tristan and Harold returned with the stipend from the Bishop and a holy relic. The Bishop was so pleased with our work that he had sent one of St. Cuthbert's fingers in a silver pendant which was encased in a casket and a priest to watch over it. Father Richard was an earnest young man. He was keen to use God to fight the Scots and he asked if he could bear the Bishop's banner. That suited me for I needed all of my knights and squires now to fight.

For half a month, we had peace and then the scouts found a trail. It was a trail from the north and it told us that the Scots had returned. The scouts saw the animal dung. They had horses. There were also the tracks of a single cart. They had come for war and not a raid. We prepared to do battle once more.

Chapter 10

The Scots had learned. With the long days of summer drawing closer, they could move through the forests more easily. Aiden deduced that they rode palfreys and not destrier and that the men they brought were more lightly armed for the tracks they left were not as deep. Most importantly they were heading for the gaps in the wall the Romans had built. There were no manors to the west of Hexham and no lords there with castles to guard the border. The castles were further south and the Scots had slipped by us without us knowing.

We left our servants with the supplies and the spare horses. Two men at arms were all that we could spare to guard our home. I asked Ralph to call out the fyrd. It was high summer and there would be men to spare. We had to use a precious palfrey for our priest who insisted upon accompanying us, swearing that St. Cuthbert would bring success to our venture. I would take any help I could get. There was a certain amount of guesswork involved in our route. If they carried on due south from their crossing points then they would hit high ground with few animals to steal. It would not be worth their while. They would have to swing to the south of Chollerford and strike at the Tyne and Wear valleys. The animals born a few months ago were now almost ready for market and it would be a perfect time to raid them. The farmers would be busy in their fields with the cereal crops they needed to tend and weed.

We headed south too with my scouts spread out in a large half-circle as we sought to catch them on the march. The rest we had enjoyed since last battle had prepared us better than I could have hoped. We had eaten well, trained hard and we knew that our enemies could be beaten. Our scouts had told us that we would be outnumbered but we had been at a disadvantage the last time and still won. Confidence was worth a hundred men.

We found their trail not far from Corbridge. They had had to use the Roman Road for part of their journey and the droppings of their horses marked their trail. I sent Edward and half of our force to the east. They rode along the old Roman Road which led to the New Castle and they rode hard. They would wait close to the castle of Prudhoe. By riding hard and fast they could reach it before the slower moving Scots. This was another castle where the lord of the manor was in Scotland but I hoped that Edward could hold it as a bastion against the Scots. I guessed that they had chosen this route because they knew that they would be unopposed. Edward, his four knights and his men at arms might prove to be a shock to them. I retained the archers. I would need them.

Aiden came galloping back. "Baron, they are two miles ahead and approaching Prudhoe."

"How many are there?"

"I estimate two hundred. They are mainly lightly armed horsemen and foot soldiers. I only counted ten knights and eight squires."

Aiden had become more proficient of late and knew the difference between knights and squires. The squires tended to wear their hair shorter. There were more knights than we had expected.

"Will they push on to Prudhoe do you think?"

He hesitated for his answer was crucial. "Aye, my lord."

It all depended upon Edward now and the speed with which he had ridden. "We ride hard!"

I threw caution to the wind. If they could make Prudhoe then they could capture a base and we were too few to assault a castle. We could hold one but not take one. We would need an army to rid the land of Scots holding a castle. Dick rode back to me. "They are but half a mile away!"

"Ride to their southern flank and harass them. Do not endanger your men but we need them halted so that Edward has the opportunity to reach Prudhoe."

"Aye my lord."

With my archers committed we moved east. There was little point in using lances for we would be fighting in woodland and so I sent the men with the lances to the rear. I halted my line. "Form a line of attack with knights to the fore." There were seven knights in the front rank. The squires, banners and the priest were in the second and then fourteen men at arms made up the third and fourth ranks. It was not a huge force but I relied on surprise.

We heard the shouts and alarm from the south. Dick had attracted their attention. I hoped that whoever led them would assume this was their main opposition. I wanted their attention to the south. I drew my sword and led the wedge of warriors. We trotted through the woods. The trees meant we could not ride knee to knee and it was a looser formation. We came upon the first body some two hundred paces into the woods. It was a Scot who had an arrow sticking through his neck. We found another three in the next sixty paces. Dick was drawing them south, away from the castle. I knew what he would be doing. Half of his men would be loosing arrows whilst the other half held the reins of their mounts. I saw the flash of colour in the woods; it was the Scottish knights riding behind a mass of men at arms as they drove towards the archers who were whittling them down. My archers could not possibly hope to defeat them but they could irritate them and draw them on.

We had our opportunity for the knights were so busy trying to get at the archers that they did not see us. The woods through which we travelled muffled the sound of our approach. As soon as we galloped they would know where we were. We did not need to ride hard; we were not using lances and we did not need a weight of warrior and horse to break a line; there was no line. We were less than a hundred paces from them when one of the Scottish squires turned and saw us. He shouted the alarm and faces turned towards us.

"On! There is no need for caution now!"

I spurred Scout and he leapt forward. I leaned out over his head. I wanted to strike the first blow. The Scottish line had turned to face us but they were still drawing swords when we struck. I brought my sword around in a wide arc to strike a red and black shield with a yellow griffin. The knight reeled but kept his seat. We needed the knights eliminating and I jerked on Scout's reins to bring his head around. As the knight swung at my shield I stood in my stirrups to bring my sword down on his helmet. It stunned him and my blade continued down his helmet and hacked through his mail and into his neck. He fell from his horse.

I felt a sharp pain in my side. I turned and saw a spear held by a man at arms. He saw the blood on the end and was laughing when Leofric jammed my banner into his neck. He died with a surprised look on his face. Nodding my thanks, I turned Scout to head towards the Scots who were now rushing to meet us. We had lost our organised ranks but I hoped that I still led mounted men. That way we could escape to Prudhoe if things went awry. The trees aided us for they hid our numbers. I knew that they outnumbered us but they had no idea how many they faced.

I saw men on foot. A sergeant at arms was trying to organise them into a shield wall. Suddenly an arrow came from the woods to my right and he fell dead. As the warriors looked to their left I swung my sword and hit one in the shoulder. He fell and Wulfric smashed his war axe into the head of another. The other five ran. I was about to order my men to charge once more when Wulfric said, "We are almost surrounded my lord, look."

I had been so keen to get at them that I had not seen that we were being drawn into a circle of swords. Ahead of us there was a continuous line of spears and shields with horses behind. They had learned and they had tried to trap us. The only thing which saved us was the band of archers led by Dick.

"Fall back!"

As I turned Scout I saw that the Scots were trying to close the neck on this net of steel. The large number of foot aided them. Dick and his hidden archers carefully picked off the men who were trying to close the gap. Wulfric and I were the last ones through and we had to smash our way through with our swords. The blows that were struck hit our mail and not our horses. We would be battered and bruised but we managed to escape. We kept going until we made the road. There were empty saddles and I knew that we had lost men. The Bishop's priest was already seeing to the wounded. Harold and Sir Geoffrey had been wounded.

Leofric rode next to me. "Baron! You are wounded."

I remembered the blow. Shaking my head, I said, "We have no time for that. Ride for Prudhoe. We can rest there."

Now that Leofric had mentioned it I felt the dull ache in my leg. Then I felt the blood as it trickled down the inside of my armour. I found that we were but a mile or two from the motte and bailey castle of Prudhoe. There were just six men guarding it. There was no banner flying. The lord of the manor was not at home. The Bishop's banner gained us admittance. The Sergeant at Arms was an old, grey-haired warrior. He bowed as I reined in, "Sir Marmaduke has taken the cross, my lord. He is in the Holy Land but you are welcome to spend the night here."

I smiled, "It may be more than a night sergeant," I pointed behind me. "There are Scottish raiders in the valley."

His face fell, "We have few supplies laid in store, my lord."

"Do not worry about that. It is shelter we need." I went to dismount and I had forgotten about my wound. As I put my injured leg on the ground it gave way and I collapsed in a heap. Leofric and Wulfric ran to my side.

"He was stabbed in the leg by a spear, sergeant."

Wulfric took off his mittens and put his hand beneath my surcoat. It came away bloody. "Get him inside." He stood and yelled, "Sir Edward, the Baron is wounded."

"I will take command. Put him in the hall. The Scots are approaching. Every man who can wield a spear, get to the ramparts!"

Just then Edward and the rest of my men arrived. I could see from the angry look on Edward's face that he was not happy to have let me down. I did not mind. It meant we had numbers once more and we could face our foes. As I was manhandled towards the steps of the keep I knew that, in my present state, I could not stand on the walls. I would do more damage than good. Edward knew how to hold a castle. I was laid down on a pallet in the small hall. Sir Marmaduke was not a rich knight. I knew now why he had taken the cross. He needed the rewards. "Get to the walls. I will be fine."

Wulfric came in with his pouch of needles and catgut. Leofric followed. "Leofric, take my banner to the walls. Make the Scots think I am there still." He looked at Wulfric who nodded. Father Richard came in with four men at arms carrying Sir Geoffrey and Harold. "Wulfric, we have a priest now. You will do more good on the walls. Go."

He was torn but he obeyed, "Aye my lord."

I looked in concern at Harold who appeared not to be moving. Father Richard saw my concern. "He received a blow to the head. He is breathing and he should recover. I have placed the saint's finger close to the wound. God will heal him."

Sir Geoffrey had a nasty looking cut to his left upper arm. I saw that his mail had been torn and an edged weapon had scored a line along the muscle. When he saw the priest threading the needle he said, nervously, "Perhaps the relic will work for me."

The serious priest said, "No Sir Geoffrey, you and the Baron need repairs; the young knight is the one who needs the intercession of the saint."

His needle was finer than that used by Wulfric and, despite his serious demeanour he had a gentle touch. I was reassured when I saw his skill at stitching Sir Geoffrey. He had to remove my mail leggings to get at my leg. I saw that the spear had struck the muscled part of my leg and missed the bone. I had also been fortunate that it had not struck an artery; if it had then I would have been dead. He cleaned up the wound and examined it carefully. "You have been lucky. It is a clean wound and nothing has been driven into the flesh. This will heal." He took some herbs from his pouch and moistened them with water. He put them to one side while he stitched. It was a sharp needle and I winced at the first stitch. "Close your eyes, my lord, and pray. The pain will subside."

It did not but closing my eyes helped. I opened them as he packed the moistened herbs around the wound and then bandaged it. All the time he had been working I had been aware of the clamour from outside. "Help me up, Father Richard."

"You need to rest your leg."

"Help me up. I do not intend to fight but I need to see how this goes. I promise I will return here as soon as I know." Reluctantly he helped me up. I saw the Bishop's banner propped in the corner. "This should be on our battlements. It will make a good support, eh Father?"

I used the staff of the banner to take the weight of my injured leg. When I reached the door, I breathed a sigh of relief. My men stood on the walls still. I could see that Edward had spread the archers out and that each knight stood with his own men on the walls. It was what I would have done. Leofric spotted me and spoke to Edward. He turned and I saw him shake his head. He said something to Leofric who, leaving my banner on the wall clambered down the ladder and ran to me.

"Sir Edward says that all is well and he has everything under control. He wishes you to return to your bed."

I smiled, "I am thinking that he used stronger words than that." He nodded. "And how goes it?"

"They have no archers, my lord, and they are wasting their spears to try to get at our men. They have no ladders and each time they try to scale the walls they are driven away. They have not attacked for some minutes."

"Good. Then I will return inside but let me know if anything changes. Here take this to the battlements. It may frighten the Scots." I handed him the Bishop's banner. As I limped back inside, I felt the pain as I put weight on my leg. I barely made it back to my pallet. Father Richard shook his head but said nothing as he continued to finish bandaging Sir Geoffrey.

"They are not closing in on us Sir Geoffrey. Sir Edward has driven them off. I believe we are safe."

"Good. I hate being in here while my men fight."

Harold stirred and opened his eyes, "Where am I, Baron?"

"We are in Prudhoe Castle and St Cuthbert has saved you." I pointed to the relic. He tried to rise, "We are in Father Richard's hands now. We rest. Sir Edward commands and all is well."

By nightfall the Scots had disappeared. We licked our wounds and counted the cost. Two men at arms and two archers had been killed when we had been surrounded. It did not make it any easier knowing that we had killed far more of them and their bodies littered the forest to the west of Prudhoe.

I ventured out to speak with Sir Edward. "I am sorry, Baron, I was late."

"It matters not." I paused. He wished to tell me the reason. "What delayed you?"

"I was careless and had no scouts out. They must have sent some lightly armed men along the Roman Road and we were ambushed. It cost me two men and we pursued them. I was angry at my loss. I am sorry."

"We did not suffer as a result but it shows that we must never let down our guard for an instant."

That night our sentries spotted the flames of burning buildings towards the east. The Scots were raiding. I held a council of war with my knights. "We will need to pursue them tomorrow and as early as possible. We have failed to do as the Bishop wanted and his people will suffer as a result. We cannot allow that to continue. We must scour the land of the Scots."

Sir Edward pointed to my leg, "You and Sir Geoffrey are both wounded and Harold is hurt."

"I can ride can I not, Father Richard?"

I could see him torn between the truth and what he wanted to tell me. Truth won out. "You can ride but you should not. You will delay the healing process."

"There and Sir Geoffrey need not fight. He can carry the banner and Leofric can use a sword." I saw my squire almost leap to his feet. "And Harold is recovered. He can fight. I know that we are fewer in number but so are the Scots and they will think that they have bested us. They have not." I waved over the castellan. "Has Sir Marmaduke lances here?"

"No, my lord but we have long spears."

"Then they will do. I want the conroi ready to ride an hour before dawn. We know where they will be heading; it will be south and east but I will send Aiden out now to be certain."

After Aiden had left us Leofric came over. "Did you mean it, my lord? I can fight?"

"You will have a sword and a shield and you will watch my right side as Harold used to. You will have your weapon and you will use it but I want no reckless heroics. If we were not desperately short of men then you would just carry my banner. I cannot afford to lose you." He grinned, "It takes too long to train up a new squire!"

Although chastened by my words he nodded, "I will do my best, my lord. I have worked hard with Harold and I am ready to face our enemies."

When I awoke I was stiff and I regretted my decision to ride. Leofric helped me with my armour. My mail legging had been temporarily repaired but I could not risk any further damage. I would have to use skill and experience. The wound had only been stitched. Another blow would open it up. I had just mounted when Aiden arrived. "They are close to Gateshead. Their camp is a few miles from there. They have camped at a small swale by a stream. They have cattle, sheep and slaves. They have been busy since they fled."

"And if they reach the bridge at the New Castle then they can hold the north to ransom. It is fortunate they did not push further east else they would hold the bridge already. Where are they camped?"

"They are on the sloping ground close to the bend in the river by the small stream and they have set sentries."

"Then we will ride to cut them off from the bridge. If they think we are still in Prudhoe they will get a shock."

It was less than a dozen miles to where they were camped and another three to the bridge. We rode hard through the early hours of the morning while it was still dark. The faint hint of dawn made me spur Scout on. My leg was complaining but the stitches appeared to be holding. I did not feel the insidious trickle of blood from a burst wound. We saw the glow from their fires as we rode to the south of them. We made the southern edge of the bridge by dawn. I sent the exhausted Aiden to the castle to warn those within of the proximity of the Scots. I told him to rest within the walls. He had done more than enough.

As we rested our horses and waited I weighed up the different strategies I could employ. If there were no captives involved then I could withdraw into the castle and wait for them to move. However, Aiden had reported that they had captives and if I did that there would be nothing to stop them from continuing their raid. If I had more archers and men at arms then I could wait on this small rise and allow them to attack us as they had at the Roman fort. It seemed to me that I only had one option. We would attack them whilst they were on the move and hope to scatter them. It was a mad idea and yet the only one which appeared to me to have the slightest chance of success.

We now had six men less than we had had when we set off. In addition, three of us were not fully fit. We did, at least, have the spears we had acquired in Prudhoe.

"We ride to the Scots' camp and, as soon as we see them, we attack. Dick, I want you and the archers to prepare an ambush between here and the place they are camped. I intended to charge them, cause as much damage as I can and then draw them onto your archers."

"We have but eighteen now, Baron."

"I know but it will have to suffice."

"And if they do not follow?"

"Then, Sir Edward, we will have failed the Bishop and he will lose his people, his animals and many of his buildings." It was a depressing thought for I could not see how we could defeat such a large warband.

We rode with the rising sun at our backs. We had but a mile or two to go. The Scottish leaders had learned their lesson and they had scouts out. As soon as they saw us the four riders turned tail and galloped back to their army. It was a chance and I took it. "Follow them and ride hard."

I gambled that the four scouts had not had enough time to count us. We were coming from the castle and it was conceivable that they might think we were a separate force. I hoped for panic. This was not a Roman Road over which we travelled. It was a track made by feet over centuries and was just hard-packed earth. It deadened, somewhat, the sound of our horses. It was also not straight and followed the river. As we came around a bend in a wedge five knights wide we saw the warband. The four scouts had only reached them moments earlier. I saw the scouts on their ponies pointing at us. There was little order in the force we saw. The vanguard was the knights with the captives and animals in the middle. There were warriors on the flanks but the bulk was at the rear. We had parity of numbers, at least for the moment.

"Charge!"

They were less than a hundred paces when I put spurs to Scout. The knights had no lances and they hurriedly tried to form a line and charge at the same time. There were just six knights but I saw twenty mounted men at arms behind and the four scouts. Their trumpets called for their rearguard but they had animals and captives to negotiate.

We struck their line. My leg screamed in pain and I knew that I would not be able to stand in my stirrups. I punched as hard as I could at the leading knight and my borrowed spear found a gap between his shield and his cantle. The head of the spear ripped into his middle and, as he fell broke the weapon in two. I swung the broken spear horizontally and it cracked into the shield of the knight to my right. As he lifted his shield to deflect it Harold speared him with his own weapon. My knights had spread out so that there were nine of us facing the three remaining knights. Sir Richard took one while Sir Guy and Sir Guiscard finished off the last two. They were leaderless.

Edward spurred his horse on and rode directly at the sergeant at arms who was busy ordering his men into a line. Edward's spear rammed into his throat and emerged from the back. My lieutenant released the now useless weapon and swung his sword at the men behind. He was like a man possessed. He was making up for his error the day before. The joy of battle seemed to have filled all of my men and I heard Wulfric screaming his war cry.

I rode towards the men at arms with my sword drawn. I saw that Leofric had done as I had asked and he was just behind me to my right. The men on foot were now flooding towards us. Their war cries and screams filled the air. The Scot who charged me had a short war axe. As he swung it I blocked it with my sword. A chip of wood flew from the handle. He tried a second swing, this time at Scout's head. I put every ounce of strength I had into the counterblow and I heard a crack as the axe handle broke. Even as he looked in disbelief at the shattered weapon Leofric ran him through. Our charge had taken us through their lines and Wulfric and his men slew the guards. The captives were freed, "Run along the river to the New Castle. We will hold them off!"

I watched as the thirty or so captives ran along the trail. I realised that there were men with them. This was unusual. Normally the men would be killed. The rearguard, who was the bulk of their band, was still trying to get at us but the animals were in the way. I had an idea. "Drive the animals at the rearguard!"

Hollering and screaming we slapped the flat of our swords against the rumps of the cattle which turned and ran west to escape the punishment. The sheep and goats that were behind them joined in the stampede. It is easier to start such a stampede than it is to stop one. The rearguard stood no chance. Six of the braver ones were trampled to death before the rest fled west. When we saw that we had succeeded we halted. Our horses needed the rest.

"Leofric ride and fetch Dick and his archers." While my squire rode away I lifted my helmet. "God was on our side today, my friends."

"Aye and the cattle helped too."

We watched as the animals, no longer being struck, gradually slowed and then stopped. Soon we would be able to collect them and drive them to the New Castle. Unbelievably our charge had succeeded. I had gambled and won.

Chapter 11

The people and the animals remained at the New Castle while we chased the raiders back to the Tyne. Dick and the archers kept their swords at their backs. They still outnumbered us but they were leaderless and on foot. We stopped when we reached Chollerford and the fort. I had left eight men at arms at the New Castle. They would strip the dead of their valuables, collect the horses and then escort the captives back to their homes. Aiden delivered a message to the Bishop informing him of the raid and the result. I still wondered why they had taken the men prisoners. The only answer I had was that they required male slaves and that was disturbing.

As Midsummer passed and late summer approached I could feel proud of what my men had achieved. We had defeated two invasions and raids with minimal loss to ourselves. Although the raiders had had little treasure our stipend from the Bishop more than compensated. We were a fine force which could hold its own against any enemies.

The next couple of weeks were spent in recovery. Both men and animals had been pushed to the limit. Now we could go back to our regular rhythm of practice and vigilance. When Aiden returned it was with another conroi. Sir Hugh Manningham had a manor high up in the Wear Valley. His ten men at arms and his ten archers were most welcome. We discovered that unlike us his reward was not money but the manor of Hexham. Odo had paid for his rebellion with his life and, having no heirs, his land was forfeit. Sir Hugh had benefitted. Hexham was a much richer manor. He and his men would use the fort at Chollerford until they had rebuilt their castle. We were no longer tied to the fort.

We had the luxury of spare men and we used it to range further afield and watch all of the crossing points on the wall. We saw occasional scouts but our presence, in numbers, discouraged them. The worst appeared to be over. As summer passed our wounds healed and our skills improved. Leofric was fast becoming a good swordsman. Harold was a good teacher and, along with Tristan, enjoyed helping the young squires. Leofric appeared to grow stronger each day. I was pleased I had not had him a good set of armour made for by the time Christmas came he would have grown out of it. By the end of summer, Sir Hugh was quite happy to take over the duties of guardian of the north. More of his men had arrived from his old manor and with the ditch repaired around his castle and walls erected, he had security once more. Hexham could control the upper Tyne.

As we headed back to Durham, all of us considerably richer, and as we passed the New Castle, I realised that the Gospatric clan was still an unresolved problem. The castle which controlled the Tyne needed a strong hand. It did not have one. We still had enemies who harboured rebellious thoughts and they were protected by the Scottish King. It was like a wound which festered. It had not gone away.

The Bishop was delighted to see us. His banner and his relic were returned to him as was his priest. He had been a dour man but Father Richard had certainly been useful. I wondered about asking for a priest to accompany us again. Wulfric was a rough and ready healer; we needed a skilled one. The final stipend was paid and we headed south. The crops we passed showed that it had been a good summer and that promised a safer winter. We had been away for many months and I wondered if I had another child yet. It had been five months since we had left home; perhaps a son or daughter was awaiting me.

When we reached Stockton, it was a momentous occasion. We would all be returning to our own manors. Our work was done and we were a band of brothers. I now trusted Sir Raymond, as Wulfstan had told me I would. I had been wrong about him and that was a lesson I had learned. We had all got on remarkably well and I was happy that we had learned so much about each other. They were all eager to return to their families and our parting was brief but heartfelt.

Adela was still with child and young William was toddling next to her. I wondered if he would remember me this time. He threw his arms open and staggered towards me. I was home and I had a perfect welcome. John, my steward looked a little portlier than I had remembered him but perhaps that was because I was used to seeing lean and hungry soldiers. He followed us into my hall and chatted to Leofric. Adela suddenly gushed out with a torrent of words and told me all that had happened since I had been gone. She barely paused for breath and, I confess, I heard barely half of it but it mattered not. She must have been lonely and the least I could do was to listen to her. William, too, just wanted my attention and I dangled him between my legs and then on my knee. When I winced, Adela stopped babbling and asked, "Were you wounded?"

"It was nothing. It is healed and you are not to worry."

121

"But I do worry. And here am I going on about things which are not important while you are hurt."

"I was hurt and now I am well. I can rest over the autumn and the winter."

She rose and kissed me, "Come, William, we shall go and organise the feast for tonight." She pointed to John who had been waiting patiently, "I think John wishes to have a word with you."

After she had left I said, "Thank you for looking after her, John. I had not realised we would be away as long."

"Do not worry, Baron. We had peace and prosperity. Our animals increased tenfold and the crops promise a great bounty. Our trade has also increased. Did you not notice more houses when you came towards the castle?"

"I confess I was too busy speaking with my knights."

"There are many more people and not just here. Both Norton and Hartburn have new settlers." He laughed, "Ethelred is now so rich that he is having a fine house built and he has asked William the Mason for some stone work."

I shook my head, "He has come a long way since I first met him. And how is the church? I hope that Ethelred's plans did not interfere with our church."

"No, Baron. The roof is on and the walls will be up before the first snows. There will be little adornment but we can worship there rather than trudging through the snow to Norton."

"Good. And we are prepared for winter?"

"As much as we can ever be prepared, aye. Much will depend upon the harvest but I believe it will be a good one. Sir Wulfstan will be pleased to see you back. He took his duties seriously and spent many hours each week travelling around the manors."

"I will thank him." I noticed that Leofric was still waiting. "John, Leofric needs mail armour. Take him to Alf. I would have him clad as I am."

John frowned, "That would be expensive my lord!"

"Nevertheless, he will be clad in good mail. We have earned enough this summer to pay for a fine suit of mail for every one of my men." He did not look convinced but he nodded. "And we will need to hire another five men at arms. I also seek more archers."

He opened his mouth as though he was going to argue and then thought better of it. "Come Leofric. Let us find Alf and get this suit of mail."

I went to my chambers. "Aelric, fetch me some water. I would bathe the dust of the road from me."

My servant scurried off and I took off my armour. It still hurt when I removed the mail from my legs. That, too, would need to be repaired. When the water arrived, I was pleased that Aelric had brought it warm. "I will see to this myself, Aelric. Have a jug of wine and a goblet taken to the west tower for me." As I washed it seemed as though I was peeling layers from my body. I had been a warrior for months and now I would need to return to being a lord of the manor. I would need to hold a session to decide all the cases which had accrued since May. Hopefully, there would be few. As I dressed in the fine linen tunic I felt better prepared to think about my duties.

I ascended the stairs to the tower. There were two towers, one to the west and one to the east. Each one would be used as a guard room but that was only in times of trouble. They were both small; they could accommodate a small table and two chairs but it was the place I could go and think. If I wished to reflect on the past I used the east tower where I could look out across the sea to my home many thousands of miles away. Latterly I had preferred the west tower for, as it was now, I could see a glorious sunset and think about the future.

The wine was there and I poured a goblet. I had soon grown tired of the Chollerford ale and this heavy red wine was like ambrosia. I cautioned myself not to drink too much. I knew that I was lucky. I had a beautiful wife and son. My men and my knights were the most loyal one could wish for and I seemed to be lucky in battle. My father and his men had always said that my namesake had been equally lucky. Soldiers never minded that. If you were skilled and had luck then that was a good thing. The pessimist in me wondered when my luck would run out. Everyone's luck did. My father's had been when de Mamers and his men had raided Norton. When would mine come? I stopped drinking after two goblets; I was becoming morose. I resolved to look for the positives and not the negatives in my life.

I left with Leofric the next day to visit with Wulfstan, Athelstan and Osric. My father's three warriors were the rocks upon which my family and people depended. I could trust them to defend my land and to manage the people fairly. I would not have been able to go to war as often as I did were it not for them.

Wulfstan's three children were all growing rapidly and were an indication of what I could expect from William and my unborn child. Wulfstan and Faren had brought them up well and they stood politely while Leofric and I dismounted. "Where is Wulfstan?"

Faren bobbed her head and pointed to the fields to the west of the hall. "He is helping to gather in the harvest." She smiled, "He has sniffed the air this morning and thought it would come on to rain."

"Come Leofric we will exercise my leg." We left the horses slurping at the water trough and strode towards the fields of oats. I saw Wulfstan amongst his villeins and men at arms. He was wielding a scythe as though it was a weapon of war and swathes of ripened oats fell at each stroke. His men gathered up the oats in armfuls and laid them in the cart. Wulfstan, like me, had two oxen to draw his cart. Both of us allowed our farmers to use the mighty beasts. They were an expense for they needed feeding all winter but they were the best draught animals we had.

He stopped and wiped his brow when he saw us. He handed the scythe to one of his men at arms, "Here William; I will speak with the Baron."

He strode over to the cart where there was a jug and some beakers. He poured two beakers of ale and held one to me. "Good to see you, Alfraed. I take it your foray north was worthwhile?"

Wulfstan was the only one, apart from Adela, who used my Christian name. He had been given the task of raising me by my father. He was still my mentor and I was still in awe of him and his skill. "Yes, Wulfstan."

He quaffed the ale in one swallow and as he poured himself another he nodded at my leg. "I saw you limping as you walked across the field. You were wounded?"

"A spear."

He stared at Leofric, "How was the Baron wounded on the side you were supposed to protect?"

Leofric coloured but before he could reply I said, "That was my fault, Wulfstan. I had him holding my banner."

"He is your squire. His job is to protect your side. You need someone else to hold your banner. You need another squire."

He was right but it still irritated me, "I will get one by and by. We have finished campaigning for the year anyway."

"You sent the Scots back from whence they came?"

I nodded, "They are good warriors but they fight as a rabble."

"It was ever the way. Do not forget, Alfraed, that your father and I learned discipline from the Emperor in the east. The Scots have only picked up a little discipline from the Normans." He wiped his face, "Come I will walk you back to my hall and you can tell me all." He put his huge ham of an arm around Leofric's shoulder, "I am sorry if I misjudged you, Leofric. Forgive an old man his hasty tongue."

Leofric smiled, "No offence was taken, my lord. I berated myself too."

I spent the morning with Wulfstan. He had been active during my absence. I discovered that he had dispensed justice without the need for sessions. Most of his judgements were a swift blow which ended most disputes. He had imposed fines for some misdemeanours and the money went to the church in Stockton. As I headed for Norton I reflected on his justice. Too many lords of the manor inflicted severe punishments for crimes. Some had those found guilty of crimes blinded or maimed. We did not. It made little sense for there were perilously few men without hurting the ones we had. In the end, it proved wise for more people wished to live on lands where the justice of Baron Alfraed was seen as eminently fair.

Osric and Athelstan had had more land cleared and drained. Although it would never make good land for crops it was perfect for pigs and Norton was fast becoming the producer of fine ham. When my hunters went hunting the boar we took the young and domesticated them. There were still more than enough wild boars for us to hunt but the tame variety ensured a steady supply all year. I was more than happy when I returned to Stockton. Athelstan had given a leg of ham to me which had been smoked in one of the new smokehouses. It was a delicacy I enjoyed.

It was still light as I approached Stockton and I rode slowly so that I could view my little settlement by the Tees. Although I had not deliberately planned it we had encouraged development along the line of huts which had been there when we had first come all those years ago. The old walls around the manor were long gone. My castle was close enough to afford protection. Ethelred's house now looked like a manor house. It was on the riverside and close to his ferry. I think he liked to stand at his door and see the storage huts by the river with the goods he traded and his main source of income, the ferry.

As we entered my gatehouse I frowned. Just outside there were two old soldiers begging. I dismounted and handed my reins to Leofric. "Stable them and take the ham to the kitchens."

I walked back to the two old soldiers. One had lost an eye. I could not see the wound which had deprived the other of his livelihood. They struggled to their feet when I approached and knuckled their heads. "Good afternoon my lord, we will go now.

We did not mean to offend you. We were travelling north to Durham to beg for alms from the Bishop."

I shook my head, "I was not offended." In many manors such beggars were beaten. Neither man looked to have had a decent meal in some time. "Do I know you? Whom did you serve?"

"We fought with you at Gainford. We served Sir Mark of Normanby. After the battle we were deemed to be of no further use and sent packing."

I remembered the Sergeant of Arms who had served Sir Mark. Like his master he had not looked after his people. Sir Guiscard had only arrived months after the battle.

"Come into my castle. You fought under my banner that day and I will feed you." They hesitated. "Come, that is a command from the lord of the manor." As we entered the gate I saw Roger of Lincoln who was the captain of the guard for the day. "Roger, we will feed and shelter these two for the night. They fought with us at Gainford."

Roger smiled, "Then they are most welcome. Leave them with me, my lord."

My men at arms had a comradeship which I envied. They were truly brothers in arms and we could never hope to emulate that with my knights. We all had our own manors and were never together long enough to form such a bond. Rolf and his Swabians had the same affinity. I saw Aiden and John his falconer. They had the cadge with Caesar and Sheba. John had grown. He had always been bigger than Leofric but he had not shown the same potential as a swordsman. He would make a good warrior. I had a sudden idea.

"Aiden, John son of Godwin, a word if you please."

John laid the cadge down carefully and they walked over. John looked worried as though he was in trouble. "John how like you looking after the hawks?"

John was an honest youth and his face showed the truth before he gave me the answer he thought I sought. "It is an honour, my lord."

Aiden was as sharp as they came and I saw the frown flicker across his forehead. He had recognised the lie too. I smiled, "Aiden, is it hard to do what John does?"

"No, my lord. It requires patience and affection. You must like the birds."

"Can you teach any to care for them?"

"So long as they have a heart for animals then aye."

"If I took John son of Godwin from you would you be unhappy?"

"My lord I hope I have not offended you!"

"Silence, John. Answer me, Aiden."

"He is good with the birds and he is strong. I would not like to lose him."

"Suppose I replaced him with two men. How would that suit?"

"You have someone in mind, my lord?" Aiden was quick.

I nodded, "If you find Roger of Lincoln he has with him two old men at arms. Speak with them and see if they could be trained. They were wounded at Gainford. The fact that they arrived here today seems to me to be propitious."

"Yes, my lord, and John…" Aiden did not want his young apprentice to be without a job.

"Do not worry about John son of Godwin. He will not suffer."

When Aiden had gone I turned to John who looked thoroughly miserable. "Do you miss the company of Leofric?"

He looked at me in surprise, "Yes, my lord. We grew up together. I envy him."

"When I took him as my squire did you wish it was you?"

He nodded, "But I knew why you chose him. I am too big and clumsy. I cannot wield a sword as well as he. He was the better choice."

"And it speaks well of you that you recognise that. Can you ride?" He hesitated, "Answer honestly. I cannot abide those who lie to get what they want."

"I am not a good rider but most horses are too small for me."

"I can see that. Go and see to your hawks and then, in the morning we will put you on a horse and see how you fare."

"You would make me a man at arms, my lord?"

The excitement in his voice and face told me that my instincts were right, "We will see."

I spoke with Adela of my plans and she approved. She knew John far better than I did. He had been in the castle all the while I had been away. "He is good with the hawks, my husband, but it is not enough for him. He would be perfect but with whom would you replace him?"

"There were two old soldiers begging at my gates. They fought under my banner. I would not have such men abandoned. Their lord was Sir Mark and they deserved a better leader."

She kissed me on my forehead. "You are a kind man, my husband. You took me in and I will ever be grateful to you for that. This was meant to be. I will find them some livery."

As I strolled along my ramparts after our meal Aiden found me. "Those men will do well, my lord. They are grateful for a roof and I have spoken with them. They are not cruel men and they can be trained. It does not need strength to carry the cadge. It is also better to have a falconer for each bird. I will begin their training on the morrow." He looked at me expectantly. "What do you intend for John, son of Godwin?"

"I will not tell another before I tell him. Fetch him now and I will tell you both at the same time."

By the time they had returned the sun had set. I walked across the bailey to greet them. "Come, we will go into my hall where there is light." The hall was empty for Adela had gone to bathe William. The fire had been lit and there were tallow candles burning. John and Aiden stood looking at me.

"John, how would you like to carry my banner into battle?"

His jaw actually dropped open. He had expected to be a man at arms and this, I could see, had been beyond his wildest dreams. He dropped to his knees. "It would be an honour, my lord."

"Good, then we need to find a horse for you and get Alf to make some mail."

Aiden said, "My lord, we have the mail we took from that Scottish knight. The huge one. I think we were going to have it melted down but I think it will fit John."

"Good. Now you will be trained by both me and Leofric. I hope you can take instruction from one who was your friend."

"I can, my lord."

"Then you had better move your things from the stable into Leofric's quarters." I smiled, "I will let you give him the news."

I suspect the only person in the whole castle who showed the slightest displeasure was my steward, John son of Leofric. "More expense, my lord, and where will you get a horse large enough for him?"

I shook my head, "John do you not realise that we need men such as John to fight for us so that you can continue to make as much coin as you do. I almost lost my life for the lack of a second squire. Think about that!"

I saw the shock on his face. He had not thought that through. "I am sorry, my lord, you are quite right."

I laughed, "Of course I am. I am the lord of the manor."

Part 3 The King's Decision

Chapter 12

My daughter, Hilda, was born on All Saints Eve. Both she and my wife were healthy after the birth and I breathed a sigh of relief. It ended a perfect time for us. The harvests were gathered and the bounty was great. The churches were full on All Saints Day to celebrate the bounty of the fields and the birth of my daughter. We had had a bell made for Norton Church and it tolled out the joyous news.

The next day I received a summons from King Henry. The most important barons in the land were summoned to Westminster. We were to be there for Christmas. I, of course, did not wish to go. I wanted Yule at home with my family in my castle. I still remembered the wolf winter and did not want them to come to harm whilst I was away.

Adela was the one who told me I had to go. "My lord, this summons marks you as a powerful lord." She held up the letter, "There are few others from the north. You are the most powerful Northern Baron. It would not do to offend the King and I will be safe."

"I shall just take my squires, Wulfric and three men at arms. The rest can guard you!"

Both Edward and Wulfstan concurred. They came, along with Harold, Edward and Richard of Yarm when I summoned them. "I know you will protect my land and my family whilst I am gone but I wish I were not leaving."

Wulfstan was in agreement with my wife. "You have to go, Alfraed. This is a great honour and your father would be proud. I know not what this means but you will be with the most powerful men in the land. It bodes well for us all. You need to listen and to make friends. This land is not peaceful yet and we will need all the allies we can get some day."

The summons had asked for us to gather by the end of the first week in December. It would take us almost fourteen days to travel south and the weather was unpredictable. Having decided to go, we left a week after the summons arrived. Our small numbers made travelling easier and we only needed two sumpters. I took Roger of Lincoln, Conan and William of Deal with me. They, along with

Wulfric, had been with me for a long time and I knew I could rely on them. I did not expect danger on our journey south but with these four men at arms, I feared no one.

The journey was not a pleasant one. It rained for the whole of the way. Had we been on my estate then it might not have been so bad but the rain permeated our cloaks and soaked us to the skin. It was fortunate that our mail was wrapped in sheepskins on our sumpters. The only good side was that John and Leofric were able to learn much from the men at arms. All of the men at arms were confirmed bachelors. None would marry and they enjoyed talking to the two squires and to have a little fun at some of their questions. It made up for the weather.

We reached London by the end of November and I found us lodgings close to the Black Friars' Monastery. It seemed we had arrived before most of the other barons, earls and counts. London would be crowded when they all arrived. I left my men to get settled and then rode to the Tower for that would be where the King would be found. I did not know the protocol but I was sure he would wish to know that I had arrived.

My livery was now well known and I was admitted to the castle. If Caen was a mighty castle, then this was a fortress. The White Tower was a symbol of the King's power. I left Scout with one of the stable boys and approached the stairs which led to the interior. Earl Robert himself opened the door and waved me inside as another shower slashed down from the skies. It was almost falling horizontally. He shook his head, "I thought Wales was wet but I seem to have brought the wet weather with me." He clasped my arm, "Good to see you again, Baron. I hear you have been trouncing the Scots again?"

I nodded, "Should they ever be led by a decent general then we will be in trouble. And you, my lord, how goes the war with the Welsh?"

"Oh, we have the lands from Pembroke to Hereford under our heel but they are the very devil to shift from their mountain stronghold. We let them have the north which is fit only for birds and sheep. Where are you staying?"

"My men and I have taken rooms at a small inn close to the Black Friars."

He shook his head, "You shall stay with me. I have a manor just north of here." He waved over one of his household knights. "Go and fetch the Baron's men to our hall. They are in the inn close to the Black Friars." After he had gone and I had taken off my cloak he put his arm around my shoulder. "My father and I will need your support. With you and the other Northern Barons behind us we can ensure that our line survives."

I was intrigued but I knew that I would be told what this was about when the time came. "I am always there to support you and your father; you know that, my lord."

"A more faithful knight I have yet to find." He smiled "And I think you will find more old comrades here too. Come we will go to the hall. There are some there you will know and others that you will not."

I heard the hubbub from within the hall before we reached it. When the doors were opened the first sight which greeted me was Matilda, Empress of Germany and my Swabian brothers. I felt a thrill when the Empress smiled at me. It was spontaneous. She was pleased to see me. I bowed, "Empress, it is good to see you."

"And you, Baron. I have been hearing of your exploits in the north. My father is well pleased with you. He has made a wise decision in appointing you his northern guardian."

Rolf and the others waited while I bowed my head and then surrounded me as the Empress left me to join the other ladies of the court. "Good to see you, Baron. And you are right about the ale over here. It is much better than that which we endured in Normandy."

I saw a handful of knights from Normandy and they scowled as they overheard Rolf's words. He was irascible and he cared not what others thought. The Earl said, "And we have other guests." He gestured towards another woman who had been seated and was attended by a young girl and a youth. "This is my guest the Lady Nest ferch Rhys."

Although approaching middle-aged Nest ferch Rhys was stunningly beautiful. She was the most famous and infamous woman of her age. She had been the lover of King Henry and she had had six children by four men. Her abduction and rape by Owain ap Cadwgan was still spoken of twenty years later.

"I think guest is a milder word than I would have chosen, my lord. I believe I am a hostage for the good behaviour of my countrymen."

The Earl smiled, "I believe you are comfortable enough here, my lady."

She nodded, "The Empress has spoken of you fondly, my Lord of Norton. Your exploits do you credit. It seems there are still noble knights who behave well."

If this was intended to insult Robert of Gloucester it did not work for he laughed. "I know the Baron is noble but he is a fierce man in a fight. The next time your countrymen prove troublesome I shall send for the Baron here and we will cow them once and for all."

The Welsh princess just smiled diplomatically. I learned that she had been used to navigating between enemies and friends since her father, the King, had been killed by King Henry.

Matilda stood, "I think we shall retire now, my lord. The King has asked me to prepare for a feast this night." She held out her hand for me to kiss. "I hope to see you again, my lord."

As I took her hand she gave it the slightest squeeze. "I am still a Knight of the Empress, my lady, and I serve you always."

I heard Nest laugh, "Perhaps I will have an order of knights and then I shall receive such honour and affection."

I found myself blushing. The Earl saw my predicament. "Come, Baron, we will go to my hall. My father entertains his Norman Barons here tonight. The conversation will be dull. We will feast with our warriors."

It was not far to the fine hall which the Earl of Gloucester had been given. The rain had eased off which made the journey slightly more pleasant. As we rode he chatted to me. "Now that we are away from prying ears and eyes I can speak more freely. My father will name my sister as his heir." I nodded. It gave me the time to digest that information. "It will prove unpopular, especially amongst the knights with lands in Blois and Normandy. The brothers Stephen and Theobald of Blois would expect to be named as joint heirs." He shrugged, "Indeed my father hinted to Stephen that he might look favourably upon him. However, there was some doubt about his loyalty."

I could have given evidence as to his disloyalty. He had tried to abduct Matilda on at least two occasions. I would not trust him despite his reputation as a fine knight.

"And your father; he still intends to marry her off?"

He nodded, "There are a number of suitors but he hopes that by making her his heir she will attract a more powerful husband."

Although I did not like this I could do nothing about it. I now understood why I had been summoned. "Is there much opposition to the decision then?"

"The knights of Normandy and Blois and those with estates in Scotland and England are looking at the opportunities to increase their lands. They worry about the husband my father may choose.

You are unusual, Alfraed. You do not seek to gain for the sake of gain. It is one of the many reasons my father likes you."

"Surely the knights who oppose him would not risk civil war!"

"The land my father rules is the richest in the whole of Europe. Everyone covets what he holds. It is one of the reasons he spends so much time in Normandy. He relies on you and me to keep his lands safe."

We reached the manor and my men were already there. They were far happier to be amongst fellow warriors. If I am to be truthful then so was I. I felt safe and secure here. I trusted Earl Robert and that was not something I would say about every knight.

I did not enjoy the next few days. Although we were happy enough in the manor of Earl Robert I was called upon to attend the court each day and I had to watch Empress Matilda being paraded like a prize cow before the lords and knights who gathered there. My only consolation was talking with Rolf and his men. They were as angered by this travesty as I was. While the other lords and knights fawned around Nest and Matilda, we would stand at the side glowering at all the false knights who paid court to them. Poor Matilda had to smile at every greasy knight who slobbered over her hand. The Earl might have thought it was a secret but Rolf knew that she would be named as the heir to the throne. He spoke it quietly and privately. Others were less discreet with the information. I now knew why I had been summoned. We were the protection for the Empress and the King. The Blois faction lurked menacingly close each time the Empress was paraded before them. My hand was constantly upon my sword.

Rolf growled, one day, "The sooner the King makes his announcement the better. Then we can close ranks and protect her. This is a nightmare. There are daggers in men's eyes and I fear they might soon be in their hands."

As the days dragged on to the announcement I prepared my men. "I want all of you sober and ready to fight until we leave London. I know not what will arise but I want all of you ready at a moment's notice."

"Trust me, my lord we will be." Wulfric was as solid and dependable as Edward. I needed not fear. I now regretted bringing so few men. The weather, like my mood, was dark and dank. It was either wet or foggy each day. This river was not the wholesome one I was used to. This Thames appeared pestilential and sickly.

One morning, when the weather was slightly better than it had been, I was summoned by Carl. "The Empress wishes to see you."

"At the Tower?"

He shook his head, "She is going to the church at Westminster to say prayers for her husband. She will meet you there."

I took only Wulfric. I needed a bodyguard I could rely upon and Leofric was just too inexperienced. Rolf and Gottfried were outside and they merely nodded as I approached. Wulfric joined them and I entered the church begun by King Ethelred. The candles gave a soft, golden light and I walked down the aisle to the kneeling Empress. She said nothing but gave the slightest movement of her arm. I knelt and made the sign of the cross. I said nothing.

"Thank you for coming." She paused, "I am in danger. My life has been threatened." I glanced over and her eyes met mine, she nodded. "One of my ladies, Judith, was poisoned. We found an antidote and she is tough but she was close to death. I need you to watch out for me."

"But Rolf and your Swabians?"

"They are warriors and will die to protect me. You are a thinker and will stop the danger."

I bowed my head, "How can I help?"

"Theobald of Blois wants me dead. My Swabians can protect me from physical harm but ..."

"But you need him diverting."

She nodded, "I knew you would understand. My brother and my father can know nothing of this for I would not have a civil war because of me."

I understood. It would not be easy. "I will do what I can. Where does he stay?"

"The knights of Blois have taken a hall close to Greenwich. Stephen also has a hall there. They believe they are safe there."

"I will do what I can."

"Do not take unnecessary risks."

I put my hand on hers, "I promise you I will not!"

I returned to the Earl's hall. I would have liked to speak with the Earl about the Empress' problem but I knew that I could not for I had given my word. I sought, instead, my men. "Come, let us walk by the river." If they were surprised by my request they said nothing.

I led them to the east of the tower and we walked along a crowded river bank. Each day more knights and barons arrived by river and they disembarked on the wharfs adjacent to the castle. Gradually the bank became less crowded and I halted at a quiet, empty wharf which was opposite the bed of the river at Greenwich.

I saw the banner of Blois flying from the top of the manor house. I could see knights moving around outside and there appeared to be guards and sentries. It would be too difficult to get to either of the brothers there.

Wulfric said, "Do you see something over there which interests you, my lord?"

These were my oathsworn and they did not need me to tell them to keep secrets however I dared not let them know the full import of the Empress' words. "Do you remember the knight with the red shield? The one who dogged our footsteps in Normandy?"

Wulfric nodded, "Aye, Baron. We saw him on many fields."

"I believe he is Stephen of Blois and he lives yonder. He is the King's nephew and I would not offend the King by accusing his nephew of treachery however I would know more about him."

Wulfric rubbed his chin. "If you wish, my lord, the four of us could take a ride south of the river tomorrow. We could scout out the manor." He nodded his head to the others, "Soldiers like to talk. If we didn't wear our surcoats we could be four men at arms seeking a new employer."

Leofric said, "What about us?"

Wulfric laughed, "The trouble is you look like a squire and not a man at arms. The four of us look as though we have seen a little of life and there are always old soldiers who wish a new lord."

"I would be careful, Wulfric. We cannot afford a bloodbath and I cannot afford to lose any of you."

"Do not worry, my lord. This will stop us being bored."

My oathsworn were the best of warriors. I could rely on them for anything. We walked back to the Earl's hall and reached there just before dark.

That evening, as I ate with the Earl, he confided in me, "The announcement about the Empress will be made four days before Christmas. By then all of the knights from Normandy and Blois will have arrived. They will be spending Christmas with the King but that will allow the rest of you the opportunity to get home for Christmas."

I shook my head, "The King does not know what the roads to the north are like. We will be spending Christmas on the road home I am afraid."

"I am sorry for that. I forget how far it is to your home in the north."

"It matters not. We will celebrate whenever we get home." We chatted about inconsequential matters for a while; the food, the wine, the inclement weather and then I asked, "The brothers, Stephen and Theobald from Blois, what do you know of them?"

He frowned, "They are my cousins. Why do you ask?"

"Oh, nothing really. It is just that I think I met the one called Stephen when we were escorting your sister back to Worms the other year."

He chewed on some venison. "But you met only enemies on that journey and my sister did not mention our cousin."

"He wore a helmet and had a plain shield."

"Then how do you know it was him?"

"As I said I was not sure but I caught a glimpse of him without his helmet and then when your father came north I saw him again. I may have been mistaken and it might not have been him. That is why I asked you the question, my lord, I was curious."

He wiped his greasy hands on his surcoat and lowered his voice. "There is a possibility you may be right but I would urge you not to voice your suspicions too loudly. The brothers have a claim to the throne. However, neither can agree which one has the better claim. We must tread carefully, my friend."

"Surely the elder has the right to the claim. Which one is that?"

"Theobald but Stephen is the clever one. He enjoys chess and strategy. That is why I think you may have been right. He would use my sister as a pawn to get what he desires." He nodded, "I am pleased that you confided in me and that you kept your eyes open. My father may be able to use this. But I urge you to keep your counsel to yourself."

I suddenly worried that I might have jeopardised the Empress, "I would not cause dissension."

"Do not worry, my friend. There will be no dissension and neither you nor my sister will be mentioned."

My four men at arms left the hall early the next day and clattered over London Bridge. If the Earl's men wondered why they rode without surcoats and shields they did not say anything. I went with my two squires to the church at Westminster. I felt we needed to pray for I was now in unfamiliar territory. The stakes were higher in this game than any I had encountered before. We were gambling on the right to rule England, Normandy and Maine not to mention part of Wales and Ireland.

John and Leofric were both becoming a little restless with our inactivity and they voiced this as we returned to the hall. "My lord, why do we have to wait here? What does the King want of us?"

"When I know then you shall know Leofric. You serve me as I serve the King. That is the natural order of things. We are not the masters of our own destinies."

"And who does the King serve?"

"A good question, John. He serves God. All kings are anointed and they all serve God."

I knew my answer did not satisfy either of the squires but I was distracted. I hated sending my men to be in danger. I did not mind leading them into battle but this was different. They were putting their lives in danger for me while I was safe. I was relieved when the four of them trotted into the manor later that afternoon.

I walked to the stables for I was eager to speak with them. "Well?"

Wulfric grinned, "They are a tight-lipped bunch, my lord, but after a few jugs of ale they loosened up a little. It seems that the Count of Blois and his little brother do not get on. They also told me that the younger one, Baron Stephen, sometimes took himself off for months at a time. He is the one who is richer."

I frowned, "Richer than his brother, the Count?"

Wulfric nodded, "I know, my lord. It seems strange to me too."

"Did you get to see them?"

He nodded, "Aye as we came away they were just returning from a hunt. I would know them both again."

"Good you have done well."

He smiled, "We enjoyed it my lord but we will keep our swords sharpened, eh my lord? His men seemed to think that they may see action soon and that it might return a healthy profit."

He was right and I made sure that my weapons were ready too. The day of the announcement saw a hive of activity as we all prepared ourselves for the great gathering. I felt quite privileged as I knew what was coming but the majority did not; they might have guessed but I knew for certain. We all had our mail and helmets burnished. We would not need our shields but it would be a mighty gathering of all the important barons from the whole of King Henry's realms. I rode with the Earl although I was at the rear of his retinue. When we reached Westminster, I left Scout with my men. I did not need to tell them to keep their eyes open. They would do that anyway.

We stood in knots of knights. Each faction was separate from the rest. I saw the knights from Blois gathered around Stephen and Theobald. They both had faces as black as thunder. I was relieved that those close to the Earl looked to be in the majority. When the

King strode in, flanked by his bodyguards, silence descended. The only sound was that of their mailed feet as they made their way to the altar where the Bishop waited. Behind him came Empress Matilda with my Swabian friends protectively gathered around her. She looked so small in the midst of their huge bodies that she appeared to be a child. How could she rule England? It was unfair of her father to make her his heir and I wished that he would name Robert of Gloucester. He could defend the land.

The King turned and Matilda stood beside him. His voice echoed in the vaulted church as he said, "Know you that I, Henry of England and Normandy, do name my only child, Matilda, Empress of the Empire, as my heir. She will rule my lands when I am gone!" There was a murmur of voices, mainly from the Norman contingent. The King jutted his chin out as he said, "Does anyone object! If so speak now or forever hold your peace!" This was a tense moment. Had anyone spoken then swords would have been unsheathed and blood spilt in the sanctified shadows of Ethelred's church. Thankfully there were none.

"Kneel and swear, in this holy church, your allegiance to my daughter Matilda. Let it be known throughout the lands of Normandy and England that she will rule after me. Swear!"

We all dropped to our knees and the walls echoed as the packed ranks of knights swore to protect Matilda, daughter of Henry. It was in that moment that any dreams I might have had of possessing Matilda disappeared. It was also the moment when civil war became inevitable and knights who knelt alongside me would be foresworn when they reneged on their sworn word. It was the beginning of the anarchy which would tear England and Normandy apart.

Chapter 13

We all bowed as the King, the Empress and the Earl left. Rolf and the Swabians nodded to me as they passed. When we emerged into the overcast, damp, London skies I saw Theobald and Stephen talking to each other and their faces showed the intensity of their discussion. The Empress had said that they needed diverting. I decided to divert them. I strode up to them and, smiling, said to Stephen. "You are the knight with the red shield who tried to attack the Empress when I escorted her to Worms and her husband the Emperor."

I think it was the last thing which Stephen expected. His face looked as though I had slapped it. He might have enjoyed chess but he could not disguise his reaction to my words. His brother obviously knew nothing about it for he gave me a look of disbelief. Stephen was not fast enough to hide his feelings and I saw it in his eyes. He composed himself and smiled back at me, "I think you must be mistaken, Baron, for I have never attacked my cousin nor would I."

"You may be right for the knight who had the red shield was obviously a craven coward else he would have identified himself so that he could be challenged. I can now see that you could not be the knight with the red shield for he ran away the last time I followed him." I laughed, "He ran so fast that hares could not catch him. Yes, now that I come to think of it, the red knight will still be hiding in Flanders and shaking in case I come for him again."

This time I had pierced the armour of Stephen of Blois. He could say nothing in reply without incriminating himself. He stared angrily at me. Had he had it within his power then he would have struck me. Theobald frowned, "I am pleased you did not accuse my brother. I would have crossed lances with you to teach you a lesson."

"Any time you wish a lesson in honour then I am your man."

Stephen put his arm between us. "Brother, this is the knight who defeated the Count of Stuttgart at a tourney in Worms. A challenge would be ill advised."

I smiled, "As would any threat to the Empress." I held the medallion out. "I am a knight of the Empress and sworn to protect her. Should you ever see the red knight again then warn him of that for I am an implacable enemy to any who would harm the Empress." I allowed my words to linger in the damp morning air and then added, "Of course we all just swore before God to protect the Empress so I am sure that you two would join me in ridding the world of her enemies eh?" They both nodded. "Well, gentlemen, I shall have to leave you. I have a long journey back to my home in the north. My work here is done. I have enough of intrigue and dishonesty. I would return to the Northern lands where I rule and I can trust the men to whom I speak!"

As I walked slowly away to Leofric and John I felt their eyes as they stared daggers at my back. I had done what had been asked of me and now I would have to pay the price. I knew that assassins would follow me north. I had insulted both of them; more than that I had told them that I would stand in the way of any threat to the Empress. They would have to be rid of me before they could bring harm to her.

As soon as I met up with my men again I said, "We are now in danger. I have upset the Count of Blois and his brother. When we ride north we ride as though we are in the middle of Flanders with enemies all around."

Wulfric laughed, "Well boys, it looks like life has become interesting once again."

I clapped my sergeant at arms around the shoulders. "It will indeed, John, unfurl our banner, let us show the world where we are!" I was pleased with the reaction of my men. They showed not fear but defiance.

We galloped north towards Watling Street. John and Leofric led the sumpters. If there were to be any fighting then it would be my four tough men at arms who would do it.

The ride south and the time spent walking around London had strengthened my leg and I no longer felt the wound. Father Richard had stitched it well and it was the smallest of my many scars. If we had to fight then I could rely on my leg and on the repaired armour which was now stronger than ever. We made good time as we headed north. We left Watling Street and took the Great North Road. The Romans had built well and it would guide us home. I knew we would be followed but the pursuit would take time to organise. I intended to get a good lead. We could not hide. Stephen of Blois knew where we were going and there was really only one way to go. The only question was where would the attack be?

"Wulfric, if you were to attack us where would it be?"

"That is obvious, my lord, Sherwood Forest and blame it on the outlaws."

"That is what I thought too. It is a pity we did not bring Dick. He would have known where the outlaws were and brought them to our aid."

Wulfric shook his head. "The last time Dick scouted for archers he found perilously few in Sherwood. They are now the stuff of legend."

We were twenty miles north of London and looking for somewhere to spend the night when we heard hooves thundering up the road behind us. In an instant, we had wheeled around to present our shields and swords to whoever was pursuing us. I relaxed when I recognised the Baron of Doncaster, Sir Roger Fitz d'Amphraville. I had met him at the Earl's hall and knew him to be an ally. He reined in when he saw us.

"We thought we had made a swift departure from London. You have ridden hard, Baron."

"We have further to go, Sir Roger. We will have to ride hard just to be home for St. Stephen's Day."

"May we ride with you? I can promise you a warm bed when we reach my manor."

"I would be delighted but that will not be tonight, I fear."

"No, but I have a cousin who lives just fifteen miles along this road. It is not a large manor bur he has a barn with a roof."

Our men fell in behind us as we spurred on our horses. I felt much safer with Sir Roger and his ten men. The Count of Blois and his brother would need to catch us alone to do us harm.

"Well, Sir Alfraed, what do you make of the King's choice?"

"He had little choice now that his son is dead. For myself I would be happy to follow the Earl of Gloucester should he be named heir."

"As would I but that cannot happen. The King's nephews would seize the opportunity to question the claim of an illegitimate son."

"You have met them then?"

"I know what they are like, Baron, and their ambition. Both seek to be king. The tragedy of the White Ship still sends ripples out from the shores of Normandy. The King plans to marry her off, you know."

"I know." I tried to keep the despair out of my voice but it was not easy.

Sir Roger was a pleasant companion and the two days spent in his company were rewarding in many ways. As we left his castle to head north on the forest road I felt suddenly naked. We had to return to looking over our shoulders. I wondered if I was wrong.

Perhaps Stephen of Blois did not think me worthy of killing. Once more we pushed hard as we headed north. The forest still stretched like an endless green blanket before us. When we had ridden through the southern portion with Sir Roger it had seemed open. Now it felt constricting and filled with danger.

It was Scout who saved us, again. The road dipped a little and he neighed whilst pricking up his ears. I needed no second warning. "There is danger! Draw your weapons! I just managed to get my shield up when a bolt from a crossbow smashed into it. It came from ahead and to my left. It was close enough for the head to have pierced my shield. Although I knew there would be other crossbows that one, at least, would take time to reload and I spurred Scout on towards the danger. He leapt towards the eaves of the forest where I caught a glint of metal and a flash of colour. A second and a third bolt hit my shield. One of them penetrated the wood a second time. That meant the ambushers were close.

I had my sword drawn already and as I caught sight of a crossbowman trying to rearm his weapon. I swung my weapon and it tore into his face. I was not worried about Wulfric and the men at arms but Leofric and John had little experience of this sort of fighting. You had to react quickly and strike as soon as you had a target. Scout had superb reactions and he pulled to the left as the man at arms with a lance galloped towards us through the trees. The head of the lance went across Scout's mane and I stabbed at him more in hope than expectation. As his horse crashed into Scout my sword entered his chest.

I continued the wheel which Scout had begun. I saw a third crossbow and this was aimed at me. I stood up and pulled my shield across my body. The bolt hit my shield but the angle made it ping off to the left and I brought down my sword on his helmet. I crushed it so hard that I am certain I drove part of it into his skull. I saw that John was using my banner like a lance and there was a man at arms being skewered even as I turned. There were, however, more of them than us. Our sudden charge had given us an advantage but our small numbers now worked against us. What we could not do was to turn our backs. They had crossbows and they could penetrate our mail. Even though it was harder, we had to face them and to fight them.

"Drive them into the woods! Use our horses!"

I had not seen any knights but these were experienced warriors. I watched as one raised his axe to try to drive it into the neck of Roger's horse. Suddenly an arrow blossomed from his neck. I had no idea where it came from but I took heart from the fact that it had been loosed at the axe man and not at Roger. Now was the time to advance.

"At them!" A man at arms charged at me. He held his shield tightly and had his sword behind him ready to swing it at my head. I jerked Scout's head around so that we would meet shield to shield. He could not react quickly enough and, as I stood in the stirrups, I punched with my shield. He had to parry with his own shield and when I brought my sword down he almost overbalanced. His arm holding the sword smashed into a tree. I heard the crack of the bone-breaking and the scream of pain at the same time. As he rode off towards the road I saw that it was over. Our saviours with the arrows had managed to reach us in the nick of time. I quickly checked to see what damage had been done to us.

Leofric and John were still in their saddles as were Roger and Wulfric. Conan was helping William to his feet. There was blood but William was moving. I searched in the forest for the men who had come to our aid. I saw no one. "Hello! Thank you for your intervention." I spoke in Saxon. If it was the men of the woods then the use of Norman might result in an arrow. A shadow moved and then a second. Five figures emerged from the woods. They looked like scarecrows.

I dismounted and took off my helmet. "Thank you! Had you not intervened then we might be dead."

The leader looked a little younger than Harold. He gave me a wan smile. "When we saw you fighting we thought to leave you for Norman killing Norman suits us. Then Alan here," he pointed to a blond-haired youth, recognised him," he gestured at Wulfric. "I remembered that you came some years ago and took some of our men: Harold Osbertson and the others."

"You are part of Robert's band?"

"We are all that remain. We were heading to the monastery close to Doncaster to beg for alms. We are starving."

"Where is Robert? This was a large band the last we heard."

"Some Normans came at the time of the Bone Fire two years ago and they managed to track and to trap us. We think there was a spy. Robert and the others were either killed or taken and hanged in Nottingham."

"How did you escape?"

"It was luck. We had been sent to empty the fish traps on the river. By the time we heard the fighting and reached our friends they were dead."

143

I saw that there were three of the ambusher's horses still loose. "Roger, capture those horses." The five young men looked lost. "Harold serves me still and he is a knight now. If you wish then you can serve me too. At least you will be fed and be warm."

Their faces told me their answer before their words. "Aye, my lord. We will follow you. The days of being outlaw are passed."

"Then strip the bodies of all that is valuable and that includes their clothes; everything is of value. Two of you can ride double." While they collected the clothes and arms I went to the tree the man at arms had hit. There, lying on the ground was his sword. It was a good sword. It was well made and it was Frankish. "Here John, fate has given you a sword." My young squire looked excited as I gave him the sword. "You may find a scabbard but if not then you can make one." The new recruits found helmets and some mail as well as daggers, shields and short swords.

We rode north until it became dark. The fight had stopped us from reaching a castle and so we camped in the forest. Luckily, we had food and Wulfric made sure that our latest recruits ate first. They would be a welcome addition to my archers. I saw him looking paternally at them. All were young enough to be his sons.

As we huddled around the fire I asked them of their life in the forest. "Our fathers did not wish to follow Branton. They were loyal to Robert. We were too young to go but we envied those who did. Life was hard in the forest. Some of our mothers had come to the woods to live with us but many found the life too hard and went to the towns to seek work. Others, like my mother and Garth's died."

"You are brothers then?"

He nodded, "This is Alan and I am Ralph. We had a younger brother, John, but he was killed in the camp with our father."

Wulfric ruffled Alan's hair. "You will like it at Stockton." He gestured to me, "The Baron here lets you hunt for him and we have a stone castle which is warm in winter." He opened his purse and spread the coins in the palm of his hand. The gold coins and the silver ones glittered and glistened in the firelight. "And you will make money!"

Ralph's eyes widened. "You are a rich man, Wulfric!"

He nodded as he put the coins back into his purse, "We all are! Even the archers!"

Ralph looked at me and said, "We will serve you well, Baron. I fear we would have all died as many did when we had the wolf winter."

I looked at Wulfric. "You had it too?"

"Aye, my lord. The cold and the wolves took many lives that year. We never recovered. I think that was how the Normans managed to attack us." he paused, "You are not Norman are you my lord?"

"No, but I fight with them and for them. If you cannot do that then we will take you to a place of safety and give you money."

"No, Baron, we know we live in a Norman land but Branton spoke well of your father and your namesake. We trust you."

Each day saw an improvement in the five young men. As we had two horses being ridden double we could not make the speed I had hoped and it was two days after St Stephen's Day when we reached the ferry. There was a shimmering of frost on the trees and a sea fret but the river was not frozen. Wulfric stood behind Ralph and Alan with a huge paw on each of them. "Well boys, there it is your new home, the manor of Stockton."

All five looked excited at the prospect. I had missed Christmas with my family but the encounter with the boys seemed more Christian somehow. It was almost as though we had been meant to find them and rescue them from a life which would have been parlous at best. The ferry proved to be a novelty to them. The rivers in the forest were all fordable. Here the tide was in and it must have seemed like a mighty sea to them. I spied Adela on the ramparts as Ethelred's men pulled us across. I saw her wave and then one of my men at arms lifted my son so that he could wave too.

I let Wulfric see to the new archers while I ran into my castle to greet my family. When my son and wife threw their arms around me I knew that I was home. London and the plots and intrigue seemed far away. I just prayed that Rolf and his men could keep Matilda safe. The last thing the Earl had said was that the Empress would be staying in London, at least until the spring. That meant her father could ensure her safety. After that…

I decided to hold a twelfth night celebration as I had missed Christmas. I took Aiden and my new archers as well as John, my squire and we went hunting on the first day of January. We went to the land around Hartburn. I knew there was good hunting there and I wanted my new recruits to become familiar with our land. John and I rode while the others hunted on foot. John and I had boar spears. Aiden's dogs soon found the scent of game and we followed the trail until we saw a stag, on his own. He was a fine beast. This was a good time to hunt stags for they had already served the hinds. It would encourage younger stags. Ralph and another of the recruits, Osbert, took down the deer and I saw that, despite their youth, they were good archers.

We found tracks of other deer but we did not see them. Aiden's dogs and Scout alerted us to danger. A sow hurled herself from under some bramble bushes. I pulled back on Scout's reins to make him rear and thrust down with my spear. It might have gone ill for Scout had not John hurled his spear into the side of the sow's head. She fell dead at my feet. While John and I tied her feet around the spears Aiden took the archers to search for the rest of the herd. They came back with six young. She had attacked us because she had young. I was just pleased there was no male close by.

"We can take them back, Baron, and raise them. This will be the start of a new herd for us." That was the beginning of a fruitful year for us and meant that the twelfth-night feast was a good one. Fortune had favoured us and our kindness with the five boys had been rewarded.

Sir Richard, Harold, Edward, Wulfstan and Osric all attended my feast. Athelstan had the winter sickness and Father Peter insisted he stay in his hall. His presence would have made it perfect. After we had eaten I told them of the oath we had made and then I told them about the Count of Blois. Edward had laughed, "That is one more Count who hates us, Baron! I think it better we stay on this side of the English Channel!"

Harold shook his head, "I think not for we make more coin when we go abroad. Will we be abroad again, Baron?"

"I know not. I will be happy just staying in my own land for a while. I have not yet had the chance to see how it fares in the summer."

The evening was perfection. I had with me those I loved the best and those who served me. What more could a lord ask for than to be surrounded by his oathsworn and his family. I might have missed Christmas but the twelfth-night feast lived long in my memory.

Chapter 14

We make plans and sometimes they work out and sometimes they do not. I had planned on a summer getting to know my children and my new men. I had planned on making Leofric and John into better squires. I had hoped to enjoy hunts with my knights. None of that happened. As Easter approached we received a summons to meet the Earl of Gloucester at Chester. It seemed that Gruffudd ap Cynan had tried to attack the rich farmland around Cheshire and Chester. Some of the Norman lords had been enjoying an extended stay with the King in London and some castles had been burned. Our success against the Scots meant that we were the first choice for the Earl and I led my conroi across the high hills towards Chester. I was less than happy to do so. My men had earned the right to some peace. This was the Earl's war and not mine.

Once again, I left Wulfstan to guard my home. With Athelstan still suffering from the coughing sickness I needed someone to help Osric and Wulfstan was the perfect choice. When I had returned from London I had noticed that he was now totally grey. He was still a fine warrior but he would not be able to stand the rigours of a campaign in Wales. He was a visible sign that all warriors either died or grew old.

I left five men at arms in my castle as well as Aiden but I took all of my archers. I now had a fine force of bowmen and they were all mounted. We made a fine sight as we rode to the south and the west. My men at arms were all mounted on fine palfreys and each one had a full set of mail. We looked more like a column of knights.

The Earl of Gloucester would meet us at Chester. This would not be a repeat of the war against Powys. Gwynedd was a mountainous region. The only flat part was the rich wheat land of Anglesey. This time there would be no fine in cattle and as the crop was not yet sown it was hard to see what we would gain from such a campaign. It was another reason for my despondency. My knights wondered the same but they hoped for riches and success. Somehow, I always seemed to manage to reap rewards. Tristan and Harold were now both experienced knights and each had a small retinue of both men at arms and archers. They hoped to increase their numbers with a successful war.

When we reached Chester, there were already many tents erected and Wulfric struggled to find us a camp which was not in the swampy area close to the river. I hoped we would not be there too long. The winter rains had left the estuary muddy and wet. I did not want the pestilence to strike my men. The Earl took me to one side as soon as I arrived.

"Alfraed you and your men will not be here long. I want you to be the vanguard. You are all mounted and have proved that you can be trusted on your own. I want you to find this Gruffudd so that we may bring him to battle quickly. The Earl of Chester managed to stop him penetrating any further north but he has taken his men towards the east and the rich farmland there." I saw him hesitate and wondered what was on his mind. "Did you deliberately upset the Count of Blois when you were at Westminster?"

I could not lie and I would not lie. "Yes, my lord, I did."

Instead of being angry he smiled. "I might have known you would give me the truth. My father was angry but tell me why?"

I took a deep breath. "I was certain that I had seen Stephen of Blois when we took your sister back to Worms. He denied it but I still do not believe him."

"You think he is a threat to my sister?"

"I know he is as do you, my lord."

He nodded, "Be careful, for Stephen and Theobald have powerful allies. There are many in Normandy who would see Theobald as King of England." He smiled as if to make it easier for me, "Anyway he is back in Blois now so you two are unlikely to lock horns again."

"He sent men to try to kill me when I returned north."

"And?" He did not seem surprised and that annoyed me.

"And they died!"

He nodded, "I would not cross you Alfraed; you do not take prisoners, do you?"

"Not the likes of Stephen I don't." He nodded and turned to go, "My lord, we have brought our warhorses. Will we need them? I would not risk such fine animals in the mountains of Wales."

"No, you are right. Leave them here. The Welsh do not use many knights and they like to kill horses." I did not want to lose Star in the mountainous valleys and summits of North Wales.

We had just the one night to spend in the damp camp by the river in Chester. We left four men to guard our war horses and my conroi set off across the east towards the flat rich plains of Cheshire.

Although the land was flatter than that which we would encounter closer to Gwynedd it still rose and fell. It made the prospect of both ambush and attack closer. Although we had not brought Aiden both Ralph and Alan had proved adept woodsmen. I could now see how the handful of archers had managed to survive after their leader was dead. They had been born in the woods and had natural skills at tracking and, more importantly, avoiding being seen. Dick was well impressed by them and the two new archers ranged far ahead of us. My captain of archers was confident in their ability. Our task was simple; we had to find and hold the Welsh and send a rider to the Earl who would then bring our army to destroy them. If we did not find any sign of them this first day then it meant we had lost them.

Alan found them within a few hours of beginning his tracking. He came riding in with a face flushed with excitement. "I have found them, Baron! They have a camp just three miles away. There is a river and a bridge. Some of the town is burned and they have taken cattle and, I think, prisoners."

Had this been Dick then I could have shown him the map which the Earl had given us but Alan could not read and had never seen a map. I would have to work this out in order to send a report back to the Earl. I knew how far we had come and where we were, roughly, on the map. There was just one bridge close to a settlement.

"Send a rider back to the Earl and tell him that we have found the men of Gwynedd close to Nantwich." I turned to my knights. "I think I know why they have chosen this place to rest. There are many places here where they make salt. They can use it to raid further afield while gathering plunder to take back to their mountain kingdom. They will slaughter and salt some of the cattle. We have a chance to catch them. They must be confident."

"If there is a bridge then that might make it difficult to take."

Ralph rode in while we were preparing to move. "I have found them, Baron."

I frowned, Alan had already done so. That meant that this was a second band. Had they split up? "Where?"

He pointed to the south. "There is a large band and they are moving south and west. They are down that road there."

"How far away?"

His face fell. He had no idea of distance and had not learned to use the Roman stones which marked distance nor had he any concept of time. "Not far."

I smiled. It was not his fault. The fault lay with me who had not taught him such things. "It matters not, you have done well. Tell me, how many men did you see?"

"As many as in the Earl's army."

"Alan, how many did you see? Was it as many as the Earl's force?"

"No, my lord." He held up both of his hands ten times; a hundred.

The Welsh had left part of their army and continued to raid with the other half. "We will need to split our force. Sir Geoffrey, take Hartness, Normanby and Piercebridge. Go to the bridge and await the Earl. Use your archers to stop them moving. I will take the rest and find this warband. Tell the Earl where we went."

"Aye Baron."

Although I took fewer knights I had more men at arms and archers than I left with Sir Geoffrey. I also had the most experienced men with me. The road we travelled twisted and turned between small rises and farms. This was not a Roman Road. This was ambush country. I kept Ralph next to me so that he could tell me when we drew close to the place where he had seen our enemy. The slight rise and fall meant that even though we would be hidden from the Welsh we could come upon them unexpectedly. Suddenly he said, "Not far now. When I saw them, they were just beyond that small stand of trees."

"Good. Dick, now is the time for your archers to do their work. Ralph thinks they are not far ahead. Find them but do not be seen. Send Aelric back to me to let me know where they are." My archers trotted off. We had five knights and seven squires. Harold and Tristan had both recently taken on a squire. Neither of them was experienced. They did, however, look like knights. With their helmets, mail and banners the Welsh might take them for knights.

"Wulfric, we will advance down this road in lines of five. I want ten men at arms behind us then the squires and the rest of the men at arms behind them. Leofric, leave a slight gap between your horses and those before you. I would have them think we have two conroi." I saw his eager face nod. He recognised the responsibility he was being given. "The front three ranks will use lances. I would shatter their first line of defence and cause confusion."

Tristan said, "But we do not know how many there are. The scout said a warband."

"You are right, Sir Tristan, but it matters not. These are raiders. They will have warriors who can be trusted to range and to ravage.

What they will not expect is to be attacked by mounted knights." I pointed to the north. "There lies Nantwich and the camp they defend. They might expect us from the west but not from the north. We charge even if it is the full army of Gruffudd ap Cynan. We are the vanguard and we have been charged with finding and holding the enemy. We will do so."

I understood Tristan's worries. This was the first time he had fought so far from home and the land was totally unfamiliar to him. He was also, like Harold, now riding in the front rank of my battle. He was nervous. If he survived this encounter then he would be a better knight.

There were hedges along the side of the road. I hoped that they would stop soon or we would be restricted in what we did. It was too late to worry about that for the die was cast. I had committed us to a charge into their ranks. Thankfully as we crested a low rise we crossed another track and the hedges stopped. Ahead of us I could see the warband as it spread like a huge stain across the plain. Here were open fields separated by ditches. I could see metal glinting in the spring sunlight. The Welsh army appeared to be largely foot although I could see that there were horsemen mounted on the small hill ponies the Welsh favoured. I could neither see my archers nor the cover they might use. Just then Aelric appeared from behind us. He came through a gap in the hedges.

"Baron, Captain Dick has the archers to the west." He pointed to another line of hedges in the distance. It looked to be two hundred or so paces from the enemy's right flank. It was the only cover he could find but the range was extreme. It was the best he could have managed. It meant that if we had to retreat it would be in that direction.

"Good, Aelric ride to the Earl and tell him where we are and what we do. Ask him to come to our aid as soon as he can. We are seriously outnumbered."

Aelric was one of my most experienced archers. I did not need to tell him about the importance of my message. As he rode off I said, "We charge their right side at the rear. I want us to draw them towards Dick and his archers. There are too many for us to destroy and they have horses. Wulfric, I want a good man in the rear rank."

"Aye Baron, it is Roger of Lincoln, he is a good fellow."

"Then let him know that he has to command the rearguard when we ride to the archers."

"Aye, my lord!"

I led us at the canter towards the rear of the warband. It was some four hundred paces away and was spread over a wide area. As we neared them I could see that, in their midst, they had some captives and some animals. What had appeared a disordered rabble now took on slightly more organisation. I also saw that they had ringed their band with riders on small ponies. At their head were about ten mailed warriors on full size horses. The mass of men in the centre were armed with a variety of weapons. This was an army like the one we had fought on the Tyne; it was just far bigger.

Inevitably the thunder of our hooves alerted them to our presence. When we were just three hundred paces away I saw the faces turned towards us and heard the shouts. We were committed. They turned to face us.

"Charge!"

I was not aiming to do more than penetrate deep into the heart and then turn away. I was trying, much as a hunting lion might do, to make the herd scatter. Their formation aided me. A dozen or so brave men turned, with their flimsy shields and pole weapons, to face us. I pulled back with my lance and punched forward. These men wore no mail and I chose an easy target, the chest. The warrior looked terrified as Scout's snorting face appeared before him and he took his eye from my lance which killed instantly. I flicked the body to the side and pulled back again. My next target had his back to me and was an even easier hit. He was a big man and a wide man. His fall broke my spear and I threw the now useless haft to one side. A warrior panicked and fell before Scout who had no time to turn. His body was trampled beneath his hooves.

There was panic amongst the ranks before us and this was exacerbated by the animals and the captives in the middle. It mattered not that we were there to save them they panicked even more and prevented those at the front from turning to face us.

I drew my sword and swung it from behind me to rip up and into the head of the mailed warrior with a shield and a sword. He tumbled backwards although not dead he was out of the battle. I glanced over my shoulder and saw that we had ridden deep into the warband. When I looked ahead I saw the warriors on the horses organising a shield wall to face us. Our horses were tiring and there was little point in risking them further.

"Norton, turn right!" I had no John to signal with the banner and I pointed to the west with my sword. The knights with me heard and began to wheel. As we galloped through the fleeing Welsh we laid about us with our swords and the shattered remains of lances.

It was as though a whirlwind had attacked a field of wheat. You could see the bloody lines of bodies behind us. It took some moments for them to realise that we had turned and we used that time well. I saw the hedge ahead of us. It was too high to jump and so we headed for the gaps. As soon as I was through the first gap I wheeled Scout around to watch the rest as they came.

Some of the riders on ponies had pursued our men. I saw the squires being attacked by them. They did us proud. Although young and inexperienced they rode fine horses and wore mail. That saved them for the Welsh riders jabbed spears at them as they closed. It was their mail which saved them from serious injury. They hacked at the spears and used the weight of their horses to force the ponies away from them. I saw John use my banner as a spear and he knocked a rider to the ground. Roger of Lincoln wheeled the men at arms to aid the squires.

I looked beyond them and saw that the Welsh leader, I assumed it was their king, had organised his men and a line of horsemen led the ponies in a line towards us. Behind them the men on foot were being ordered into lines ready to advance towards us.

I said nothing to Dick for he knew the range better than I did.

"Position yourselves close to the gaps. Dismount. We will face them on foot. That is where they will come through."

I saw that we had lost at least two men at arms but my knights appeared to be unscathed. I saw Tristan and Harold congratulating each other. I understood their pride. They were young knights and they had acquitted themselves. They had done well. Already we had scattered the Welsh army and halted their plundering. It was all that the Earl could have hoped for. Now we had to hold them until he and the army arrived. I hoped it would not take too long.

I was next to Wulfric at the central gap in the hedges. "They are piss poor soldiers, my lord."

"Aye Wulfric but now they are angry. They have seen how few we are and that makes a man fight harder. This will not be easy."

The men at arms were formed on either side of me. John and Leofric hurled themselves from their horses and stood behind me. "Make sure they see my banner, John son of Godwin."

"Aye my lord." I heard the pride in his voice as he raised the standard.

"Release!" The thirty arrows soared high over the hedge and even as they reached their apex a second flight was on its way. I knew without counting that they would release five and then begin to aim. To the Welsh on their small ponies it must have been like stepping from a house into a blizzard save that this storm was deadlier. Ponies and men fell as though scythed. Inevitably some got through for they were attacking on a wide front. The gaps were not large but two or three ponies could get through. I deflected the spear of the first rider who burst through the hedge and swung my sword. He jerked his pony's head around and my blade bit into the skull of the beast which reared in pain. The rider was thrown and the pony fell to the side. I stepped forward and killed the rider where he lay. The dead animal effectively blocked the gap and the other riders struggled to make their ponies climb over. Wulfric and my men at arms stepped forward and began to lay about them with their weapons. Ponies and riders fell. Most had no armour and could not stand against such disciplined men.

I heard a trumpet and the Welsh fell back. They left behind a bloody pile of ponies and men. We had held them; for the moment.

"Wulfric, see to the wounded. Dick, send a rider to the Earl and tell them that we have stopped the Welsh but we need help." I turned to Leofric and John as my men attended to their duties. "Come we will ride towards the Welsh. Bring my banner."

We rode west to the departing Welsh. Although I had done as ordered I did not want the Welsh to slink off and escape the wrath of the Earl. I could see that some of the Welsh lived still. John looked aghast at some of the wounds the men had endured and yet they lived still. "Many of those will have their pain ended, John, but we have other duties to perform."

"Will the Welsh not attack us, my lord?"

"They may do although I doubt it. It is more likely that they will talk for they will be curious about me. My banner is unknown, I think, in these parts. If this is the Welsh King who leads them then he will have been surprised by our ambush." I pointed to the huddle of knights, "See how they hold conference. He is asking his men for advice. We have piqued their curiosity."

We halted some two hundred paces from the Welsh. We were still close enough to our own lines to ride back if we had to and I knew, without looking, that Edward would have my knights ready to ride my rescue if it was needed. I sensed the nervousness of my two squires. "You two did well but John you need to learn to ride with the banner in your left hand and wield a sword with your right. We cannot have my banner broken because you have used it as a spear."

"Sorry, my lord, but the blood was in my head."

"I know but better you keep a calm heart and a mind which thinks. You will live longer."

There was a pause. I saw the Welsh leaders still arguing. "I am still learning to ride, my lord."

"You need to practise riding without using reins."

"That is magic, my lord!"

"No, you use your knees. You will need to know your horse better than you know Sheba and Caesar." I was just talking to fill the silence for both of them were nervous.

I heard Leofric say, "I did tell you."

Just then a trumpet sounded and a knot of mailed knights with banners rode towards us. They bore the standard of Gwynedd. "Now keep quiet and listen. If this is a trick then I will tell you to ride back to Sir Edward. Do it instantly."

The five knights stopped twenty paces from us. They were as wary of a trap as we were. I removed my helmet to show that I was here to talk and they did the same. Their leader, who bore the dragon on his shield, spoke, "I am Llewellyn ap Gruffydd and I command this army of Gwynedd. Who are you?"

"I am Baron Alfraed of Norton and I command the vanguard of the army of Robert Fitzroy, Earl of Gloucester and Lord of the Welsh Marches. You have come where you are not wanted and raided our people. You must pay." I saw some of his knights look over their shoulder as though the Earl might appear like some vengeful angel.

"We outnumber you, Norman! Surrender and we will give you terms."

I almost laughed but my father had taught me that was not polite. "We bar your way home. If you wish to drive us hence then do it and do not waste words."

"Who says we wish to return home? We have retaken the land your people stole from us."

I nodded, "Then stay and the Earl will drive you hence. And I am Saxon, not Norman. My land was taken by the Normans too but I have learned to live with that. Perhaps you and your King should too. Remember what happened to Powys when King Maredudd ap Bleddyn dared to threaten England. I have heard that the men of Powys have forgotten what beef tastes like." I suddenly realised that this knight was talking Norman. He had served under a Norman lord. I stored that information. Perhaps the Earl knew of him.

"If you stay then we ask permission to carry off our wounded and dead. You may have the same courtesy."

I smiled, "Thank you for the courtesy but none of ours lie on the field. You may carry them hence. They died well."

"Thank you," he paused and smiled, "Saxon. I will remember you."

"And I, you."

As we rode back Leofric asked, "Why did you allow them to carry off their wounded and dead, my lord?"

"It affords the Earl more time to reach us and it does not harm us. Our horses are resting and when they move we can still follow."

When I reached Edward, I saw the relief on their faces. "Well, Baron?"

"They carry off their dead."

"And then?"

"And then they have two choices. They either return to their camp at Nantwich or they ride west. Both bring them into contact with us. If they return north they meet the Earl and if they head west then they have to shift us."

Edward nodded, "The Welsh are a poor people. We found little on their bodies and their weapons are useful only as ploughshares."

"I know. And their King is not with them. It is not like King Henry who lives hundreds of miles away; their King lives in Anglesey. A leader should fight with his men."

We waited while they collected their dead. They had to come quite close to us. As they did so I had a chance to examine their men at close quarters. We saw no mail on those who were sent to collect the bodies and the helmets were simple affairs; they were pieces of metal attached to a rim and one central cross piece. All had left their shields behind but their swords were also crudely made. I could not see how they would stand against a determined charge by a large number of horses. Our vanguard had been simply too few in numbers to destroy them but we had seriously damaged them.

Their eyes flicked to the dead ponies as they collected the bodies. Wulfric looked at me and I nodded. It was a small gesture but we made it anyway. Taking his sword Wulfric hacked off the hindquarter of a pony and gave it to one to the Welsh soldiers. His face lit into a smile and he nodded his thanks. We did not understand his words but guessed they were thanks.

156

As night fell the Earl had still to arrive. "Dick, send a couple of archers a little closer to watch them. I do not want a sneak attack on us."

My men had a fire going and the ponies that had died had been butchered and were now roasting on the fires. My conroi was made up of practical soldiers. You never knew where your next meal was coming from or when; you ate when you could. If we had to leave in a hurry then they would take the half-cooked meat and devour that.

Aelric arrived, "My lord, the Earl has captured the men at Nantwich. He says he will join you on the morrow."

I was both surprised and disappointed. The Earl had taken the easy route of a quick gain. Had I led the army then I would have destroyed the Welsh first and returned later to the Welsh camp. We had just eaten and were contemplating camping when Garth the archer rode in, "My lord, they have broken camp and are heading south quickly. Griff of Gwent follows them. They have left their captives." He hesitated, "They have slit their throats."

Dick had done well; he had sent one of our Welsh speakers to watch them. "Aelric ride to the Earl and tell him the Welsh have broken out. Wulfric, mount the men. We follow."

I was angry. If the Earl had come when I had sent for him then we could have attacked and the captives might have been saved. Equally, Gruffudd could have just left them. He and I would need to cross swords. Edward said, "They will turn west."

"I know." Although it was dark we could see the shapes of the mountains in the distance, a black shadow which rose like a wall to the west. "If they make the mountains then we will have the devil's own job to catch them."

John brought me Scout and I mounted. We were lucky not to be encumbered by too much captured weaponry and we would be able to move swiftly. However, we had to find our way to the south and west over unfamiliar land.

"Dick, send all of the archers south and west. We need a road and we need to find the Welsh." The archers rode off.

Wilson arrived back within a short time. "My lord, there is a track which heads south-west. It is wide enough for four horses. If you would follow me I will take you there."

We picked our way across the fields until we came upon the track. It was rutted but we could, finally, move more quickly. Dick had sent the archers out in pairs and gradually, over the next few chilly hours we received reports. The Welsh were almost running back to Wales. They were well ahead of us. The delay in leaving and the early, difficult terrain had given them a lead. We could do nothing else but follow as quickly as we could. The Welsh were moving swiftly; they were a warband with no order and that gave their legs more speed. They had no captives to slow them down and they were heading for safety. I knew there was an old fort called Wrecsam. It had been destroyed by William, the Earl's grandfather, but who knew if it had been rebuilt.

As dawn broke and the weak spring sun made us feel marginally warmer we saw that we were close to the foothills of the mountains. Our scouts had kept us informed of their movements and we now knew that they were not heading to Wrecsam. It had not been rebuilt. They were heading for the mountains and the safety of the rocks and gullies there. I knew that we were tired. We were riding; the Welsh also had to be exhausted. When I had seen them, collecting the bodies I had seen how squat they were. Compared to our men they were almost dwarves but they were hardy and that hardiness was showing now. The advantage of daylight was that we could push harder. After we had stopped at a stream I summoned my knights.

"We need to put our spear points in their backs. I know our horses are tired but so are the enemy. We push harder. If they reach the high mountains then we will have the devil of a job to shift them."

They looked unhappy for their horses were valuable to them but they obeyed. We had been tasked as the vanguard and with that honour went responsibility. As we neared the foothills we began to catch glimpses of the black shadow which oozed west. Most of our scouts had returned to the main body for we were now on the same road. This was a better road and looked to have been made by the Romans although it was in a poor state of repair. Ralph of Wales and Griff of Gwent were the two scouts who dogged their trail. The other scouts reported that the rear of the column, the stragglers, was spread out well behind the main body.

Despite my need for speed we still had to halt every hour, dismount and rest the horses for a short time. I was lucky; Scout was a strong horse but Sir Geoffrey and Sir Guiscard's mounts were struggling. I made a decision. "We will divide our conroi in two. Sir Geoffrey, you command the half of the vanguard whose horses are struggling. I will take Sir Edward, Sir Harold and Sir Tristan with me. I will keep all of the archers and half of the men at arms. Rest your animals for at least an hour and then follow."

Sir Richard protested, "We can go further. Our horses have some life in them yet."

"But if you push them then they will not. I intend to ride hard, attack their stragglers and make them halt. They will be as tired. When you join us then you and the others can attack for your mounts will be fresher." It was not a matter for discussion and Sir Richard knew it. They would obey. I was their lord.

Once the slower beasts were left behind we made much better time and we actually cantered down the road. We came upon the first of the stragglers after we had passed through a small gaggle of huts. Perhaps the Welsh had looted them and been delayed; I know not but the result was that they died. As we came through we saw thirty more of them struggling up the road. They were not a rearguard. These were the weaker warriors. As soon as we saw them we charged. It was not a charge in the true sense of the word but we hit them hard and they fell. Even my archers used their swords as we swept through them like a whirlwind and when we had passed over them their bodies littered the road. We knew that the main body could not be far away and our sudden success had spurred our ambition. We had a chance to halt them sooner rather than later.

The road was rising and I saw rocks and clumps of scrubby growth on the sides of the poor land. There was heather and there was gorse. We had to keep to the paths. That slowed us down more than our tired animals. The actual rear-guard was now less than a mile away. Before them were the last of the stragglers. As soon as we appeared I heard a wail of despair from those who were the closest. The rearguard ran. I could see the skyline ahead. That was where they would make for. It was somewhere they could defend and we could not attack. We had done all that we could and could go no further. Had the Earl and the army been with us then we would have had a chance to destroy them all.

"Dick, be ready to dismount. They will halt soon and we cannot charge uphill. We will take these warriors at the rear and wait for Sir Geoffrey and the rest of our men." I would have to rely, as always, on my own men.

"Aye, my lord."

"One last push!"

We spurred on our weary mounts and they lumbered and laboured up the slope. The Welsh before us were as tired as our horses and so we gained on them. There were fewer this time for some found our blades gave their legs extra power and they joined

159

the rearguard. When the first arrows flew from behind the rocks then I knew we had come too far. Sir Tristan was slightly ahead of us and he and his horse were showered with arrows. His horse fell dead. Sir Harold kicked hard and leapt up the slope while the rest of us held shields before us and began to back out of range. Dick and his archers were already stringing bows to reply to the unseen archers.

Tristan had been wounded but he still stood his ground defiantly. He raised his good arm and, with his foot in the stirrup of Harold's horse, he clambered on his back.

"Fall back!" I began to back Scout down the slope. I kept facing the hill side to watch for danger. Harold and Tristan were a tempting target for Welsh warriors who had been fleeing for almost a day before us. Now was their chance to turn the tables and wreak revenge on knights. Dick and his archers were now keeping down the heads of the Welsh archers and I thought we had escaped further losses when two Welsh warriors rose from behind a bush and ran towards Harold, Tristan and the weary horse. I thought we were all too far away to help when Leofric suddenly spurred his horse up the slope. As his mount knocked one to the ground he swung his sword and took the second in the neck. He wisely turned to the right so that he could use his shield to protect himself. The three arrows which came his way were taken on his shield and Dick's archers sent a flurry of flights toward the ridge.

I breathed a sigh of relief when Tristan, Harold and Leofric returned safely and unscathed. They had been lucky.

"Wulfric, see to Sir Tristan. The rest of you dismount and prepare to be attacked."

If I was Gruffudd I would have used that moment to charge us. He could easily see how few we were and here, on this rock strewn, gorse filled slope our horses would be of no use for they were exhausted. I waited and I watched. "Well done, Leofric, that was bravely done."

"Sir Harold is my friend, my lord, and he was brave too. I could not allow him and Sir Tristan to be butchered."

The man who had been knocked to the ground by Leofric's horse staggered to his feet to be pierced by two arrows. He fell dead. We stood, a huddle of knights and men at arms, with our archers behind us. We could do no more. The Earl had let us down. He had asked us to find the Welsh army and we had succeeded. He had taken the easy victory of capturing their camp and their supplies. We had been left exposed. It was a lesson I would learn and I would risk neither my men nor myself again.

"Where is the Earl, my lord? If the Welsh choose to charge us then we cannot stand here nor can we run."

If Leofric could see the danger then why could not the Earl. "I know not but we shall sell our lives dearly and, besides, we have the rest of the conroi on the way. They will be here shortly."

Sir Edward shook his head, "Let us hope they do not find just our bones."

"Let us prepare to receive them." We had found a piece of ground which was flat and had a slight dip before it. It was little enough but we would use it. If the Welsh came they would have to climb to reach us. I prayed that they were as tired as we were.

Miraculously the Welsh did not come immediately. When they did come they did not bring their horses, which was a blessing, and they came in a mob, hurtling down the slope towards us. Those two factors saved us. We presented a solid wall of spears. Behind me our banners bravely fluttered. Our archers were tightly tucked behind the squires. As the Welsh charged us, expecting, no doubt to sweep us off this hill side, my archers released their arrows. They had to conserve their arrows for we had left the bulk of them at Chester with our war horses. Even so they managed to fell a large number of the enemy. Others overran themselves and I saw at least two tumble and crash into the rocks which littered the side of the slope. The arrows, the falls, their headlong charge all contributed to a thinning of those who ran headlong on to our spears. We were able to despatch the first eight easily. Then it became harder.

The next warriors down the slope threw themselves at us. Their bodies broke as did our spears and they crashed into our shields. If Wulfric and the men at arms had not braced their bodies behind ours then we might have been knocked to the ground and slaughtered. As it was things became desperate. I drew my sword just in time to slice across the chest of a warrior. Edward also stabbed a Welshman as spears were passed to the men at arms behind us and their points became a thin barrier before us.

Dick and his archers loosed their remaining arrows and then dropped their bows, took out their short swords and joined the fray. I fended off an axe with my shield, dropped to my knee and thrust upwards at a mailed man at arms. The first to reach us had been the lighter men without armour. Now we faced Welshmen who had mail, shields, helmets and long swords. Even as I knelt I saw a double-handed sword swing towards the head of Harold who was fending off two spearmen. I gave a wild and hopeful strike at him. It was not a full blow but it succeeded in tearing through the tendons behind his knees. His sword fell from his hands as his support went. Tristan smashed in his head with the edge of his shield. This could not go on. We were encircled.

Then I heard, "Baron, it is Sir Geoffrey and the rest of our men!"

They might have been charging uphill but the reinforcements were mounted and held lances. The Welsh at the rear who were attacking Dick and his archers fell to a man.

"Hold them!" I punched forward with my shield as I stabbed blindly into the mass of men before me. My sword sank into something soft. I twisted as I turned and a man fell dead. My knights and squires took heart and we held. As my conroi flooded around the side of the Welsh, they began to fall back up the slope to the safety of the ridge. My men had ridden hard and their horses could go no further.

"Withdraw down the hill. Take our wounded and our dead with us!"

We had been hurt. There were more dead Welsh lying for the buzzards and the foxes but we had taken too many wounds for my liking. This had been the nearest we had come to a defeat and none of it was our fault. We had been betrayed and I was angry.

As Wulfric dressed the wounds of those who had suffered Sir Geoffrey dismounted. "I am sorry we waited so long, my lord."

"It was not your fault. I should have disobeyed my orders. The Earl has abandoned us. We will wait until dark and withdraw back to Chester."

Sir Richard shook his head, "You cannot do that, Baron, the Earl expects you to keep the Welsh within sight."

"And I have done so. We found these more than a day ago. Where is the Earl?"

Just then we heard the sound of trumpets. John son of Godwin pointed to the north and shouted, "It is the Earl's banner! He has come!"

As we watched we saw the rest of the army galloping along the high ground from the north and the east. With banners flying they fell upon the flank of the dispirited and exhausted Welsh of Gruffudd ap Cynan. Half of the men of Gwynedd were still struggling up the slope while the other half had their attention upon us. It was slaughter on a massive scale. I took off my helmet. We would fight no more that day.

"There my lord, the Earl came!"

"Yes, Sir Guy," I pointed to the six bodies laid in a line, "but he came too late for those."

We looked at the straggle of bodies which lay on the slope before us. Those men had died far from their homes and would reap no reward. All that they had was a cold and bare grave on a remote Cheshire hillside. I felt my anger, like bile, rise in my throat.

Chapter 15

We waited at the bottom of the hill for the Earl to join us. He took some time to come and we buried our dead and said our farewells. My men at arms stripped the Welsh dead of the little they had about them and we waited for the Earl. He eventually made his way down to us. He beamed at us as though the whole thing had been well planned by him.

"What valiant knights are the men of the Valley! I knew I could rely on you!"

We all bowed but I could see that he realised how displeased I was. He turned to point to the ridge. "We destroyed this warband and now we will go and demand reparations from the Welsh on Anglesey. Baron, you have done well. Take your conroi back to Chester and await us there. We will reward all who took part in this glorious campaign!" He turned and rode up the slope. Like his father, he dismissed us easily. It showed our true worth.

My knights all looked at me, expectantly. I had to become their leader once more and put my own anger behind me. "We have a hard ride ahead of us if we are to be at Chester before dark but at least we sleep in a bed this night."

My men could tell how angry I was and none, save Edward, approached me. He was the only one who could do so. Had Wulfstan been there then he would have done so but he was back on the Tees. We had ridden north for some miles when he nudged his horse closer to mine and spoke quietly to me. "The Earl of Gloucester is the King's son, my lord, and you cannot upset him. We survived well and have gained great honour once more."

"We lost men because of him and his tardiness."

"He is our master and we obey. Can I speak openly, Baron?"

"Of course! I am no tyrant."

"You were brought up well by your father but did he not tell you of his service with the Varangians?"

"Aye he did and I know what you are going to say. They were used by the Emperors." He nodded, "The difference was that they swore fealty to the Emperor and they defended just the Emperor just as my father, when he was a Housecarl, protected the King."

"And the Earl is his representative."

I shook my head, "The King tasked me to protect the Tees, not the land adjacent to that of the Earl. We were making life easier for the Earl and leaving my lands unguarded."

For the first time Edward looked thoughtful, "You mean the King might not have sanctioned this?"

"I mean that we have left our home undefended. We were the only conroi summoned. I think we are being used to strengthen the hand of the Earl. There will be a rat race soon. Rolf told me that. Many people will seek to become the ruler of this land when the King dies."

"But you wanted the Earl to become the next king!"

"I did but..."

"You need to be careful, Baron."

I laughed sardonically, "I was brought up in Constantinople and I knew how to put on two faces at once. I do not like it and I thought when I came here I could be honest. Patently as I cannot I will prepare a face to meet the other faces."

He shook his head, "I was a hired blade for many years until you saved me, Baron. I know there are some injustices you have to accept. The Earl is part of a tide against which you cannot stand."

We made Chester just after dark and I was in no mood to camp again in the pestilential swamps by the river. We stayed inside the walls. I drank far more then was good for me and had to be put to bed by both Edward and Harold. The Earl did not return for two more days by which time I had recovered some of my composure.

The army arrived back with horses laden beneath ransom and coins. The Earl had punished the men of Gwynedd for their impudence. The Earl was greeted like a conquering hero and the bile came once more into my mouth. They had destroyed an army weakened and exhausted by my men. I believed now that he had deliberately delayed in order to ensure complete victory for himself.

He smiled at me as he entered but it was not the warm smile of a friend; it was the cold smile of a conqueror. This must have been the look his grandfather had adopted. He too had been a ruthless man. Perhaps this land needed such ruthlessness. One of his household knights told us that there would be a celebratory feast that night but the Earl wished to see me in private before the rest of the knights joined us. I idly wondered if he had rested us to allow us to perform another task for him. I was summoned to his quarters. He sat behind a huge table with piles of coins and documents upon it. He dismissed his clerks, priests, officials and knights so that we were alone.

He leaned back and stretched, "Alfraed you and your men ensured our victory the other day and I wish to thank you for that."

I nodded and he frowned, "That is all? You nod like some obsequious Greek?"

I realised that he must be trying to upset me by calling me a Greek but I did not react. "I know what my men did, my lord. You and I have fought alongside each other before and we have always won." I paused, "This time I thought that I might lose."

"It worked out well, Alfraed. We reached the Welsh in time did we not?"

I sighed. Despite what I had said to Edward I could not keep my counsel. "If I had known what you had planned, my lord, I could have acted differently and the result would have been the same save that my men would still be alive."

"No, Baron, there you are wrong. Your men needed to die because that drew the enemy on and weakened them so that we might win. And we did win." He waved an arm at the coins. "It is like a game of chess. Sometimes we sacrifice a pawn to make a capture. You lost none of your knights, did you?"

"My men are as important to me as my knights."

"You cannot believe that."

"It was the way my father brought me up." I genuinely believed that. It was the reason so many of my father's men had followed him to England. He had made them as important as any general or strategos.

I saw that I had confused him. He did not understand this care and my sincere concern. "Then I am sorry for you. Your life will be much harder if you worry about every archer and warrior who fights for you."

"Perhaps, my lord, but we cannot change our nature."

"You are right there, Alfraed." He stood. "I will have your conroi's share of the ransom sent to you on the morrow. The campaign here is over and I daresay you will wish to return home?"

"Thank you, my lord."

With that, I was dismissed. That night the way he viewed me changed and it would be many years before it returned to what it had been. He laughed and joked with those he had led to defeat the Welsh and we were left like lepers on the edge of the feast. We left after we had collected our war horses and loaded our sumpters with the weapons and the coins we had won. We headed north back to the land where I could be what I wished to be; a northern knight.

We reached my lands when they were at their best. The fields were filled with growing crops and the hillsides were dotted with young animals. I quickly forgot the way I had nearly been betrayed and I threw myself into the running of my lands and my estates. I determined to make life for all of my people from the knights to the villeins, as good as it could be. The summer fayre we held was the grandest anyone had ever seen in this part of the country. I held a tourney and presented a golden hawk to the winner. I did not take part. I wanted my knights and squires to be rewarded and I wanted to watch them. They all fought well but Sir Richard proved the best and he won the hawk. His son and Harold both did well but their time would come. When the old became weaker they would become the strength we would use.

We also held an archery competition and, surprisingly it was not Dick who won but Ralph of Sherwood. Dick took the defeat magnanimously and did not begrudge the young archer his silver arrow. The festivities lasted two days.

My council met two days after that and when I entered the hall where they held the meeting I was applauded. The meeting was filled with suggestions for other ways of drawing visitors and new trades into the burgeoning town. All of the burghers had done well from the Fayre we had held. Alf asked me if I was out of pocket for he and the others would recompense me.

I laughed and shook my head, "I did this for my people, Alf. If I wanted to do it for gain I would have taxed the stalls and the entrance to the tourney. Do you not know me yet?"

Alf was crestfallen, "I am sorry my lord, it is just... you are right to chastise us. We should all trust you." He glared at Ethelred whose mercenary nature had obviously made him mistrust my motives.

We held a short session later in the summer and then I enjoyed myself and spent a week hunting. It had been some time since I had indulged myself and it felt good to ride my lands without armour in the company of my squires, Aiden and Wulfstan. Life was worthwhile once more.

When the Church was ready to be consecrated the Bishop sent his personal representative to do so and I felt that, at last, civilisation had reached my lands. I think that summer, in the year of Our Lord eleven twenty-seven, was one of the most contented I could remember. After the close encounter with death in Wales, the world seemed better somehow. We all appreciated the beautiful sunrises and glorious sunsets. The food we ate tasted richer and our land seemed more precious. A brush with death always made the world seem sweeter. Our success led to more men at arms and archers seeking to serve me. After I had filled my ranks I sent the others to my other knights and they improved their own retinues. The world I ruled was a better one.

The black cloud on my horizon was that Athelstan, one of my father's oathsworn, was ill. He had the coughing sickness. There were just three left from my father's retinue and with Wulfstan ageing as well as Osric I worried over each of them. They were as close to me as my family. I decided I would need to spend more time with the three of them while I could.

And then the raiders came from the west. This was not an invasion of Scots lords who wished to increase their lands. This was not a rebellion of men who wanted power. This was a raid by an army of brigands and outlaws who had come from beyond the sea to raid the fertile valley filled, if one believed the troubadours, with streets paved with gold. Our success meant that stories were told of us. As with all stories they were exaggerated as they were spread. By the time they reached the western isles, and Orkney as well as Ireland they spoke of my valley as though it was the Holy Land. We were close enough to all of them for them to make a short sea crossing and then follow the line of the wall through half-deserted lands before descending like wolves into my valley. They came with enough men to destroy us. The army who arrived had heard of our success against the Welsh and the Scots; they believed they would defeat us.

It was Sir Hugh Manningham, Lord of Hexham who told me of their arrival. A rider galloped into my castle with a horse so lathered with sweat that it looked almost white. "My lord of Hexham sent me. There is a large band of warriors; Irish and Vikings, and they are heading for your valley. There are almost a thousand of them."

"How do you know?"

"We captured one and after we broke him he told us. We lost some men as did the men of Carlisle but these are a swiftly moving band and they skirt the castles. The last we heard they were this side of the castle at Barnard ravaging the high farms. I stopped to warn the Bishop and he has called out his fyrd."

"Thank your lord."

After he had gone I sent riders to warn my knights. We had little time to waste. John, my steward, asked me, "Why did not the lords of Hexham and Carlisle come to our aid rather than sending a message?"

"There are too many in the warband. If they attacked with their small conroi then they might risk losing all of their men and then their lands. Besides, they now guard the north against the Scots. Do you not think that the Scots would take advantage if the knights there headed south?"

"Is that not true of us too, my lord?"

"No for with all of the estates close by we can present an army of almost two hundred; more if we call upon the fyrd."

"But the harvest!"

"Do not worry, John, I will not call upon the fyrd. What I need to do is to find them first but you need to prepare for hard times. Have the supplies in the castle and the town replenished. If we have to we will sit behind our walls."

"But if we do that then they will rampage through the valley!"

"I know and we shall not do that unless all goes against us and we fail. Now go!"

I took out the map of the valley. I hoped that Sir Guy and Sir Geoffrey had not yet been reached by these barbarians. Although they were the closest to the line of attack they were both stronger than they had been but not strong enough to withstand a thousand barbarians. If the enemy were close to Barnard then they could be at Gainford within a few days. I wondered if the Bishop might send men and then dismissed the idea. He would want all of his men protecting the Palatinate. If the raiders destroyed us then they could take their time and capture the riches of the Palatinate. This would be a task for me and my men. This time it would be me making the decisions and not the Earl of Gloucester. I found myself relishing the prospect.

The knights arrived in swift succession. Wulfstan had hurt his leg hunting wild boar and could not come. Of that I was glad for I knew that he was now too old to fight the fast battles we would expect and, if we failed, he might be able to save my family. Edward and Harold were the first of my knights to arrive, being the closest. They had brought all of their men and emptied their manors. Both knew that a sudden summons from me was an indication of danger. Sir Richard and Sir Tristan brought most of their men but they had left some to guard their family. I understood that. Sir Guiscard and Sir Raymond now had the largest retinues and they arrived last. I held a council of war for we would ride west to meet with our remaining knights.

"We will needs must ride hard and ride fast. A warband moves swiftly."

Sir Raymond ventured, "But if they have no knights then surely they will be easy to defeat."

Sir Edward snorted, "Do not make that mistake. It would not do to underestimate them. These are old fashioned warriors. They may not ride horses nor use lances but each one could be a knight if they chose. These are not like the Welsh or the hired swords we have fought before. If they are of Viking or Irish blood then they will be sworn to fight to the death for their leader. They may be Christian now but they believe that it is better to die honourably for an oath than live in shame." He looked at the younger knights. "There will be no ransom from these enemies."

I waved a hand to the west, "Come we waste time. Our enemies are yonder and our people in great danger. We ride hard. I would reach Gainford by dark. Dick will command the archers and Wulfric the men at arms." They all nodded, understanding the need for a single command.

Adela came with my children to see me off. "Take care, my husband. Each time you ride away I fear I shall never see you again."

"But each time I do return and I will do so again. If there is danger then bring the people within these walls. The men of the town can protect you."

"Fear not; your castle and your people will be here when you return."

I sent Aiden to ride as fast as possible and reach Gainford. As we passed the farms the farmers and their families knew that something was amiss. We told them all the same as we passed. "Enemies are coming and we go to fight them. Be prepared to move to safety in case we fail."

There was fear on the faces of the women and the old as I told each farmer the same but determination on the faces of the men. We had faced wolves and enemies such as this before. My valley would survive. Sir Geoffrey of Piercebridge caught up with us close to the estates of the Bishop of Durham some five miles west of Stockton. He had ridden hard.

He rode next to me so that we could speak; my message to him had been succinct. I had urged him to make all haste but I was surprised to find him this close and so soon. "I had thought you might have followed the river west to Sir Guy at Gainford."

He shook his head. "I had many of my men with me as we were going to Durham to make a pilgrimage to the saint. My men wished to thank him for saving us from the Welsh. We were already on the road north when your rider found us."

I nodded; Sir Geoffrey and his men lived an almost monastic life. None of them were married and they were deeply religious. It would not surprise me if he did not take the cross one day and go to the Holy Land. "We have barbarians to deal with. Sir Guy and his men are in danger. They were at Barnard yesterday. We could meet them at any time."

"How many do we face?"

"The reports said a thousand but these do not fight as we do. It could be a far greater or a far smaller number. Whatever the number we will be outnumbered."

As we passed Sadberge, one of the Bishop's manors, we took the opportunity of telling the reeve there of the danger. This was an undefended manor. The Bishop had many such as this. The reeve collected the taxes for the Bishop but he was in charge of the fyrd.

"Robert of Sadberge, there is a warband of Vikings and Irish to the west of us. Prepare to defend your manor."

The poor man, who looked to be of an age with the ailing Athelstan, almost shook with fear. "My lord, we have neither knights nor men at arms!"

"Then call out the fyrd or if you need to then go to Hartburn or Stockton. There you can be defended."

He nodded his thanks and hurried off. We had travelled no more than two miles when Aiden galloped in leading a horse with a wounded warrior. I saw, for he wore no helmet, that it was Sir Guy's youngest son, Hugh. Aiden spoke while Wulfric tended to the young squire's wounds. "Gainford has fallen, my lord." He pointed to the west and I now saw the pall of smoke in the distance.

Hugh of Gainford struggled from Wulfric's grip. "We did not receive your message until it was too late, my lord. My father saw buildings burning in the distance and called out his men. They headed north for the smoke and your rider arrived. We were ambushed close to the hamlet of Ingleton. They were wild men with axes and they fell upon our horses. My father commanded me and your archer to ride to you." He lowered his head, "Your man, Paul of Stockton, died when four enemy scouts caught us. He slew three before he fell and I received this wound. I owe him my life."

I nodded. Paul had been with me since the start and had been one of my best archers. Dick would be saddened by his loss but if he had saved young Hugh and given us warning then his death had not been in vain. "Where are they now, Aiden?"

"They were five miles in that direction when I saw them." he answered my unspoken question without me asking it, "They were still north of the river. They are heading in this direction."

I stood in my stirrups and looked around. Sadberge was on a slight rise but a warband could sweep around us. "Is there anywhere west we can stop them?"

Sir Geoffrey said, "Aye, Baron. Close to the Skerne, there is a steep slope. We could use that as a stand. It is like the place in Wales where the Welsh stood but this is flatter at the top. It is like an island. The Skerne is nothing but, at this time of the year, it is boggy and will slow them up."

"Then lead us there."

I noticed that Gille, Hugh's cousin and Edward's squire spoke to Hugh and comforted him. The two were the last of their family. We had suffered our first serious loss since my father's death. My world was changing once more.

We rode as though charging into battle. We had to find a place to halt them or we would be swept away. If we could not reach this place before the warband then we might suffer the same fate as Sir Guy. We were now weaker by almost forty men. It was a grievous loss. As we rode I looked at the faces of my knights. This was our first serious setback. Until this moment we had enjoyed victory after victory. Even in Wales, we had lost neither knight nor squire and now we had lost both. They now knew that we were not invincible. This coming fray would be a test of their character and their mettle. If any had any doubts about the skills of these barbarians they had been destroyed along with Sir Guy

When we reached the high land above the Skerne I saw that Sir Geoffrey had been correct. The small river which led to the Tees was some six hundred paces below us and the land fell away steeply. Sadly, unlike Wales, this was not a rock and gorse strewn slope; this was land with animals grazing upon it. It would be easy to cross. The farmer, whose hut topped the rise, looked in fear at us. "Gather your animals and, with your family, drive them east. Enemies come and we will have to fight them. They have called out the fyrd at Sadberge. You can reach there."

This was the palatinate and he was one of the Bishop's subjects. I hoped that my message had reached Flambard but I had no confidence that aid would come from that direction. Perhaps my success had made everyone else complacent and they thought that I could deal with any danger in this land. The farmer and his family grabbed their meagre possessions and began to drive their animals east. I hoped that they would make it.

I spied a small stand of willows adjacent to the river. "Wulfric, have our men cut down the willows. Make a palisade of sharpened stakes before us. Leave a gap in the middle five horses wide."

He grinned as he visualised what he had to do, "You draw them into a fish trap, my lord!"

I smiled, "Aye for this pike may be a dangerous fish and I would not have him twist and turn."

As I dismounted, Leofric, who was holding my horse asked, "Why do you not put a wall all around us, my lord?"

"For if I did so then the enemy would come between the stakes. We have not enough to make a solid wall. There have to be gaps. By making one big enough for a large number of men through then we force them there. We can face whoever they send with an equal number and our archers can rain death upon them. Men, like fish, always choose the easiest route unless they are well-led. This is a warband and we use that weakness to our advantage." I sounded more confident than I was. I was clutching at straws. This defence was all that I could come up with. I prayed it would work.

We had brought our warhorses and I had them taken to the rear of our lines to rest. When we needed them, we would have to ride hard. Until then we would remain on foot. Sir Geoffrey had found us a perfect place to defend. The warband could not get to the rich valley without first defeating us. We could fall upon them whichever direction they chose. Of course, when they saw us they might choose to head south or north or even return west but we could follow them. That was where our horses would give us the advantage. If the numbers had been exaggerated them they would move west otherwise they would attack us and I hoped to make them bleed to death.

Wulfric and the men at arms worked swiftly. The thick willow branches they cut were all different lengths and girths. My men made them roughly the height of a man and they sharpened one end before driving them in at an angle. My archers then used small hatchets to sharpen the stakes. Had we had time we would have fire-hardened the tips but we wanted a barrier to slow them down and they would have to suffice the way that they were fashioned. The slower the barbarians came the more my archers would slaughter before they arrived.

As the men at arms finished I said, "I want the knights and the squires in the gaps. The men at arms will be in two lines behind them and the archers behind those. Plant our banners in the ground. We do not retreat and every man fights!"

While we waited I made sure that the men ate and drank. Another advantage, however slight, which we had, was the fact that we would be fresher than this warband which had had to move across the spine of the country. They would neither be rested nor refreshed and the slope up which they came, after a boggy crossing would sap and suck the energy from their legs. At least, that was my hope but I still had little idea of true numbers. I knew that although he and his men had all fallen Sir Guy would have extracted a high price from these enemies. I waited to see their numbers.

Aiden had the sharpest eyes and he suddenly shouted, as he spotted them, "There my lord, to the west!"

A mile away, on the other side of the Skerne, descending the gentler western slope was the warband. I could see why we only had a vague indication of numbers. It did not merely move, it swarmed. The sun glinted off spear points, helmets and mail. One could not begin to estimate numbers for they did not fight as we did. They fought the way they had since before the Romans had come to these lands. It did not matter how many men the enemy had; it could be tens of thousands but we had to stop them. Our families, our homes and our lands depended upon us. Every man fighting for me was fighting for something personal. This was not the same as fighting in Wales or the Borders for the Earl or the Bishop. This was personal and that would make all the difference.

I stepped forward into the gap and faced my men. I still held my helmet and my coif was hanging from the back of my head. I wanted them to see my face and know I spoke the truth. "The men of Gainford bought us time with their lives so that we might prepare here. That sacrifice will not be in vain. This warband thinks to sweep us from this hillside and take all that our people have gathered. They will take our women and our children if we let them. They will raze to the ground all that we have built and all that we hold dear. That will not happen this day. We fight neither for gold nor glory; today we fight for us and our people. Let none of this rabble leave the field alive. I would the buzzards feast on their flesh and only a memory returns to their heathen homes across the sea. We will show them that we are true warriors and that God is on our side. What say you?"

There was a huge roar from my men. As I turned to return to my place, I saw that the enemy host had halted across the valley. A mile separated us and whosoever led them was contemplating our position. I saw a huddle of warriors beneath three banners. Two of them were mailed; they would be from Orkney and Dublin. The third was not. I suspected he led the Hibernians. This was an unholy alliance. These were the last remnants of a bygone age. This was a meeting of two worlds; the old and the new.

I pulled my coif over my head and fitted my helmet. Behind me were John, son of Godwin, Leofric son of Tan and Hugh, the youngest of the line of Sir Guy of Gainford. I turned to them. "The three of you are to watch my back. Do not step before me, Sir Edward or Sir Harold." I saw Gille nod to his younger brother as though to confirm his words. "But you will use your spears in the gaps to stab any flesh you see. You jab into any face for the enemy wear little mail and shun the aventail and the coif. If they are before me, they die."

Hugh of Gainford nodded, "We will avenge my people my lord and we shall not let you down!" I saw the pride in his elder brother, Gille's, eyes.

These were young men and this was a crucial battle. Soon they would be under the greatest pressure they had ever experienced in their lives. This would be a charge by the most ferocious foot soldiers anywhere. These were the same kind of warriors my father had led and I was under no illusion. This would be a hard-fought encounter. My father had fought at Stamford Bridge when the last Viking invasion had been ended. I had heard the story of the three berserkers holding off the whole of the Saxon army so many times I could recite my father's version word for word. These men did not surrender for ransom. They fought until you took off their head.

There was a movement and I saw their plan. They came in a huge wedge of Norsemen flanked by the wild Hibernians. The Norse would try to force the passage between the stakes while the Hibernians would use their speed to surround us. This was the way they had fought for centuries. The overlapping shields and the spear points would normally drive through any enemy. I was pleased we fought on foot. Our horses would have been of little use against such a formation.

"Wulfric, Dick, do you see?"

"Aye, my lord."

"Aye, Baron."

"You know what to do, Dick?"

"This time we have arrows aplenty. God will give our arms extra strength."

Dick would target the mailed warriors until the lighter armed men closed and then he would shift targets. Wulfric and his men at arms would be the barrier which held the enemy form the archers. I could now estimate their numbers. There were not a thousand as had been suggested but it looked to be well over six hundred. I estimated that from the wedge. Each successive line added another two warriors. There appeared to be nineteen ranks in the wedge. There could be almost four hundred Norse alone. As they made their way down the slope the sunlight glinted off the front seven ranks. They were mailed. The rest were not. We had forty mailed warriors to eliminate. Dick's words made me realise that I needed a priest with us. When we had fought with the Bishop's priest my men had had the comfort of the cross.

I could tell that the Hibernians on the flanks of the wedge were champing at the bit. The wedge had to move slowly or lose cohesion but the Hibernians just wanted to race at us and get it over with. They reached the boggy stream which was half a mile away and I saw that they became a little disordered as they slipped and struggled across the sticky, muddy bottom. It was tempting to risk sending my archers to loose arrows at them but I knew that the Hibernians were fast enough to catch my bowmen no matter how swift-footed they were.

As the wedge began to labour up the slope some of the wilder, younger Irishmen decided to forget their orders and get amongst us. Forty of them suddenly raced up the slope, alarmingly quickly. I need not have worried. It took but fifty arrows to kill them. They shunned armour and our arrows were well made. Their bodies were now a human obstacle to the wedge which would have to cross their corpses and it was forty fewer men for us to deal with. The success of the archers raised the spirits of my men who cheered wildly as though we had won the battle. Wulfric growled, "Shut your noise! Anyone would think you were Frenchmen! Wait until they are all dead before you crow!"

The dead bodies also acted as a mark of the range of our bows and I knew that the attackers would begin to get nervous once they came within range. I saw the wedge as they squeezed together more tightly. The Irishmen were hanging back a little on the flanks and we all knew what that meant; they were preparing to charge. One of them sounded a horn made from an animal horn and the warriors on both sides of the wedge leapt forward to close with us. Almost a quarter of them had already been killed but there was still nearly two hundred who hurled themselves quickly through the stakes.

These were agile warriors and the stakes did not slow them up. It did, however, prevent them coming at us in a line.

Dick and the archers began to pick off Irishmen. They had no armour and each arrow struck a body. Wulfric and the archers had all spread water between the stakes and when they reached the stakes and began to dodge and twist some of them slipped and brought down others. Dick and his archers picked them off at their leisure. The handful that made it through were despatched by Wulfric and his men at arms. They came at us piecemeal; it was a waste of warriors. Almost without a pause, the archers shifted their aim to the wedge which was now within their range and picking its way across the bodies. They did not aim their arrows at the front ranks who wore mail but those behind who had but a helmet and a shield for protection. They were not looking to the skies for they had to step around the dead bodies.

Whoever led the Norsemen, and I saw two candidates in the third rank of the wedge, had not allowed for the narrowness of the channel we had created. The men had to bunch after the fifth rank had entered the staked maze. Their numbers would not help them. We had nine knights to face them. We filled the gap and the column, no matter how big could only face us, nine men, wide. We would outnumber the first five ranks and I hoped to make a barrier of their bodies. Dick and his archers were now working their way in from the flanks and death rained upon those who were at the rear.

I concentrated upon those at the front. They had put their best three warriors as the point of the wedge and the two leaders were behind those three. The first Norseman was a giant of a man with a full-face helmet and byrnie down to his knees. He had his shield slung at his back and he wielded a double-handed Danish axe. The two behind him had long spears. The axe was being spun in a figure of eight. It was almost mesmerising. It was so long that it extended beyond the spears of his two companions.

I spoke in Saxon, "Edward and Harold, take the two men behind this giant. Squires go for his knees. He has no armour below them."

I heard them all chorus, "Aye Baron!"

The wedge tried to run the last ten paces. It was not successful. The slippery ground did not afford good grip for their boots. I saw the axe being swung as they ran at us. I had to time this well. I angled my shield as I punched forward with my spear. My arm and my shield shivered with the force and shock of the axe but the angle of my shield deflected it down the side. My spear tore

177

through the links of the Viking's mail, his padded tunic and into his stomach. I saw a spear come from behind me and it jabbed into his knee just below the kneecap. I heard a scream of pain as the spear was turned. As the giant dropped to one knee I withdrew my spear. The spear in the knee shattered when his body fell upon it and a second spear struck him in the throat.

We had no time to enjoy our minor victory for, although Edward and Harold had killed the next two warriors there were now five men facing us and two of them were leaders. Both wielded swords. I stabbed forward with my spear and it began to penetrate the mail of one of the leaders. The warrior next to him swung his own sword and took off the head of my spear. It cost the warrior his life as Edward stabbed him in the throat but I would have perished as I tried to unsheathe my sword if it was not for Hugh of Gainford whose spear came to my aid. He disobeyed me and did not go for the knee or for flesh but for the weakened links of the mail. He pulled its bloody head back and, as I drew my sword, I punched the warrior with my shield to buy myself some time. He stepped back and I drove my sword through the hole made by Hugh and out of his back. I put so much force into the blow that it penetrated the thigh of the next warrior.

We were winning the battle in terms of casualties caused but now their sheer weight of numbers began to tell and we were faced by nine warriors. They began to push their wall of shields towards us. It was no longer a wedge we were fighting; it was a column of men. A sword came from out of nowhere and I tried to pull my head away. I partly succeeded but it still tore through my coif and into my cheek. I tasted salty blood. The joy of the wielder of the sword was short-lived as an arrow suddenly blossomed from his face and, as I stabbed forward, I found that the men before me no longer had mail.

This was a chance. Our weapons could wreak havoc on men without mail. "Come! We have them! Now we push them back! Men of the valley, on!"

I felt my squires pushing from behind me and took comfort from the three spears which surrounded me. I looked to my right and saw, not Edward, but Wulfric. "I was fed up with watching my lord! No, you don't!" He brought his sword down to split the helmet and skull of a shocked Norseman who had been poised to stab me with his spear.

I could now see daylight where there had been merely bodies. Dick and his archers had continued their work at the rear of the column and, while we had absorbed the blows of those at fore, those at the back had perished. Their tiredness now showed for we had renewed energy and hope. We had weathered the storm of their better warriors and now it was those who had hoped to enjoy the spoils of victory. They were more tired than we and although our blows lacked the power they had had at the start, theirs had none at all and every swing brought a wound or a death. Willow can be amazingly strong when bent but there comes a point at which it shatters in two. That happened to the Norse. One moment they were whole and fighting hard and the next they dissipated and disappeared like morning mist. It happened when we found ourselves beyond the gap we had created. As we burst through our numbers began to tell and my men at arms swarmed through and beyond those of us who had fought at the fore for so long. Their arms were not tired and their legs were fresh. My men fell upon the warband with savage strokes and hard blows. The raiders fled down the slope.

I turned to Wulfric. "Mount the men at arms and pursue them. We will join you." We could catch them quicker on horseback and I wanted them destroying.

"Aye my lord."

He shouted, "Men at arms, to horse and let us make merry with these barbarians!"

I turned to my three squires. They were all bloody but it was not their blood which covered their amour and their surcoats. It was our enemies. "You did well. Get my horse and your own."

I looked at my knights and saw that there were just three of us still standing. Sir Richard and Sir Raymond were the only ones who would ride after the enemy with me. I knew not if the rest were wounded or dead but I would have to leave that for we had to finish off these wild men of the west. We had thwarted the enemy, now they needed eliminating.

I mounted Star. I knew that he was ready to go to war for he stamped his hoof and tossed his head. Leofric handed me a lance and then mounted. I led the eight knights and squires after the men at arms. I could see that Wulfric had them spread out like huntsmen in a wide semi-circle. We passed the wounded and dying enemy. Dick and his archers were already moving amongst them to end their pain. When we reached the Skerne, I saw how difficult it would have been to cross on foot. Star ploughed through the water and, shaking himself, galloped up the other bank.

Already we were catching some of the men at arms who had poorer mounts than we did. The fleeing enemy should have turned to face us but their panic meant that with their leaders and heroes dead they just ran. These were not the oathsworn we pursued; these were the glory hunters and those who sought to find treasure. We had drawn them to us with our success and poor Sir Guy and his men had paid with their lives. It gave impetus to my arm as I swung it on unprotected backs. Some heard me coming and turned to raise a feeble arm in defence. I felt no mercy. They had come to take all that we had. They would have slaughtered our families or enslaved them had we not held them at the Skerne.

Here and there minor chiefs tried to rally their men and hold us off. We found knots of weary warriors with a handful of men who stood in small shield walls. Our lances tore through their defence. With no armour to slow them the heads ripped through bodies and were unbroken. Their dead bodies marked where they had fulfilled their last oath and died with the chiefs. The warband bled to death on that race across to the Tees at Gainford.

Chapter 16

We reached their camp at Gainford. There we found their booty and their slaves tethered by the neck and hands to trees. Star was tiring and I halted by their camp. My faithful squires all dismounted too and joined me. John son of Godwin looked shaken, "My lord, that was not war, was it?"

"No, John, but it was necessary."

Hugh spat out, "I would have inflicted more pain if I could." There were tears in his voice and I saw where he looked. There outside the burnt-out shell that had been Gainford was the head of his father and his brothers, each one arrayed on a spear. His brother dismounted and came to join us. He put his arm around the shoulder to comfort him.

"John, Leofric, go and take them down." Hugh went to go too. "No, Hugh, you stay here with your brother. Until you become a man you will be as a son to me and I know your father would have you do what I asked my squires to do. Stay here." He obeyed, albeit reluctantly. "Go and free those slaves and tend to their hurts. They were your people and they look to both of you."

Hugh nodded and went off to attend to the terrified and shocked villagers of Gainford with his older brother to guide him. Wulfric and my men at arms rode in just as the grisly remains of Sir Guy and his sons had been reunited.

"We caught the last of them, although some may have jumped in the river. I think we may find their bodies washing up close to our castle. Sir Richard and Sir Raymond went back to the Skerne. They were both worried about their squires."

I nodded, "I am afraid we will have to bury the dead here. Have the dead raiders piled together and we will burn them. I hope they have left a priest alive I don't know the words to say over our own dead."

I led Star towards Hugh and Gille. I saw one man who looked different from the others standing to one side. Gille was viewing him with suspicion. "He is not one of my uncle's people and he was not tied."

"You think he is one of the raiders?"

"He could be although he had this around his neck." He showed me a thrall's yoke.

I approached the man and tried Saxon. "Who are you?"

"I am Oswald son of Harold. I was taken in a slave raid when I was but four summers old."

"You have lived in Orkney all of this time?"

"No, my lord, I was taken from Man to Dublin."

"Who were these warriors?"

"My master was Magnus Fine Hair. He brought me to translate. He was keen to find out where the treasure of Alfraed of Norton was."

I smiled; he did not know who I was. "I am Baron Alfraed."

He dropped to his knees, "I am sorry, my lord, I meant no offence."

"None taken, you were not to know. And who were the others?"

"The Irishman was the young son of the head of the O'Neill clan, Padraig. He wanted to show his father that he was a better warrior than his brothers and that he should be named as heir. The Jarl from Orkney was Harald White Eye."

"It seems a long way to come for slaves."

"It was treasure they sought. There are stories told in Dublin of how you and your father came from the court of the Emperor in the East with his treasure. There were tales of how your father and his men had crept into the palace and stolen it. It was said you could not return to the east for there was a price upon your head. It was said that you had built the castle in Stockton to protect all of your gold."

"But I have no more gold than other men."

He shrugged, "That was the story we heard and it was also told in Orkney. They say that is why you are the champion of the Empress of the Germans."

"I am no champion; I am one of her knights that is all."

"There are many stories about you, lord. You defeated the Welsh King and took all of his cattle. You fought the finest knights in Germany and defeated them all."

"I did none of those things."

"I am just repeating the stories that we heard. I am sorry."

He looked fearful as though I might punish him for telling me the truth. I smiled, "Well you are free now. What would you?"

"I would like to live amongst people who speak my language and where I am safe."

"You may return with us to Stockton and then choose your home. You will be safe in my land." The look of relief on his face was a sober lesson for me. His past would have been my people's fate had we failed.

We found that they had left the priest alive and he helped us to bury the dead of Gainford. The dead enemy were thrown on to a pyre and the smoke filled the air. Those who had survived went nervously back to the remains of their homes. They knew how close they had come to death. "I will have the men of Piercebridge keep watch over you and should you need aught then send to them." I looked at Gille and Hugh and they both nodded. They would not forget.

We rode wearily back to the Skerne as darkness was beginning to fall. Sir Richard had organised the burning of the enemy and our dead were laid out. There were fewer of them than I had expected but the losses were still grievous. None of our knights had been killed but all had wounds which would keep them within their halls for a month or so. It was the squires who had suffered the most. Only my three had survived and Gille had survived. Harold had lost his squire and was distraught. Sir Edward's wound was the least serious. A war hammer had caught him a glancing blow on the side of the head and he had been knocked unconscious. Had it occurred earlier then he might have fallen to the advancing Norse but it had been in the last moments of the battle. Gille had ensured that he was still alive and then joined his cousin. Harold had a badly gashed arm and Tristan's foot had been speared. None of the wounds were life-threatening but we knew we had been in a battle.

Sir Geoffrey took his men back to Piercebridge and promised to watch over Gainford. He spoke with both Gille and Hugh before he left. He and Sir Guy had been friends. I knew that the manor was in safe hands until the King appointed a new lord. We returned to Stockton for no one wished to stay at the charnel house on the Skerne. It was pitch black when we crossed our bridge into my castle. We were home. It was the first battle I had fought so close to my home that I could see my family at the end. It showed me how close we had come to disaster. I decided I would visit with the Bishop and ask him if his knights could keep a better watch on my borders.

I was stiff the next morning. I had fought longer than I had for some time. I prayed that my fighting was over for this year. Adela asked me about the battle; I had been in no mood when I had returned. I told her and she burst into tears when I told her of Sir Guy.

"Poor Hugh! He has no one save his brother?"

I shook my head, "I have said I will take him as my squire and train him to be a knight. It is what his father would have wished. He will live here with us."

She put her hand on mine. "That is the Christian thing to do. What of the manor?"

"That is up to the King but I will plead for the rights of Hugh. Perhaps he will hear me." I stood, "And now I will walk among my people and put their minds at rest. They will have worried when we left so swiftly and there will be gossip. I would have them know the truth and not the exaggeration."

I had told her what Oswald son of Harold had said. "How can men believe such nonsense?"

"There are some men who always believe that there is an easy route to riches and to power. They know not that you must work for it."

"Could I walk with you in the town as I once did? I have missed it."

"Of course."

As we left the keep she asked, "What of this Oswald? What will happen to him?"

"He wants a life amongst his own people and safety. I cannot blame him."

"I will see if I can find a place for him. It seems he was sent for a purpose."

It was only when I walked around my town that I realised we had security. Gainford had all but gone. It could be rebuilt but it would never match my town. I had achieved much. I began to wonder if I had now achieved all that I was born to achieve. My father's old nemesis, *wyrd*, came to prove me wrong. As we turned to return to the castle a rider hurtled to a halt next to me.

"My lord, Father Peter sent me. You must come quickly; Lord Athelstan is dying. He must speak with you."

I left Adela and ran to the stables. Leofric and John were there. "Saddle Scout, now!"

I threw on my cloak and waited impatiently as they tightened Scout's girth. I jumped into the saddle and galloped as hard as I could. The journey was short but seemed to take forever. The gates of Norton were open and I galloped in and jerked Scout to a halt. A sentry said, "They are in the main hall, my lord, and you should hurry! Father Peter is administering the last rites."

I gave him the reins and ran into the dimly lit hall. Osric stood by Athelstan's bed while Father Peter held Athelstan's hand. He murmured something into his ear. I dropped to my knees next to his bed and the eyes of my father's oathsworn opened. He gave a wan smile, "You have come, my lord. I knew you would."

"It is Alfraed, my friend, and I would have come sooner had I known you were so ill."

He shook his head. "It is my time, Alfraed. I have seen the angel of death and I am not afraid but I wished to speak with you before I join your father and his oathsworn." He flicked a nervous look at Father Peter, "I will go to heaven Father?"

"You are a good man and I have absolved you of your sins. Soon you will be without pain. You will go to heaven." He looked at me. "You wished to say something to Baron Alfraed?"

He nodded and then coughed up some blood. "Your father and I buried something in the garden of our old home near to the palace in Constantinople. It is beneath his favourite lemon tree in an urn."

I glanced at Osric but he looked blank as though this was the first he had heard of it. "What is it, Athelstan? Why did he leave it there?"

He closed his eyes and carried on. I wondered if he had heard me. "When King Harold fought at Stamford Bridge his sword was damaged and the pommel stone came loose. It was left with Aelfraed's uncle for safekeeping. He gave it to your father." He coughed up more blood and Father Peter dabbed it away. He looked at me and shook his head. "He did not want to bring it back to England in case we found ourselves outlaws. He told me he did not want Harold's enemies to have it. It is a symbol of life before the Normans came."

He was silent. I looked at Father Peter who leaned in and then nodded, "He lives still but not for long. You had best ask any questions quickly."

"What should I do, Athelstan?"

He opened his eyes, "That is for you to decide. You are now Baron and you are the keeper of the secret. He told me one night before he died for he felt his time was coming. My time is coming and the secret now is yours. I have done my duty and passed it on. I can tell your father, when I see him, that I was oathsworn until the end."

He smiled and looked totally at peace. His eyes closed and, with a soft sigh, he died.

I looked at Osric who shook his head. "I thought that I knew all there was to know about my friend Athelstan and yet I did not. He was truly oathsworn." He held Athelstan's dead hands in his and said, "Goodbye old friend. I shall see you ere long." Father Peter made the sign of the cross and we bowed our heads. The priest put his arms behind us and led us into the light.

I turned to Osric. "Did you know of this stone?"

"I knew not that it had survived but, in the Guard, we all heard the stories from the housecarls who had known King Harold that his sword had a blue stone in the pommel. That was the reason for the star on your father's standard. The blue star was for King Harold." I nodded. "You remember the lemon tree?"

"I do. It was where my father would sit and talk with me in the evening when I was growing up." I shook my head. "It stopped when I grew and I miss those talks."

Father Peter smiled, "We can all look back and regret things we did when we were young. The trick is to not make those same mistakes when you are older."

I was silent as the secret filled my head.

"What will you do, Alfraed?"

I looked at Osric, "About the stone?" He nodded. "I know not. It should be safe enough, at least for a while. It would be a long journey to get it. And it is no secret now; three of us know it."

Osric and the priest looked at each other. Father Peter said, "It is a secret still. A man's last words are like the confessional."

"And I am oathsworn to you, Baron. The secret is safe. It dies with me."

I clasped both their arms. "Thank you both. I will send for Wulfstan and we will bury him by the church."

Osric pointed to a large elm. "While he was ill he liked to sit beneath that elm. It looks east and he liked to sit there."

"Then we shall do it. We shall bury him there." Wulfstan arrived and dismounted stiffly from his horse. The wound from the hunt still bothered him. It was another sign of the age of my father's men. Their time was coming to an end and soon I would be the last of the band that had left Constantinople.

Under the light of the moon, we buried Athelstan beneath his favourite tree. We buried him in a stone-lined grave with his sword, shield and armour upon him. We laid stones on the top and I told Father Peter that I would have a special stone made by William the Mason. Athelstan and his fidelity would be remembered. I took my leave of Osric who suddenly felt frail as I held him tightly to my chest. There were tears in the old man's eyes as I mounted Scout. I rode back to Stockton with Wulfstan. I chose to tell him Athelstan's words. He too was one of my father's oathsworn. He seemed happy

186

that he had not been told the secret. "We were all oathsworn. I think there may have been secrets your father confided in me and not the others."

"Should I know them?"

"You know all that I know. I have no secrets to tell you on my deathbed." He looked at me searchingly, "When will you fetch it?"

"How do you know that I shall?"

He laughed, "Because of all of your father's oathsworn, I know you the best. That is the last true secret I hold, Alfraed; I know your heart and you will travel east and bring back this stone. You will do it even though you do not know what to do with it once it returns. It will gnaw away inside you until you travel back to the lemon tree. The only thing I do not know is when."

"Perhaps I do not know when either."

He nodded, "That I can believe. Then leave it to *wyrd*. That will decide when." We rode in silence and then he said, "The Vikings you defeated believe that there are three witches called the Norns and they sit in a cave spinning webs. They are complicated webs and our lives run through them. The Norse believed that they are the ones who decide what we will do. Perhaps the Norse are right. It may be that they decide what you will do. I know it is not Christian to believe such things but I have seen strange things in my life and some cannot be explained away by a priest." He shook his head, "Do not worry about this stone. If you are meant to fetch it then you will. The decision will not be yours."

And he was right. Wulfstan was incredibly wise. In the end, it was not my decision.

Epilogue

It was September when I was summoned to London with Sir Edward and our squires, now augmented by Hugh of Gainford. I knew not the reason save that the letter, from the Earl of Gloucester, spoke of fulfilling our oath to the Empress. As we made our way south I wondered what it would entail.

"Perhaps we are to guard her now that she is to become the next Queen of England."

"I would not relish that prospect, Edward. I have a young family. If we have to guard the Empress then it will take us many miles from my home. The Empress would not relish the north. I suspect it will be another journey back to Normandy. I know that she has many enemies there."

"Not least the brothers Blois, eh Baron?"

"Exactly." The two brothers, Stephen and Theobald, were now like a thorn in my side or, more appropriately, a nagging ache in my tooth which came and went but the threat was always there. A thorn I could remove but not this nagging spectre of Norman enemies.

The journey south was swifter than the one north had been and this time we were to be accommodated close to the royal apartments in the Tower. Our star, it seemed, was on the rise. Perhaps this was the influence of the Empress. I had no doubt that there would be a chilly reception from the Earl of Gloucester.

The Earl greeted me stiffly when we met. He had still to forgive me for my outburst in Chester. Some men did not enjoy the truth. I preferred honesty. I had learned that, while the best of the earls, Robert Fitzroy was still acutely aware of his position. He might be the illegitimate son of Henry but he was the most powerful man in England. I had questioned his judgement. "It is good to see you Alfraed. You did well to defeat those raiders."

I nodded, "And Hugh here is the last of his family. His father and brothers fell."

He looked at my new squire. "I am sorry for your loss."

I took the bull by the horns. "I have made him my ward until he comes of an age and can take over the manor of Gainford."

The Earl's eyes narrowed, "That would be a decision for the King."

I smiled, "Then I shall broach the matter when we meet. I take it I am to see him this visit. If not, why was I summoned?"

I could see that he still rankled with my attitude after the battle in Wales. "You are right; he does wish to speak with you. We will go and see him now for he has a task for you to perform." He looked at the squires. "You four stay here. This is for your masters only."

Edward and I followed the Earl as he hurried through the castle to reach the King. He was with the Empress and she looked tearful. There were others in the room and when we entered, they were peremptorily dismissed; all except for a priest whose hand was poised over a wax tablet. King Henry looked much older since the last time I had seen him but he looked genuinely pleased to see me. Perhaps his son had not told him of my words. That would make sense for he would not want his father to know of a rift between us.

"Baron! My strong right arm from the Northern Marches returns. Bishop Flambard speaks well of you and I have heard that you destroyed a large warband which would have laid waste to the north. That was nobly done!"

"Sir Guy of Gainford and all of his family, save his son, Hugh and nephew Gille, died. I took it upon myself to watch over Hugh until he becomes old enough to manage the manor himself."

Unlike his son, King Henry did not dismiss the idea out of hand. "How old is he?"

"He has seen sixteen summers."

I saw a pained look come over the face of Empress Matilda and King Henry said, "What do you think of him?"

"He has a good heart and a strong arm. He will make a good lord of the manor and the people there love him still. I have my steward watching over the manor for taxes and for their well being."

"Good! Then I shall confirm this." He nodded to the priest. "Father Abelard, make a note of that. And now, gentlemen," he smiled, "I have a task for you. Tomorrow week we travel back to Normandy." He leaned forward, "This news is for your ears only, "My daughter and heir, Empress Matilda, is to be betrothed to Geoffrey the eldest son of Count Fulk of Anjou."

Once more my heart fell but I had known, all along, that the Empress could never be mine. However, this was just confirmation that the King had made a decision. "Congratulations, my lady." She nodded and dabbed her eyes.

"She is a woman, Baron, ignore her tears. They mean nothing. As you and Sir Edward here are Knights of the Empress you will act as her bodyguards until the announcement is made. There are those who plot and plan still to prevent a safe succession. King Louis still puts forward William Clito whom the French King has had made Count of Flanders." He rubbed his hands. "This alliance will protect our southern borders and make us more powerful. Now we can take on France and Flanders."

I saw a thin smile on the Earl's face. He could only gain from this. A thought came to me, "Your majesty, what of Count Fulk?"

He smiled, "The Count, it seems, sees his future in the Holy land. Once the marriage has taken place and his son established he will leave for his lands in Outremer." He lowered his voice. "He has ambitions to be king and there he can achieve those ambitions."

I could now see why there was urgency and why the marriage had been arranged. King Henry could not afford to have enemies to the south and the north of Normandy as well as the French in the east. I nodded, "I will need to send a message to my family to tell them I will be absent for a while."

He waved an absentminded hand, "Just so long as you keep the secret from your wife. Now you may escort the Empress to her quarters. All this sniffling and weeping is annoying!"

Once we left the hall the Empress said to Sir Edward, "I would speak with the Baron alone Sir Edward."

He smiled, "I understand and cheer up, my lady. It cannot be as bad as you seem to think. At least it is not his father to whom you have been betrothed!"

I know that Edward meant well with his joke but it set her off to weeping again. He shrugged and fled down the empty corridor. Matilda threw herself upon my shoulder and began to weep. This was not the place for such a display of emotion. "Where are your rooms?" She pointed to a door at the far end of the walkway. I took her and led her inside. Her ladies, Judith and Margaret, looked up as we entered. The Empress waved a hand and they left.

She looked up at me with red-rimmed eyes. "You do not understand. This is far worse than you can possibly imagine."

I smiled, "I know you do not wish to be married again to someone chosen by your father but surely you expected this. What is wrong with this Geoffrey of Anjou? Is he so ugly that you cannot bear to look upon him?"

She stepped back, "Alfraed, this Geoffrey of Anjou has seen thirteen summers, I am twenty-five. I am almost old enough to be his mother! He is a child and he behaves like one. At least the Emperor was a man. I am now to look after a child all so that my father's lands may be protected."

Now I understood. The tears were for a loveless life with a man half her age. She was going from a cold man who did not love her to a child who knew not what love was. She threw herself at me again and this time I enfolded her with my arms. I held her sobbing body tightly until she stopped her tears.

"Fear not, my lady. I swear that I shall be by your side and I will do all that I can to help you."

She smiled at me. "And you are the truest of all knights. Even in my darkest hour, I know that I can depend upon Baron Alfraed of Norton who will put me first always. You are my hope in the darkest of nights." She leaned up and kissed me softly on the lips.

I would not be travelling to Constantinople to fetch back a relic. I would be travelling east to Normandy to give away the woman I loved to another. Such was my fate. Perhaps Wulfstan had been right. I was not the master of my own destiny.

Wyrd!

The End

Glossary

Angevin- the people of Anjou, mainly the ruling family

Battle- a formation in war (a modern battalion)

Breeks- Trousers

Cadge- the frame upon which hunting birds are carried (by a codger- hence the phrase old codger being the old man who carries the frame)

Conroi- A group of knights fighting together

Demesne- estate

Destrier- war horse

Fess- a horizontal line in heraldry

Gambeson- a padded tunic worn underneath mail. When worn by an archer they came to the waist. It was more of a quilted jacket but I have used the term freely

Gonfanon- A standard used in Medieval times (Also known as a Gonfalon in Italy)

Gruffudd ap Cynan - King of Gwynedd

Hartness- the manor which became Hartlepool

Maredudd ap Bleddyn- King of Powys

Mêlée- a medieval fight between knights

Musselmen- Muslims

Outremer- The Frankish kingdoms in the Holy Land.

Palfrey- a riding horse

Pyx- a box containing a holy relic (Shakespeare's Pax from Henry V)

Sea fret- a coastal mist

Seggesfield- Sedgefield

Strategos- Byzantine general

Surcoat- a tunic worn over mail or armour

Sumpter- packhorse

Tagmata- Byzantine cavalry

Ventail – a piece of mail which covered the neck and the lower face.

Wulfestun- Wolviston (Durham)

Historical note

The book is set during one of the most turbulent and complicated times in British history. Henry I of England and Normandy's eldest son William died. The King named his daughter, Empress Matilda as his heir. However, her husband, the Emperor of the Holy Roman Empire died and she remarried. Her new husband was Geoffrey of Anjou and she had children by him. (The future Henry II of England and Normandy- The Lion in Winter!)

Norman knights were the most successful warriors of their age. Time and time again they defeated much greater numbers. Hastings was the closest they came to being beaten. The Hautevilles conquered Sicily and Naples with just a handful of knights. They, briefly, threatened the Byzantine Empire itself. In Ireland, five hundred knights conquered the whole country. In one battle one hundred Norman knights defeated over five thousand Irishmen. Perhaps it was their Norse blood which made them so successful. My books reflect that success in battle.

The Scots were taking advantage of a power vacuum on their borders. They were a constant threat to the lands in the north of England. William the Conqueror had claimed lands which were felt to be Scottish. The line of Hadrian's Wall was often regarded as the border between the two countries. The border between England and Scotland has always been a prickly one from the time of the Romans onward. Before that time the border was along the line of Glasgow to Edinburgh. The creation of an artificial frontier, Hadrian's Wall, created an area of dispute for the people living on either side of it. William the Conqueror had the novel idea of slaughtering everyone who lived between the Tees and the Tyne/Tweed in an attempt to resolve the problem. It did not work and lords on both sides of the borders, as well as the monarchs, used the dispute to switch sides as it suited them.

The Scots did, according to chroniclers of the time, behave particularly badly.

"an execrable army, more atrocious than the pagans, neither fearing God nor regarding man, spread desolation over the whole province and slaughtered everywhere people of either sex, of every age and rank, destroying, pillaging and burning towns, churches and houses"

"Then (horrible to relate) they carried off, like so much booty, the noble matrons and chaste virgins, together with other women. These naked, fettered, herded together; by whips and thongs they drove before them, goading them with their spears and other weapons. This took place in other wars, but in this to a far greater extent."

"For the sick on their couches, women pregnant and in childbed, infants in the womb, innocents at the breast, or on the mother's knee, with the mothers themselves, decrepit old men and worn-out old women, and persons debilitated from whatever cause, wherever they met with them, they put to the edge of the sword, and transfixed with their spears; and by how much more horrible a death they could dispatch them, so much the more did they rejoice."

Robert of Hexham

When the civil war began Matilda's half-brother, Robert of Gloucester (one of William's bastards) declared for Matilda and a civil war ensued. The war went on until Stephen died and was called the anarchy because everyone was looking out for themselves. There were no sides as such. Allies could become enemies overnight. Murder, ambush and assassination became the order of the day. The only warriors who could be relied upon were the household knights of a lord- his oathsworn. The feudal system, which had been an ordered pyramid, was thrown into confusion by the civil war. Lords created their own conroi or groups of knights and men at arms. Successful lords would ensure that they had a mixture of knights, archers and foot soldiers.

The manors I write about were around at the time the book is set. For a brief time, a de Brus was lord of Normanby. It changed hands a number of times until it came under the control of the Percy family. This is a work of fiction but I have based events on the ones which occurred in the twelfth century. A manor was just a farm initially but when a knight took over such a manor he would, normally, fortify it and try to increase his power. Powerful lords were allowed to hold sessions where they would dispense justice. They had to collect taxes for the king. Part of the taxes was their due. Most lords were very religious and built fine churches to assure life after death.

Matilda was married to the Emperor of the Holy Roman Emperor, Henry, in 1116 when she was 14. They had no children and the marriage was not a happy one. When William Adelin died in the White Ship disaster then Henry had no choice but to name his daughter as his heir, however, by that time she had been

194

married to Geoffrey Count of Anjou, Fulk's son and King Henry was suspicious of his former enemy's heir. His vacillation caused the civil war which was known as the Anarchy. However, those events are several books away. Stephen and Matilda are just cousins: soon they will become enemies. I have the Emperor dying in Worms- he actually died in Utrecht. I am continuing the thread I began in book 2. The other aspects: the Archbishop getting the insignia form the Empress and then Matilda taking her Imperial jewels with her are all true. Lothair of Supplinburg did hate the two of them and he became Emperor. The Emperor died in May 1125 of cancer. His heir was Frederick who inherited his estates. Matilda left her estates in Germany to join her father. Lothair was elected Emperor and he hated both Matilda and her husband, Henry. The accounts of the attempts on her life are my fiction. When King Henry died the Empress was in Normandy and Stephen of Blois, the nephew of Henry, sailed for England where he was crowned king. A number of events happened then which showed how the politics of the period worked. King David of Scotland who was related to both Stephen and Matilda declared his support for Matilda. In reality this was an attempt to grab power and he used the Norman knights of Cumbria and Northumbria to take over that part of England and invade Yorkshire. Stephen came north to defeat him- King David, having lost the Battle of the Standard fled north of the Tees.

In the high middle ages, there was a hierarchy of hawks. At this time, there was not. A baron was supposed to have a bustard which is not even a hawk. Some think it was a corruption of buzzard or was a generic name for a hawk of indeterminate type. I have used hawks in my book as they were a symbol of a knight's status. Aiden finds hawks' eggs and raises them. The cadge was the square frame on which the hawks were carried and it was normally carried by a man called a codger. Hence the English slang for old codger; a retainer who was too old for anything else. It might also be the derivation of cadge (ask for) a lift- more English slang. Similarly, all hunting, including that of rabbits as well as deer, was reserved for the lord of the manor. The penalty for poaching was blinding at best and death at worst.

Gospatric was a real character. His father had been Earl of Northumberland but was replaced by William the Conqueror. He was granted lands in Scotland, around Dunbar. Once the Conqueror was dead he managed to gain lands in England around the borders. He was killed at the Battle of the Standard fighting for the Scots. I had used this as the basis for his treachery. He was succeeded by his son, Gospatric, but the family confirmed their Scottish loyalties. His other sons are, as far as I know my own invention although I daresay if he was anything like the other lords and knights he would have been spreading his largess around to all and sundry!

I realise that some names are used repeatedly. I am afraid that is just the way it was in the 12th Century. There were at least three Matildas. It might explain why the Matilda who figures most prominently in my books was known, until she died, as the Empress. Matilda herself was the daughter of a Henry, married a Henry and had a son called Henry. There were two Roberts, Henry's illegitimate son and his brother, Curthose whom he imprisoned. There were several Williams: The Conqueror, Adelin (Henry's son who drowned in the White Ship), and Clito, the son of Robert Curthose. Those names were very popular and were given to many children. I have tried to use, 'son of' etc, whenever possible.

Hartburn is a small village just outside Stockton. My American readers may be interested to know that the Washington family of your first President lived there and were lords of the manor from the fourteenth century onwards. In the sixteenth century, they had it taken from them and it was replaced by the manor of Wessington, which became Washington. Had they not moved then your president might live in Hartburn DC!

Books used in the research:
The Varangian Guard- 988-1453 Raffael D'Amato
Saxon Viking and Norman- Terence Wise
The Walls of Constantinople AD 324-1453-Stephen Turnbull
Byzantine Armies- 886-1118- Ian Heath
The Age of Charlemagne-David Nicolle
The Normans- David Nicolle
Norman Knight AD 950-1204- Christopher Gravett
The Norman Conquest of the North- William A Kappelle
The Knight in History- Francis Gies
The Norman Achievement- Richard F Cassady
The Times Atlas of World History

Griff Hosker April 2015

Other books by Griff Hosker

If you enjoyed reading this book, then why not read another one by the author?

Ancient History

The Sword of Cartimandua Series
(Germania and Britannia 50 A.D. – 128 A.D.)
Ulpius Felix- Roman Warrior (prequel)
The Sword of Cartimandua
The Horse Warriors
Invasion Caledonia
Roman Retreat
Revolt of the Red Witch
Druid's Gold
Trajan's Hunters
The Last Frontier
Hero of Rome
Roman Hawk
Roman Treachery
Roman Wall
Roman Courage

The Wolf Warrior series
(Britain in the late 6th Century)
Saxon Dawn
Saxon Revenge
Saxon England
Saxon Blood
Saxon Slayer
Saxon Slaughter
Saxon Bane
Saxon Fall: Rise of the Warlord
Saxon Throne
Saxon Sword

Medieval History

The Dragon Heart Series
Viking Slave
Viking Warrior
Viking Jarl
Viking Kingdom
Viking Wolf
Viking War
Viking Sword
Viking Wrath
Viking Raid
Viking Legend
Viking Vengeance
Viking Dragon
Viking Treasure
Viking Enemy
Viking Witch
Viking Blood
Viking Weregeld
Viking Storm
Viking Warband
Viking Shadow
Viking Legacy
Viking Clan
Viking Bravery

The Norman Genesis Series
Hrolf the Viking
Horseman
The Battle for a Home
Revenge of the Franks
The Land of the Northmen
Ragnvald Hrolfsson
Brothers in Blood
Lord of Rouen
Drekar in the Seine
Duke of Normandy

Northern Knight

The Duke and the King

Danelaw
(England and Denmark in the 11th Century)
Dragon Sword
Oathsword

New World Series
Blood on the Blade
Across the Seas
The Savage Wilderness
The Bear and the Wolf
Erik The Navigator

The Vengeance Trail

The Reconquista Chronicles
Castilian Knight
El Campeador
The Lord of Valencia

The Aelfraed Series
(Britain and Byzantium 1050 A.D. - 1085 A.D.)
Housecarl
Outlaw
Varangian

The Anarchy Series England
1120-1180
English Knight
Knight of the Empress
Northern Knight
Baron of the North
Earl
King Henry's Champion
The King is Dead
Warlord of the North
Enemy at the Gate
The Fallen Crown

Northern Knight

Warlord's War
Kingmaker
Henry II
Crusader
The Welsh Marches
Irish War
Poisonous Plots
The Princes' Revolt
Earl Marshal
The Perfect Knight

Border Knight
1182-1300
Sword for Hire
Return of the Knight
Baron's War
Magna Carta
Welsh Wars
Henry III
The Bloody Border
Baron's Crusade
Sentinel of the North
War in the West
Debt of Honour
The Blood of the Warlord (Feb 2022)

Sir John Hawkwood Series
France and Italy 1339- 1387
Crécy: The Age of the Archer
Man At Arms
The White Company

Lord Edward's Archer
Lord Edward's Archer
King in Waiting
An Archer's Crusade
Targets of Treachery
The Great Cause (April 2022)

Northern Knight

Struggle for a Crown
1360- 1485
Blood on the Crown
To Murder A King
The Throne
King Henry IV
The Road to Agincourt
St Crispin's Day
The Battle For France
The Last Knight

Tales from the Sword I
(Short stories from the Medieval period)

Tudor Warrior series
England and Scotland in the late 145th and early 15th
century
Tudor Warrior

Conquistador
England and America in the 16th Century
Conquistador

Modern History

The Napoleonic Horseman Series
Chasseur à Cheval
Napoleon's Guard
British Light Dragoon
Soldier Spy
1808: The Road to Coruña
Talavera
The Lines of Torres Vedras
Bloody Badajoz
The Road to France
Waterloo

The Lucky Jack American Civil War series

Northern Knight

Rebel Raiders
Confederate Rangers
The Road to Gettysburg

The British Ace Series
1914
1915 Fokker Scourge
1916 Angels over the Somme
1917 Eagles Fall
1918 We will remember them
From Arctic Snow to Desert Sand
Wings over Persia

Combined Operations series
1940-1945
Commando
Raider
Behind Enemy Lines
Dieppe
Toehold in Europe
Sword Beach
Breakout
The Battle for Antwerp
King Tiger
Beyond the Rhine
Korea
Korean Winter

Tales from the Sword II
(Short stories from the Modern period)

Other Books
Great Granny's Ghost (Aimed at 9-14-year-old young
people)

For more information on all of the books then please visit the
author's website at www.griffhosker.com where there is a
link to contact him or visit his Facebook page: GriffHosker at
Sword Books

Northern Knight

Made in the USA
Middletown, DE
17 May 2022

65870534R00116